"Irony of ironies, the more separations we experience, one from another, the more stories we have to tell— and the more pressing becomes the need to tell them."

—SUZANNE LIPSETT
Surviving a Writer's Life

for Paula—
Who obviously appreciates
great Literature!

love Jiv

saving gracie

A NOVEL

JILL TEITELMAN

FREESTYLE PRESS
Boston, Massachusetts

FREESTYLE PRESS

For information regarding permissions, visit
www.saving-grace.com

Cover art copyright © 2012 by Harry Teitelman
Book design by Kathleen Westray

ISBN 978-0-9858887-0-1
10 9 8 7 6 5 4 3 2 1   12 13 14 15 16
Printed in the United States of America
First printing, November 2012

FOR MY PARENTS

I See My Friend Everywhere

she nearly touched my hand
yes I said you were still alive

—GRACE PALEY

I.
satori

IT'S 1984. I'm sitting on my fire escape staring down at midnight Second Avenue between Twelfth and Thirteenth streets, and the particularly aromatic grass I'm smoking is helping me cope with my latest identity crisis.

I'm almost forty. I intended to be a famous writer by now — a straight East Village version of Gertrude Stein, maybe. I should have aimed a little lower, but my privileged adolescence left me with unrealistic expectations.

Of course I was supposed to bring home a suitable fiancé to repay my parents' investment, but I needed adventures worth writing about. I hitchhiked to Crete in Henry Miller's footsteps, spent time in Andalucía à la Hemingway, and taught English at the Sorbonne. Then it was time to trade my expatriate identity for that of East Village poet.

The lonely stretches between lovers were good for my soul.

These days I teach English 101 to lovable, Mohawked art students. In my copious free time, I spin my motley relationships into poignant short stories and publish them in obscure literary magazines. When I read my poetry at St. Mark's Church, the applause sounds sincere. But despite minor success and a not-bad body, I usually climb into my loft bed with only books for company.

Too much freedom is starting to feel as bad as not enough. Why did I jump on the Liberation train without asking where it would take me?

Even Gertrude had undying love. Where's my Alex B. Toklas?

Someday he'll come along? I've lost my faith in Gershwin.

      *   *   *

ONE BY ONE, my single girlfriends have abandoned me for lovers, but there was always good old Rhonda. A few days after Bookstore Bert (my ex-boyfriend and her then current one) introduced us years ago, we flew to Jamaica where we snorkeled naked, drank ganja tea, and had deep conversations under the stars. She and Bert broke up, men came and went, but Rhonda and I have gone steady ever since.

Until she started nursing a partner at her law firm through his ugly divorce, a guy who seemed destined for the discard pile.

"Reggie's dull," she kept saying. "He watches the worst junk on TV. We're just friends." But as soon as his court date was over, Reggie turned into the man of Rhonda's dreams, sort of.

I tried to get over my jealousy and be happy for her, but it wasn't easy. We still saw an occasional movie together and kept in touch by phone, but I was demoted to second fiddle.

Then things got worse.

"Career schmareer!" Rhonda the hotshot attorney crowed at our favorite café on Bleecker Street. "I'm pregnant!"

You can't do that to me, I wanted to scream. I choked on my scone, which gave me time to hide my distress — OK, my horror — and faked some enthusiasm. "Wow" was the best I could come up with, but Rhonda was too ecstatic to care.

I should have seen it coming, but I was in denial. Had my friend settled for such an unexciting guy because her hormones were choosing for her? Reggie had been dead-set against kids, but Rhonda can be very persuasive.

I can hardly say the b word without wincing. Rhonda's brain and body will go to hell and she'll start talking *baby talk*.

There went our plan to bike in Vietnam. At least there's no fancy wedding to go to. They had a quick ceremony at Reggie's parents' convalescent home in Florida. Rhonda wore the Mexican peasant dress I made her buy in Oaxaca so no one noticed the obvious.

She and Reggie have moved uptown to Babyland. And instead of jazz clubs and art openings, a weekend date with Rhonda means pushing her top-of-the-line baby carriage through Central Park. And listening to her gush while she breast-feeds gorgeously dressed little Julian.

"Who's the most amazing baby in the universe?" she coos. Whatever universe she's talking about feels far away from mine. My friend has reached a strange nirvana and left me in the dust.

      ⁑   ⁙   ⁘

I HAD TO TAKE two subways to get to Rhonda's new neighborhood, hoping for some sympathy. I'm recuperating from another crash landing after a brief flight with a sculptor. His Giacometti-meets-David-Smith structures were almost as huge as his ego. Why am I so susceptible to narcissists?

"Our conversations were fascinating," I whine.

"Grow up, Ruth!" Rhonda interrupts me, exasperated. "Life isn't a movie. Forget about romance." She practically spits out the word that used to be our religion.

Grow up? Abandon my search for a man who'll read my poetry and trek through Tibet with me?

"Who do you really think will come along?"

I try to absorb the blow.

"*This*" — Rhonda holds her little prince aloft as if he's the Holy Grail — "is real love."

Blame my own less-than-idyllic infancy, but I've always wondered just what people *see* in babies. Motherhood always seemed like a masochistic Olympic event others competed in for unimaginable reasons, like wrestling, or the luge. *My* mother certainly didn't thrive on it. "I should have been an architect," she once confessed, "or a librarian."

If you want a life, don't reproduce, preached the Women's Movement, or the one I gravitated to. I want to be remembered for my aesthetic vision, which takes nonstop discipline. Being a small person's slave would block my progress. No one in my pantheon of heroines — Emily Dickinson, Virginia Woolf, Germaine Greer — spent herself on children.

Baby Julian is an alien creature, a repulsive, red-faced screamer. But when I hold him, more tenderly than I knew I could, he stares at me as if he knows me better than my shrink does. As if he's warning me: *You're about to miss the boat.*

I feel a twinge of frightening desire, the one I've buried the deepest. All I see on the subway downtown are mothers whose angelic broods clutch them with tiny hands and mysterious trust. I've never belonged to anyone that fiercely. A kid is the closest I can come to forever.

The small stone I didn't know was in my heart has suddenly rolled away.

2.

contact improv

THE BABY IDEA IS probably far-fetched at this point. But just in case, I need a boyfriend. Finding someone to inspire me who's also a potential dad won't be easy, but I'm a glutton for hopeless challenges. The domestic guys I never wanted are all taken by now, and when I flip through my mental Rolodex of old boyfriends, even the divorced guys are already working on their second families.

I've read a few Have-Your-Own-Baby books, but solo adoption and sperm banks seem too daunting. I've squandered all my fertile years tilting at sexual windmills and now it's too late. How can I exorcise this sudden, crazy idea from my consciousness?

＊　＊　＊

AN OLD FRIEND from college calls the next day. "Can I crash at your place?"

I have a great rent-controlled apartment, so I'm used to a steady stream of visitors. (My real estate karma's a lot better than my relationship karma.)

"I'm on my way from Denver to Tel Aviv," Tanya says. "It'll be great to catch up!" We studied creation myths with Joseph Campbell at Sarah Lawrence and she's been following her bliss ever since. These days she calls herself a "spiritual anthropologist."

"I'm studying love in other cultures," she informs me while we lug her suitcase up my five long flights. "The Inuits are fascinating. I can't wait to study the Bedouins."

"Have you thought about having a kid?" (My only topic right now.)

"I don't need to," she laughs. "Abe already has them."

I find out that her much older lover — an amazingly wise Kabbalist rabbi — is still married to the mother of his five wonderful children, and Tanya's part of the family. I try not to look askance. Why judge another's ecstasy?

"I'm the only single person I know," I mumble pathetically.

"You're a free spirit, Ruth. We've got to find you some male energy."

"Tanya," I remind her, "we're in Manhattan."

"I only know one guy in New York," she says, deeply concerned. "Jake tutored me in statistics at UCLA."

She studies the phone book while I cook dinner. "Here he is," she shouts. "Jake Rosen. West 111th Street. The guy's brilliant." She leaves him a message.

*   *   *

"JAKE'S COMING OVER after his dance class," Tanya announces when I get home from work the next day.

"That's cool," I say, feeling a touch of dread. Tanya and I have different tastes when it comes to men, but I don't want to seem ungrateful.

"Jake's dance studio's in your neighborhood!" she chirps.

A mathematician who takes dance classes sounds intriguing, but maybe he's gay. I've been through too many misalliances to get excited, but I run out for wine and Brie just in case he's worth it.

Jake is hetero as they come. Tanya neglected to mention he was gorgeous: medium height, olive skin, wild, dark curls, and I detect a perfect physique beneath his classy suit.

"Do you miss the weather in L.A.?" is all I can think to ask him.

"Weather is so irrelevant," he says, his gaze intense but flattering.

A man who craves meaningful conversation? I rummage around in my brain for the right subject. "I went to an amazing past-life regression workshop last week," I start.

"What did you find out?" Instead of dismissing my weirdness, he seems genuinely interested.

"OK. It'll sound strange, but I was a poet in medieval France, thrown into a dungeon for speaking the truth."

"Then what happened?" Jake asks sympathetically.

"I went mad. It doesn't mean this actually happened," I add. "It's just interesting to see how you imagine your former existences."

"I've always had the feeling I was a galley slave in chains."

We're off and running. "Let's hope we're both in for better luck this time around," I say, pouring us large glasses of wine. My voice has softened into an alluring tone I haven't used in a long time. Thank God I'm wearing my clingiest skirt and eyeliner.

After Tanya and her friend reminisce over cheese and crackers, I put on the Rolling Stones, roll a joint, and turn down the lights. Soon the three of us are gyrating around my candle-lit living room, solo at first, then contact-improv style. It's been a while since I've danced this unselfconsciously, but my Martha Graham technique comes right back. Thank God for the pot.

Even though Jake hardly tokes, he gets right into the beat. After a few songs, he flings off his suit and shirt, revealing a shiny black unitard—and the muscles I imagined.

Tanya was right, he's the Renaissance type. As soon as she

goes into my tiny guestroom to sleep, Jake's eyes lock onto mine. We slow dance to "Wild Horses," then we sit on my fire escape to cool off.

After our second bottle of wine, I read him my most recent poem:

On a frigid February 14th
I cross 11th Street to avoid my last lover,
the kinky psychoanalyst in training.
I pass the blues bar on 13th where we met.
"Someone should tie you up," he said.
I buy roses for myself this year
Almost slipping on the ice.

"Hmm," he says thoughtfully. "An expanded haiku." How perceptive. "I love tragic voices."

My forte! His questions are deep, his answers wise.

I watch the moon — or maybe it's a streetlight — reflected in Jake's eyes until he pulls me to him and we breathe in unison for a long time. Our lips just barely touch. We talk nonstop: Native American spirituality, his love of the desert.

"We should go there," he says. "We could purify ourselves in a sweat lodge."

"Sounds better than a *mikveh*." Even though Jakes's a hardly-Jewish Orange County Jew, this makes him laugh.

Our first real kiss makes me quiver and the second one leaves me out of breath. He's been searching for this, too. By dawn we're drunk on our mutual fortune. There's one star left to wish on.

Let it finally be my turn.

I sleepwalk through my classes the next day. As soon as I get home, Jake calls to make a date for the following night—a record seven hours and thirty-five minutes since our tender farewell.

"Don't thank me," Tanya says when I put her in a taxi to JFK. "You simply got out of your own way."

        ※   ※   ※

NEW YORK MEN DON'T call you every day, especially after you sleep with them. Jake lives two long subway rides away in a gloomy, overpriced studio on a seedy block near Columbia. Since he works—and dances—in my part of town, he comes over often, bearing pastrami sandwiches, pierogies, or curry so we can stay in. He loves my rent-controlled East Village treasure, an impossible coup for a newcomer to the city like him. Five long flights up, then five more steps to my loft bed.

Jake's past relationships haven't lasted any longer than mine. His most recent breakup sounds ugly, but who am I to judge? My life is full of wreckage, too. I'm so swept away I can barely grade my students' essays and prepare my classes. All my friends are on hold since my new lover isn't ready to meet them.

Jake and I both have flexible schedules, so we indulge in one another frequently. There's a cinematic quality to our fervent rendezvous: Rohmer or Godard. He reads my stories and wants to know everything about me. We compare unhappy childhoods and (as a result?) our ill-fated attempts at lasting love.

No guy since seventh grade ever said he loved me so fast and so seriously. Even when we laugh, we end up in tender tears. No one has ever *gotten* me the way Jake does. I feel as lucky as the couples I envy who kiss on the subway.

"I've always wanted to take care of an artist," he assures me. "You have so much to say."

And—what a relief—he's been *shrunk*. Back in L.A. Jake was in group therapy with movie stars.

I'm writing upbeat poetry.

I float to work and try to concentrate on my students, but we end up discussing our love lives instead. On the way home I pick up aphrodisiacal artichokes, oysters, and budget caviar.

Rhonda leaves me frantic messages. "Don't keep me in suspense."

How can I explain what's going on when I don't have a clue? I think my news is good, but Jake and I are the only inhabitants of a tiny planet that has broken away from the solar system, so I can't be sure.

"He's a biostatistician. Don't ask me what that is, but he wants his formulas to help humanity."

She's not impressed yet.

"He actually makes a living," I add. Unlike all the creative types I've dated.

"Is he dad material?"

"Did I ever say I cared about that?"

"I'm saying it for you."

"OK, so he'd be *great*."

"That's fabulous, Ruth."

I wish Rhonda would shut up about babies. After my cat finally died, I confess I felt relieved of the responsibility. When the infant in the apartment below mine squalls nonstop, I get a headache. The parents look haggard and oppressed. I love hitting the streets whenever I want, sleeping all day after a night of frantic creativity or barhopping. I've always thought a kid would turn me into a resentful, unfulfilled domestic servant, use me up, then leave me forever.

Then I remember how baby Julian looked at me. *You'll miss the boat.*

I've hiked through the Samarian Gorge and walked past exploding Katyusha rockets during the Six Day War.

Can I conquer my fear of the scariest mission of all?

"I'm doing cartwheels for you," shouts the friend who's lured me into this terrifying metamorphosis. "You have to bring him for dinner."

"I searched the world for the right man," I say. "Then I found him in my living room."

3.
equanimity

"I THOUGHT YOU WERE a genius," I tease Jake because I'm surprised he can't program my VCR. Suddenly he's wounded to the
quick and we have to deconstruct the misunderstanding.

"If you think I have problems now," he eventually explains,
"you should have known me *before* I had all that therapy."

We hit frequent turbulence, then find our way back to decent
weather. I have my moods, but his are dramatic. He's adorable,
brilliant, compassionate. He's also prone to flaring, imaginary
hurts, and he frequently spins into darkness.

After arduous hours of processing, we deepen our mutual
understanding, apologize, and are laughing again. "Soul mate"
always sounded ludicrous to me, but I don't know how else to
explain our closeness. Our heat and hunger, my relief at such
acceptance. We're stunned at our luck.

"He's willing to process things," I tell my therapist, Rose. "He's
in touch with his feelings."

She can hear my silent "but" and waits.

"Well, there are a few *issues* . . ."

Her eyebrows rise.

"When my phone rings, Jake doesn't want me to answer it. And
if I stop to chat with someone on the street, or even banter with a
waiter, he gets annoyed."

"All that drama sounds draining," she empathizes. "Can I ask
why you're putting up with it?"

Because Jake and I are supposed to have a child together. My therapist will think I'm crazy.

"I guess I haven't told you." I take a pregnant pause to muster courage. "I'm thinking about having a baby."

For the first time in our five-year relationship, Rose is speechless—but smiling.

"I can't explain how I know this. But Jake will be an amazing father."

"You'll be just as terrific a mother. I'm thrilled for you, Ruth."

"Will it be too hard with this difficult man?"

"He does seem willing to work on himself," she finally says, her sacrosanct requirement. "But you'll have to hold your ground." Rose is the wise maternal voice I never heard, so I listen carefully, crying and blowing my nose. "It's not easy with anyone. But I promise you'll never regret it."

On the way down in her elevator I feel weak with relief.

      ＂   ＂   ＊

A SWEET MOOD'S in the air when I get home. "Let's make an omelet," Jake says. I pour us some extra-strong beer and we curl up on my couch to watch Kurasawa's *Seven Samurai*. My last boyfriend complained about subtitles, but the more obscure the film, the better Jake and I like it.

"How was your shrink session today?" he says, in the middle of a bloody battle scene.

"Fine." I'm keeping the dangerous news to myself for now. After the tragic film ends, in a graveyard scene, Jake and I climb up to the loft.

"I love cooking together," I tell him. "What a great idea to put capers and peppers in with the cheese."

He kisses the back of my neck, then wants to chat some more. *A man who likes to talk in bed.* "I'm here all the time," my paramour says softly, his wonderful torso against my back. "Don't you think it makes more sense for me to give up my apartment and move in?"

What? Already? I try to hide my alarm. I know I have my own pretty serious agenda, but I'm in shock anyway. We've only been "going out" (mostly in) for about six weeks. The brief gaps between Jake's visits let me recuperate from our heady and bodily together-ness. Living together sounds dangerous.

"That's so sweet that you want to really share my life," I say. "Let's think about it."

"We can take some great trips with the money I'll save on rent."

He knows my magic buttons. But I don't want to ruin what we have. I give him a massage to change the subject until he falls asleep smiling.

I've had this wonderful womb of an apartment all to myself for years, not counting a few brief live-in boyfriends. I love being here alone, lowering all the shades and cranking up the air conditioner on brutally hot summer days, playing New Orleans jazz and drink-ing beer. I love getting up in the middle of the night and writing my heart out, having wild parties with artists and musicians on my roof, weekends with my girlfriends ordering in meals and figuring out our lives.

I'm glad Jake's so committed, but he still has no idea about my latest agenda. The baby's still such a dreamy concept, I haven't even thought about actually living with its moody prospective father. First, we need to get through this dramatic stage. And then we'd have to find a bigger place. So what's the rush?

The next morning, Sunday, I leave my lover aloft and race to my

Kundalini yoga class, a grueling three-hour Warrior Workout with Siv Sivaranda (né Stuart Shapiro). I chant myself into trusting that everything will work out. What choice do I have? All men come loaded with near-fatal flaws. According to the profoundly practical Rhonda, "Men are long-term projects. Just find someone who'll let you work on him."

Jake can definitely use some renovation, but he has great bones.

      ▪   ▪   ▪

THE CLASS ENDS with some pranayama breathing through alternate nostrils to clear my spirit. Jake and I have been unleashing so much infantile energy at one another, I've kept the baby issue buried deep inside me. But now that he's lobbed his ball over the net, it's time to hit it back.

We're pushing our way through a dense Village crowd after seeing *Waiting for Godot* when I hear myself blurt out, apropos of nothing, "I'm starting to want to have a baby." I have to shout it to be heard, which feels great. If he goes nuts, the surge of humanity is here to protect me. (At least I haven't put too much heat into the situation by dropping this bomb while we're making love.)

Jake stops, dumbstruck, and leans against a building. I watch the jolt of electricity go through his system. He'd be less surprised if I wanted us to move to Vermont and raise goats, or take up couples' ice dancing. His vision of our life together is winning respective MacArthur genius grants for mathematics and poetry, then moving to the South Pacific.

"Why would anyone choose the punishment of parenthood?" he wants to know. We're walking on quieter streets now. "Families are obsolete."

"Mine wasn't great," I say. "And yours sounds even worse." My father said mean things to me, but Jake's father *did* them. "But we can get it right when it's our turn."

He tries to change the topic back to Beckett's brilliantly dismal humor, but I stick to my agenda. Now that I've broached forbidden territory, I'm undaunted. I've seen my lover cradling our feisty, pink-faced daughter in a dream. This isn't a rational or even a conscious decision — more of a primal instinct. I need to love someone from the start so we can both begin.

"It would be healing to raise a child with so much love she'll know her worth," is the line I've rehearsed. "The idea never even occurred to me for years, but now that it's almost too late, I have to try." Can he tell I'm still trying to convince myself?

I've upped the ante considerably. We walk all the way home in silence. "Just think about it," I say in my gentlest voice. How can he refuse the greatest gift I've ever offered?

I practice the superhuman art of patience while the subject hangs between us, a solid wall. The next day, before he rushes out the door for a dance class, Jake announces, "Kids are cute, but eventually they say 'fuck you' and leave." He's just read an article in the paper about a gang of young boys in Chinatown.

"So you think we'll have a little thug?"

"Why give up your art for a blue-collar job?" he asks over dinner that night.

"Lots of writers have been mothers." One of my favorites these days, Grace Paley, wrote amazing stories about her kids. (I'm pretty sure Jake doesn't know about Sylvia Plath and Anne Sexton, suicides who left their broods.) "I know I'm rushing things, but it took me so long to figure this out. Besides, I have the rest of my life to make my literary breakthrough."

If I weren't so biologically driven, I'd feel compassion for the guy, but I can't retreat from my crucial campaign. I want to move uptown to Rhonda's neighborhood and swirl my baby in the YMCA pool with all the other late-in-life moms. I want to teach my child what I finally know, read her the wonderful books my mother never read me, and adore her the way my parents would have adored me if they'd known how.

※　※　※

"RUTHIE, I HAVE a great idea," says my cousin Gert in San Francisco after hearing my latest installment. "You're overdue for some inner clarity. Come with me to a silent meditation retreat. Ten days in the Mojave Desert! It'll be amazing."

"No talking for *ten days*? Are you kidding?"

"It's exactly what you need. Talks by inspiring Buddhist masters. And every few days you have an interview with one of them. You're ready for it, kiddo, and it's such great timing."

Being so alone with myself sounds terrifying, but I'm on an emotional roller coaster and maybe this will help.

"It won't be easy, but you'll thank me when it's over."

I knew Jake would be distressed about my sudden plan to go so far away. "I respect Eastern religions," he assures me. "But why can't you just meditate here?"

"My work isn't happening at all," I say, leaving out that I need some distance from us. He says he understands; he even says he admires my courage, but he pouts while I pack my most meditative outfits: gauzy pants, long, flowing skirts, and an Indian shawl. "You'll get so much done without me trying to drag you to movies," I add.

"That's true." He's quiet for a while. "Forgive me, Ruth. You're an explorer. So go. Find out something new."

Two days later I fly to Southern California, then get a bus to a place called 29 Palms in the Joshua Tree National Park. The ten-hour trip leaves me pleasantly exhausted. Gert has gone on these retreats before and raved about the results, so I'm glad she has pulled me out of my left-brained Manhattan world into her spiritual one. Our dorm rooms are at opposite ends of a low-slung stone building surrounded by sand, scattered rocks, and scrubby, prickly vegetation.

We eat salad and cold noodles in the dining room, noisy for the last time, then wash our bowls. Our official silence is about to start. "I'd better call Jake," I tell Gert, ducking into the pay phone.

"Now I understand what you love about the desert," I report. "I feel like I'm on another planet."

"I spent all day looking for my *Statistical Abstracts*," he changes the subject.

"It's in the file under the hall table."

"I looked there already."

"Did you turn on the light?"

"Oh." Even after he finds his precious journal, he's in a sour mood. I'm supposed to be at his side, keeping track of his misplaced journals.

"We're about to start. I'm a little nervous about getting through this," I confess.

"You can always leave, right?"

"I was hoping for a little more support."

"Well, it does seem a bit extreme."

A loud gong forces me to end our conversation before we get back to being nice. I try to hide my tension, but Gert gives me a concerned look as we enter the geodesic meditation dome. Thank God we don't have to talk. I take off my sandals and sit cross-legged on my round, hard pillow. Not exactly comfortable. I wonder if I can score two or three more.

For our first *satsang*, a renowned Tibetan monk talks about compassion for the self, and I listen hard. Then we sit for forty-five minutes, which is only a warm-up. My heart won't stop pounding long enough for me to hear my breath. Everyone I sneak a peek at looks already blissful.

Comparisons, I remember, are always a bad idea.

*   *   *

WE'RE GONGED RUDELY awake at five the next morning. After herb tea, apples, and toast, we shuffle back to our pillows for the first entire day of submission to the rules. Every so often we're sent outside for *very* slow walking meditation through the sand and scrub grass. I'm used to jaywalking across Fourteenth Street. Moving by inches is impossible to master.

Nothing calms me down, even for a few seconds. I'm in more trouble than I've wanted to admit.

I'm bombarded with thoughts, locked into my obsessive monkey mind.

What was I thinking? Life shouldn't be this difficult. A kid will make things a million times worse. I've been racing blindly toward a dangerous dream, but now that I'm so close, how can I give it up? The harder I try to be here now—no past, no future, only breathing, accepting, letting go—the more intensely the battle rages. This masochistic experiment is only making things worse.

My stomach growls loudly and I'm fidgety, but I stay in my seat until lunch: watery vegetable tofu soup, tasteless crackers, and carrot salad, which we're instructed to eat mindfully. Smell, pause, taste, pause, chew while thinking about chewing. Drink slowly, feel the water going down my throat.

I imagine I'm eating a roast beef sandwich with Russian dressing. I've always liked the *idea* of asceticism, but the real deal leaves a lot to be desired. By the end of the next two-hour sit, I feel shooting aches in my upper back and neck. I squirm and shift position a hundred times, trying to breathe through the pain as I've been instructed. Whenever it subsides, my worries swarm around me like hornets. I have no idea who I am anymore. How much can I blame on the baby thing?

"I'm a mess," I whisper to Gert the next day.

Every time I shoot my cousin a desperate *please talk to me* look, she refuses to make eye contact. When I volunteer to chop vegetables during her shift in the ashram kitchen, where some talking is allowed, all she'll discuss with me are carrots and garlic.

I'm afraid of losing my mind—even if I'm supposed to. Was I in such bad shape before Jake came along? I must have been, or I wouldn't have pulled in such a challenging partner.

The days are interminable. Nonstop harsh judgments of myself. Nagging fears. Why didn't I go to law school? What makes me think I can take care of a helpless infant, or even get through pregnancy and labor? If Tanya hadn't come to town, I'd be free of my conflicting obsessions. Jake's all light or all dark, like the moon. I'm a spiritual failure.

"My back hurts," I tell my meditation teacher during my ten-minute interview.

"Your body's telling you to listen to your hurting heart," the lovely African-American female monk tells me. But I'm drowning in negativity. The next time I'm out in the desert, I race to my dorm room and grab the joint and matches I brought for an emergency.

I'm hungry for escape, dizzy from all this anxious navel-gazing. A baby with Jake, a baby without Jake, Jake without a baby, myself without either. It's hard to pay attention to where I am—which I'm no good at anyway. I try to follow what looks like a trail through low bushes, past enormous boulders. The cacti look fake.

I should have taken a map. The trail fades out, but I assume I'll find it beyond the clutch of prickly Joshua trees. They're supposed to look like the prophet reaching toward heaven, but even he couldn't help me out right now. The desert's dusky; time to turn around.

I inherited a terrible sense of direction from my parents. Whenever they started bickering on our car trips (*You told me to turn right. No, I said go straight . . .*), I knew we were lost again. I always forget about this disability until it's too late and it's so goddamned symbolic.

Gert's on her deep, inner journey and won't notice I'm gone until I've turned into a fossil out here. Someone mentioned poisonous snakes and even more poisonous spiders. It should be easy to find my way back to the only building for a hundred miles, but I've lost sight of it. The sky's an amazing purple I can't appreciate right now.

Why couldn't I just stay on my pillow like everyone else? Cold and sweaty, I sit on a flat rock and notice some stars but no moon. My breathing's rapid. When I make a weak attempt to ask—the universe?—for help, the silence is deafening.

First, find yourself. The voice I hear is unfamiliar, but my own. My compulsive agendas evaporate into the desert air. Real fear has chased away the imaginary kind.

Then I get the message: I'm not really lost.

I remember passing the boulders where the trail ended. I walk, then race toward each group of those strange trees until I spot the boulders. The trail's invisible now, but I'm calm enough to keep going. Soon I hear otherworldly chanting and follow the sound. The dimly lit meditation dome looks like home instead of prison.

Safe in my bunk, I feel both courage and acceptance. If I let go of what I only *think* I have to have, I can find myself.

The last few days of the retreat fulfill Gert's promise: the windows in my mind are open to air and sunlight. My breath is steady and I walk gracefully between sits. When a thought intrudes — *I'm too old to have a child; I don't make enough money; I hate that watery soup we get for lunch* — I gently let it go. The simple meals are what my body craves.

I don't want to leave this sacred space and time.

"Are you sure you want to have his child?" Gert asks during our final embrace.

"I'll be all right whatever happens."

"If it doesn't work out," she says, "come to California and we'll raise the baby together."

*   *   *

I'M SURPRISED JAKE helps me up all five flights with my suitcase. "I'm sorry I was in such a bad mood when you called," he says humbly. He's broiling us a steak, which I could probably eat raw. "I was angry that I missed you so much. It made me feel dependent. I guess it's good, but I have to get used to it."

I tell him about losing and finding myself. We've fire-walked our way back together, too wired and tired to make love, but just as close.

IT'S ALMOST THE END of the semester and my students are finally working hard instead of blaming me for insisting on draft after draft of their final papers. I love teaching artists to use language as a visual medium. When my essay, "Painting with Paragraphs" is accepted by an academic review, Jake takes me out for Afghani food.

We're the best thing that ever happened to either of us, until our baby comes along and steals that prize.

4.

the last boat out

AFTER LESS THAN three months together (so much has happened between us that it feels like three years), we have our first catastrophe: I'm pregnant — accidentally — after switching from my annoying diaphragm to the newfangled birth control sponge that sounded so *comfortable* I had to try it. After the longest five minutes of my life, the test-kit verdict is in. Jake has no idea I even bought it.

My heart pounds in a thrilling kind of terror. Everyone has warned me how hard it will be to conceive at my age, but we did it by trying not to. I wash some dishes to compose myself and gather courage. Jake notices I'm too quiet. I'm supposed to be grading student papers and writing semester reports and he wants me to finish so I can edit something of his.

"What's up?"

"I guess the right answer is, my fertility."

He reacts calmly, scientifically, when he hears about the test we've just passed. I'm surprised he doesn't make me take it again. He studies the pamphlet that came with the newfangled sponges. "I can't believe I didn't read these bogus statistics before I let you try one of these things."

If it were his body, would I be this detached?

"Look, I'm in shock, too, Jake. But I've been dreaming of doing this, so it's just a change in the timing." I hope he can't detect my panic. Raising a child still feels like something other women do, women who fussed over their dolls and rocked them to sleep. (Did I even have dolls?) Women with motherly mothers, aunts, and grandmothers. Now that I think about it, I come from a long line of pretty non-maternal females.

"We should sue the pharmaceutical company," Jake mumbles. "How did those things get past the F.D.A.? It's preposterous."

I stare at him in disbelief until he notices.

"Ruthie. Darling. It's just too soon. Let's pick a more sensible time to have a baby."

I want to beat the shit out of him, then run out the door forever. But the faint heartbeat inside mine drowns out his horrifying suggestion. "No," I mumble. *"No."* He puts on his coat to go to work. *"You* have other options. I don't."

After he leaves me whimpering, my panic takes over.

I have less than eight months to get in touch with my still-buried instincts, and what if I can't? Those hormones already coursing through me are supposed to help. But what if they don't?

On the other hand, if I can handle Jake, I can deal with our innocent creation.

I call Rhonda.

"Give him a few days off," is her advice. "Stay away from the entire topic."

Impossible. I work on Jake night and day. All I've ever known for sure is that he and I will have an amazing kid. Why let our miserable childhoods deprive us of this chance at rebirth?

"I'll do most of the work," I hear myself promise, as if I know what I'm talking about. I'll make any deal I can get away with. "You have no idea how much you're going to love our baby."

I get through the next few days by giving my students extra conference time and taking yoga classes. "I'm searching my soul," Jake tells me during our fifth or sixth discussion. I start to feel optimistic until he adds, "But honestly, Ruth. Having a baby sounds like climbing Mount Everest. I understand the desire, but I'm just not ready to sign up for the trip."

"No one's ever really *ready."* (Thank God I remember the line Rhonda used on Reggie, who was just as down on the baby idea and now wants another one.)

Rose is worried. "Didn't Jake say he'd go back into therapy?"

My shrink needs a reality check. She's been married so long, to the kind of *mensch* who's now extinct, that she has no idea what a wasteland it is out there. At my advanced age, you don't give a handsome, faithful lover reasons to jump ship. Most of the men I've slept with are light years from their emotions and wouldn't go near a shrink if their life depended on it, but at least Jake's a believer.

"I want to accomplish so much more than simply *reproducing*," Jake tells Rose in the emergency session he agrees to. "Ruth and I both have important work to do." I'm relieved he includes me in that sentence.

"Children inspire great science." Rose tells Jake about her husband, a Harvard-educated physicist who considers their children the secret of his success. They help balance his life. In fact, he thinks parenthood is essential for any scientist.

Jake takes a deep breath and his face softens as if he's suddenly under a spell.

"I realize Ruth doesn't have a lot of time," he says. "I guess I don't want her to miss what could be her only chance to have a baby."

Rose and I are stunned at this startling display of generosity.

The real Jake is finally speaking, open to what simply is. This is why I love him. The man can grow.

"You've got a decent deal here, Ruth," Rose says to me during my next session. "Let him move in."

Even if she's calculating all the couples therapy sessions we'll need, it's blessing enough for me.

"I'm your last boat out of Communist China," Jake says, climbing loftward with a bottle of champagne.

I hear Ella singing Gershwin. Our love is here to stay.

* * *

JAKE HAS HAPPILY given up his apartment and dumped two dozen cartons of books and papers into mine. His elegant suits look great in my closet, but since we hardly go out anymore, he only wears them for business meetings. I don't fit into my best outfits these days, anyway. My idea of a great evening is reading baby-name books together. Odysseus would be Ody for short. Lulu. Persephone.

"I'll be done with this report in a few days," Jake promises, flipping through stacks of pages with nothing but numbers on them.

Time is of the essence.

A few months ago *I* was of the essence, but now my lover has different priorities. The meter's always running; I can practically hear Jake *ticking*. When he's finally too tired to work anymore, I get his full attention. If I can stay awake that late.

It takes me a while to realize that, in his opinion, shopping, cooking, and cleaning are negligible time-wasters. At first our commingled laundry thrilled me: his charcoal grey jockeys and tees swimming gracefully among my colorful panties and sports bras. I'd joined the conjugal world I'd yearned for. What was a little extra housework?

Now I'm tired of treating my paramour like a weekend guest and washing his sweaty dance outfits. After lugging our clean clothes up five flights and ringing the buzzer in vain one Saturday morning, I put everything down to hunt for my key and drag everything inside. Still on the phone, just as he was when I left two hours ago, Jake gestures that he's on a business call (what else?) and needs utter silence.

The apartment's still a wreck. "You said you'd vacuum," I snarl loudly enough so his client can hear me. He shoots me his evilest scowl. "I have deadlines, too." I dump his clean shirts and pants on the dirty floor and storm out again.

When I come back after walking all the way to the East River, trying out ultimatums, Jake's as furious as I am. "You're the one who wants a baby, so I'm working harder to make that possible. I thought you understood that when you said you'd pick up the slack for a little while."

"You spend most of your time writing statistical papers. What's that got to do with improving our lifestyle? You're not the only one around here who's trying to get published." My overdue tantrum feels exhilarating.

Steam's coming out of Jake's ears by now. "My clients won't hire me unless they're impressed with my publications. Why can't you understand that?"

My teaching salary is pathetic, and my published stories haven't made me a marketable commodity. I've sent my first collection, *Sailing Around Manhattan*, to a dozen literary agents in vain. All I write these days are mean journal entries about the last-resort sperm donor I found in the nick of time.

"I want to make my mark on the world before we have this baby, too," I wail at him. Jake's most seductive line comes back to me: *Your work is very, very important to me, Ruth.*

"I want to take good care of you and our family," he says. "But someone has to be the actual provider."

He's got me there. Whenever it comes to money, which is frequently these days, Jake holds all the trump cards. As soon as he started mowing lawns when he was twelve, his parents charged him rent. Compared to him, I've had a practically free ride: arty summer camps, an expensive college (instead of being proud of me for getting in, my father bragged that he paid cash for it), lots of traveling.

And the therapy I needed to recover from getting cash instead of love.

After counting every penny and buying cheap hamburgers during the Depression, my parents launched Pool Paradise, a leap of faith in the late fifties. Palatial homes were blooming all over Connecticut and my dad was the friendliest salesman in the state. *Turn your backyard into the Riviera. Make your neighbors envious.* My mother kept the books. Business — and therefore life — was good.

"Don't worry about the money," they told me when I wanted to quit my tedious copy editing job at *Cosmo* and go to graduate school in Paris. I stayed in Europe for three years, taught at the Sorbonne, worked for a London barrister, and supplemented my pay with the checks my parents sent to American Express.

Writers need experiences, so I collected them, often in the form of boyfriends. A Polish one in Paris, an Irish one in Andalucía. Back in New York, I dabbled in television news, wrote travel articles and comic books.

There was a bill for all my wanderlust, which I still pay with shame.

"Don't worry about money," they said. Unfortunately, very unfortunately, I listened.

I retreat from our argument, giving my lover — the one with

the actual money-making skills, who waited tables through college and graduate school — the benefit of all my doubts.

And, as if he's rigged the game, Jake marches in the next day victorious; he's snared a new client. He hands me yellow roses. (I don't like *any* color roses, but I'll tell him another time.) "How did I get so lucky?" he asks, pouring us *Entre Deux Mers* while I cook shad and asparagus.

I don't ask if he's referring to me and the baby or to his new project, because I know. But I want to reach forgiveness. I fill the bathtub and light a joint. The medical studies I've read about marijuana's effect on the fetus conclude it's safe enough. "Good for de momma and good for de baby," my Jamaican student, a mother of three, has assured me.

I remember the desert and that all will be well. I have Jake's best version of love, and he'll never leave me. I'm *his* last boat out of solitude. My real life has finally started. Our child is already leading me toward the self I've never known. Both of us — all three of us — will be brand new.

       *   *   *

TIME TO BITE the bullet and let my parents meet my new boyfriend — before I look pregnant and they panic because I'm having their grandchild out of wedlock. They're coming to town to take me out for my birthday. If my faultfinding dad knew about my latest achievement, he'd have a field day. Even if Jake were an acceptable fiancé — which he certainly isn't — Irving has offended every boyfriend I've made the mistake of letting him meet.

My father is Grouchoesque, a brutally funny man whose sarcasm knows no bounds. He humiliates anyone in his line of fire. I'm his favorite target. No matter what I tell him about myself, it's more proof I do everything wrong. And despite all my therapy, I still get sucked into pointless father-daughter battles. I'll never get what I really want, which is his respect. He puts me down and I explode in vain; my mother begs us to stop and runs for cover. Once, in my twenties, I kicked Irving in the shins after he called me a horse's ass. My mother knew he deserved it, but all she said was, "Don't be so sensitive. He doesn't mean it."

Did she really believe that crap?

How was I supposed to navigate the tricky straits of love? So I found boyfriend after momentary boyfriend. Who wanted anyone to stick? That could be dangerous.

■　■　■

MY PARENTS AGREE to drive into the city all the way from New Haven to meet my live-in boyfriend. Irving always gets a headache in my neighborhood. "Don't ask us to climb all those stairs," he groans. "We'll have heart attacks." He doesn't see the charm of what he calls my slum apartment, even though my building was once an elegant Yiddish actors' club. "Is there something wrong with elevators?" he asks me. "Why live like this?"

And now I have to let him meet Jake, who has all the makings of a provocateur. I'm sorry I've told Jake my story. My dad's social graces are limited to wisecracks, and Jake lacks that kind of humor. But I'm ready to walk through fire to get this ordeal over with.

"*You'll* have to be the adult," I warn the father of my unborn child while we wait in front of my building for my father's Mercedes to pull up.

"So you're the guy Ruth thinks she loves this time," Irving lobs as soon as we climb into the back seat. I elbow Jake to shut up while directing my father toward the Lower East Side.

"Manhattan is so exciting!" my mother says as we creep through traffic.

"If you like getting mugged," Irving adds. We finally get to Sammy's Romanian, and I convince my dad his car won't be stolen if we park on Chrystie Street. I'd rather take that chance than hear him complain about the price of a garage, but it's a toss-up. I'm hoping Sammy's *heymish* atmosphere, the klezmer music and insulting waiters will save us from a catastrophe. At least my dad will love *schmearing* chicken fat on his rye bread.

I'm praying we can keep up the polite façade until the high-octane slivovitz takes effect. "Ruth has always had man trouble," Irving tells Jake. "I guess her father's a tough act to follow."

Despite my begging, Jake grabs the bait. "That's interesting," he fires back. "She hasn't told me one good thing about you."

"What's the matter, the guy can't take a joke?" My dad has always been aggravatingly perceptive.

I have no appetite for my tenderloin. "Did anyone ever say you look like Cary Grant?" my mother asks Jake, to keep the conversation rolling.

"No," he says. "Because I don't."

"Jake has his doctorate from UCLA, and his consulting work is really taking off," I try.

"Actually, I never got the doctorate," he corrects me. "My thesis advisor was a moron." At every other table people are having the time of their lives. I order myself another glass of slivovitz. Somebody has to celebrate my fortieth.

As if his potential nightmare of a son-in-law—or something like that—will try to beat him to it, Irving grabs the check dramatically and groans when he sees it.

"I'd love to meet your parents," my mother tells Jake while we're putting on our coats.

"I haven't seen them in years," he informs her.

"Never put me in the same room with that jerk again," my lover mumbles after my parents zoom toward the safety of Connecticut, my futile mission sort of accomplished.

My heartburn won't be from the chopped liver, but I know enough not to discuss the unfortunate evening. Stressed out from all the changes I'm putting him through, my lover retreats into darkness for a few days.

"That guy's a beaut!" my father says when I finally call.

"Oh, Irving!" On another phone, my mother tries to change the subject. "Don't listen to him, Ruth."

"Everyone will get along once the baby's born," Rhonda assures me. But her husband is well-mannered and her father was her biggest fan, so what does she know?

5.
hurricane

WHEN A BEASTLY Manhattan July strikes, I convince Jake he'll be more productive in the peaceful country. Instead of teaching summer school, I've vowed to finish my collection of stories. We could have shared a beach house in the Hamptons with my friends, but Jake insists we rent our own place. We end up stranded on Long Island's more affordable North Fork in a falling-apart monstrosity that reminds me of Grey Gardens.

I love living at the beach, but there's no one to talk to besides Jake, who's always working. I'm writing a story about Harris, the man I wanted more than anyone, who never wanted me. I spend the rest of my time on the phone with commiserating girlfriends or reading about pregnancy and nutrition. And I sleep a lot.

Once in a while we play tennis or ride our bikes, but, except for sex and meals, we hardly see one another. I've made the mistake of thinking we're on vacation, a foreign concept to Jake. "You have no idea how hard a normal person has to work to make ends meet," he says when I try to get him to go swimming.

Jake is always happy to remind me of my unrealistic expectations. When I feel too woozy to stand up one night, my lover gallantly volunteers to make us a salad for dinner. I'm touched by his tender gesture — until I taste sand in the lettuce he didn't bother to wash. "I'm eating dirt!" I scream.

He flies into a rage: "You never appreciate how much I do for you. I'm sorry to say this, Ruth, but being pregnant is making you selfish."

If only I were selfish enough to leave you right this minute, I think bitterly. But our child needs its father, so I have to find a way to resurrect the man who so excited me with his grand vision of life on the night we met.

Was that the last time we danced?

It takes us several exhausting hours to figure out that Jake's upset about work. When I find out his newest client didn't like the report he put a hundred hours into, I'm sympathetic. We promise one another we'll get better at this.

Thank God for the hurricane. "It's raining in the living room," I yell up to Jake, who's wonderful in an emergency. We've taped sheets of plastic over the windows and hauled in food, batteries, and candles. After we lose power and Jake can't work, we ride out the dramatic storm by giving one another massages and making daytime love. I catch a glimpse of his strong body and my graceful, still lithe one in the mirror. When we smile, we look like we belong together.

The storm over, we generate another squall. Something to do with my sudden craving for fried clams when we already have hamburgers. I walk on the rocky beach and reassure myself out loud. *We've been ambushed by this startling pregnancy. We'll work everything out. But first things first. We're going to have a baby.*

※　※　※

ONE QUIET AUGUST night, a group of my pre-Jake summer buddies appears in our driveway to surprise me. I haven't seen my old beach gang in ages. "We're finally taking you up on your invitation for dinner," they tease me. Thrilled, I put on loud reggae while Susie, Paul, Annie, and Jeff march in with bags of lobsters and corn. Jake seems to like this excuse to kick back and pours everyone wine.

We find the lobster pot, lemons, and butter and strip the corn. Soon we're all laughing and Jake has finally joined my world. I'm wearing a short pink skirt and my tank top barely contains my extra cleavage; I feel sultry in the moonlight. A short while later, I notice Jake tossing lobster shells and corn husks into the trash even though some of us are still eating. Party time is clearly over.

"I guess we'll head back to the South Fork," Susie says, taking Jake's not-so-subtle hint.

"Promise you'll come again," I say before they drive off.

"I can't believe what a mess they made," Jake complains.

"Does it matter that I had a fabulous time?" He's inspecting a possibly recent cigarette burn on an old porch table. I wash the dishes, sweep the floor, then fall asleep on the couch, as far away from our bedroom as possible. Jake doesn't come and get me the way he did the last time we argued.

After Jake leaves the next day on a business trip, I call Rhonda at her summer house on the Vineyard. Reggie's building a tree house for the kids and growing vegetables. "We have the best salads for lunch," she says. I'm sure Reggie washes every lettuce leaf. "Can you feel the baby move yet?"

"I thought I did a week ago, but now I'm not sure. My breasts don't feel tender anymore."

"Being pregnant makes you worry about everything. How are things with Jake?"

"He's away, so they're good right now."

The next day Jake calls from Southern California. The client he's working for is close to where his parents live. He hasn't spoken to them in years, a scary fact in the back of my mind. Proud he's about to be a father, he planned to tell them the big news and make peace with his past.

"It's time to set things straight between us," he said before he left. Jake once told me, in tears, that his father hit him—often. "I got away as soon as I could," he said, "at sixteen."

I'm proud of him for wanting to see his parents, but his agenda sounds more like a showdown. "Are you prepared for that kind of conversation?" I ask.

"What kind of question is that?"

Jake has apparently given his parents an hour's notice. "Maybe you should start by forgiving them." A foreign concept, I know.

"Frankly, Ruth, I thought you'd be more supportive." He practically hangs up on me.

When he calls back later, he's in a panic. "I said they'd almost ruined my life. Then, you won't believe this, they both just stood up and ran out of the restaurant. Before our food came. I never even told them they're going to be fucking grandparents!"

I'm as sorry for the man I think I love as I should be for myself.

And for our kid, who's lost his or her chance to have two sets of grandparents.

   ❧ ❧ ❧

A MICROSCOPIC HEART is supposed to be thumping in the tiny body inside mine, but it doesn't feel that way. I have no strange cravings and plenty of energy. I'm not peeing more than usual, and I can blame my decreased libido on other things. Am I in such good shape from all the yoga, biking, and swimming that gestation is no big deal? It's easy to put my anxiety on hold all summer, but as soon as we get back to the city I make the scary appointment with Dr. Spencer.

At first he reassures me that everything's fine, but after he examines me internally and orders an ultrasound, I know something's wrong.

"I'm so sorry." Spencer looks down at his expensive shoes and shakes his head. "It's a blighted ovum."

I stare at him.

"Very common at this stage," he reports, his compassion weak. "It's really a good thing. Your body detected something was wrong with the fetus."

I'd finally absorbed the *good* shock. What do I do with the horrible kind?

"You can try again in three or four months," the nurse says cheerily. She makes my miscarriage seem like nothing more than a rained-out baseball game. The dream I didn't have until it was almost too late is over forever.

I wish I'd never had it in the first place. I stare bitterly at every mother and child on the interminable bus ride down Second Avenue. Who did I think I was, trying to beat the clock? Why did it take me most of my life to figure out what I was supposed to do with it? The miracle was a mirage.

Jake's kind enough to hide his relief at this reprieve, and doesn't even remind me that our almost-child was badly timed. "We'll have a baby," I think I hear him mumble. *"When we're ready."*

Nature does away with imperfections, according to the books I read. "Spontaneous abortions" are common. Our future child has an excellent chance of being born. I'm supposed to grieve, create a ritual: bury rose petals and pray for a stronger soul next time around. "Truly felt pain carries us forward," says Rose, who miscarried once herself.

Jake and I weren't supposed to have a baby so fast, but we

already almost *did* have one. I've fallen into a dark, barren limbo where nothing matters. He tolerates my moping for a week, until his sympathy expires and we start snapping at one another again.

                    ⅏   ⅏   ⅏

FALL, THEN WINTER stalemate. I'm writing a story, called "A Route of One's Own," about finding a lover while traveling alone in the Lake District. It's nice to float back to my adventurous past, when life seemed so much simpler.

"You have to create your own destiny," Jake enlightens me. Easier said than done. Our kid would have had his analytic mind and my imagination. She—I was sure we'd have a girl—would have had the sense of humor I've lost forever, and she'd have danced better than we do. Or did. I want her back. I'll never ask for anything unlikely again.

After teaching classes all day, I drag myself uptown to Rhonda's, who orders in Chinese and helps me strategize.

"Go away for a romantic weekend," she decides. I'm drinking the brandy Reggie poured me before he disappeared to read the kids a story.

"Too extravagant. Jake would never go for it."

"So treat him." Rhonda convinces me that this is one of those times when money should be no object. That I need to keep my eyes on the prize.

The next day I make Jake's favorite chicken soup with dill and garlic. "What about taking a few days off between projects?" I ask while he sips the ambrosia.

"You're joking, Ruth. Did you forget I have two grant applications due?"

"What about after you finish them?"

"I have to write that paper for the biostat conference in Cleveland."

"You always have your best ideas when you go away." I unwrap éclairs from Veniero's. "Didn't you tell me your brilliant T-cell formula came to you while you were hiking in Yosemite?"

"That was fifteen years ago." When Jake let himself enjoy a casual California life. I drop the subject. I have fifty student essays to read: *Write about someone who has made a strong impression on you.* Grandparents, ministers, camp counselors. Ralph Vinatella, who fought in Vietnam and now operates an elevator, writes about his hero, Picasso, who *believed in himself, and let nothing stand in his way.* Ralph never knew either of his parents, grew up in foster homes, and went through various rehabs. Now he's raising a family and becoming a graphic designer. Where does he get his tenacity?

I love my students, even the unappreciative ones who don't care if their sentences say anything. When I help them express their ideas more vividly, they swell with pride and thank me for making them work so hard.

A few weeks later, a bioengineering firm in Cambridge hires Jake for a prestigious project. He's sure this will put his career over the top so he can design his own studies. What a great time to get him to leave town.

"Maybe that's not such a bad idea," he says. "What about two nights?" I was hoping for three. I admire his almost superhuman drive, but we need more balance.

Rhonda knows the perfect place on Nantucket, overpriced, but remote and charming.

"It's a bargain this time of year," she assures me. "You'd never get a reservation in season." I was thinking about a motel in Montauk, but since Rhonda has two children, I might as well take her advice.

The first Friday in April, we take a taxi to LaGuardia and fly directly to the exclusive but increasingly corporate former whaling capital. Another taxi takes us to a weathered inn overlooking the pounding grey Atlantic. It's too dank to go outside for long, so we make a fire, eat the picnic dinner I've packed. And go to bed early.

Jake's proud of his latest assignment, and optimistic about his career. I've gotten excellent student and faculty reviews, so he's proud of me, too. Things go well between us in our pre-season, rose-covered Siasconset cottage, where we recreate our child. This time on purpose.

   ※ ※ ※

As soon as I find out, I want to call everyone I know and have a wild party, but I settle for one slow dance at home with Jake. He's satisfied with our efficiently timed accomplishment. We're ready for some smooth sailing.

Soon I'm nauseous all the time, and I almost kill myself racing down the loft stairs to the bathroom several times a night. My body's so busy my mind has never been this calm. The bitter city winter feels mild, even when I'm blasted with gale forces walking through midtown wind tunnels.

After Dr. Spencer gives me a Polaroid of our blob of pulsing ectoplasm, Jake and I go to Little Italy to discuss our options. I play with the wax dripping down a Chianti bottle while he tries to convince me we've got plenty of room for an eight-pound baby in my apartment. "You said babies can sleep in a dresser drawer," he reminds me.

"Sure, but not *forever*." Generations of mothers have raised large families in tiny walk-up apartments, but it doesn't sound easy. Bigger places in Manhattan cost way too much, so we're destined for the far reaches of Brooklyn or Queens, i.e., Siberia. Or even farther. *Life is change*, according to my Kundalini teacher.

I'm mildly queasy when I order my dinner. By the time the waiter brings our food, the smell makes me sick. *"Buon appetito,"* I yell, running outside to find a taxi. "Bring my dinner home. No point wasting the *osso buco*."

I make it up seventy-five stairs to the bathroom just in time and heave cathartically. I lie on the cool tile floor and enjoy the blue, fluffy-clouded *trompe l'oeil* sky my artist boyfriend, Tony, painted on the ceiling. Then the phone disturbs my reverie.

"I was just about to call you, Mom." Time to fill her in. "Are you sitting down? I've got big news." I hear her brace herself. *What is it this time?*

"I'm going to have a baby." Dead silence.

"That's so exciting, darling." She sounds more confused than enthusiastic, but my parents gave up on grandkids so long ago I'm sure she's in shock.

"Irving!" she shouts over the television. *"Pick up the phone!"*

I was hoping he was out and she'd update him for me. "Hi, Dad. Jake and I are going to have a baby."

"So when's the wedding? I'm not crazy about the guy, but he's better than nothing."

"Well, we're kind of postponing that for now." I want to hang up before his inevitable tirade: How can I do such a terrible thing to my parents? Is this what they get for being so good to me? The guy's annoying, but I should marry him anyway so Irving and Stella can hold their heads up in New Haven.

I'm still doing my life all wrong. What else is new.

Such a serious undertaking with Jake is a scary gamble, but I'm grabbing my final chance to do, sort of, what my parents always expected me to, and all I get is disapproval. Pretty hard to weather on top of the nausea, but I resist the urge to slam down the phone. "We'll probably get married. Eventually," I pander. "But right now we have other priorities."

More silence. I should have left out the "probably," but I don't want to give them false hope.

If Jake weren't such a loose cannon, if our partnership were a little more solid, we *would* get married. He actually wants to, and even offered to take a long lunch break and do it at City Hall. "Someday," I've told him, "when we're ready."

"We have to find a place to live," I say, since Stella and Irving are waiting for more data.

"So *this* is what it takes to get you out of that terrible neighborhood?" And here comes the spiel I know by heart. "I suppose we'll have to help you. If we didn't work so hard, your life would be an even worse mess than it already is."

"Irving!" Stella chides him. "He doesn't really mean it, Ruth."

We both know he does. But if Jake and I don't move soon, I'm going to ask the man who delivers my groceries to carry me up the stairs as well.

"You'll appreciate Jake eventually," I tell them, and thank them for standing by me — sort of.

As soon as I've put that fire out, the other one walks in the door.

"I just told my parents." I search Jake's face for compassion, but the best he can do is hand me a doggie bag. "Don't go in the bathroom until I clean up."

"Stop worrying," Rhonda reassures me. "Reggie and I couldn't stand each other during both my pregnancies. But everything will change as soon as you have your baby." So far, she's always been right. But as soon as Rhonda was pregnant, she and Reggie moved into an apartment with a washing machine and a dryer.

The next several weekends Jake and I go apartment-hunting

in Hoboken, Flushing, and Flatbush. It's the middle of my second trimester and the best place we've seen is a basement apartment in Williamsburg, which hasn't been discovered yet.

Then Jake comes home excited. His client in Cambridge, Massachusetts, wants to hire him full-time. Boston trumps Brooklyn; and there are so many colleges there, maybe one of them will hire me.

More good news: I call an old poet friend named Donald who's now a pediatrician at Boston City Hospital. "I'll book you in with a great obstetrician," he says. "She'll let you push for hours."

I guess that's supposed to be a good thing.

Maybe Jake and I are bringing fortune to one another after all, because I finally get The Call I've been waiting for all my life, from a prominent literary agent. "Ruth Kooperman? It's Riva Rosenholtz. I love your stuff. Let's get together."

Halleluiah. Wearing a new pair of lacy black tights and a black-and-blue-striped tent dress, I drink Perrier in Riva's office, pinching myself. "I should have good news for you very soon," she assures me. After nothing but dashed hopes for years, I've been discovered. Who would want to be married if they could be published instead?

6.

you bet your life

JAKE AND I TAKE the train to Boston where he sails through his interview at a biotech company near MIT. He looks great in a new suit and his manners improve when he wears one, so I'm full of hope about our imminent new life. We stay with my friend Donald in Jamaica Plain, where the lilac-scented Arnold Arboretum feels like Eden compared to noisy, swarming Central Park. It only takes us a few days to find a ground-floor flat in a Victorian house near Jamaica Pond, an amazing bargain compared to anything we could rent in New York. We're in sync with the universe and even with each other.

Then the reality hits me: I actually have to move far, far away. Extricate myself from my entire *life,* abandon my rent-controlled haven in my beloved neighborhood, the only place I've ever belonged. How can I leave glorious Gotham, the pulsing, electric universe whose power keeps me *on.*

I won't be able to meet Rhonda and her kids in the park, or have smashed tuna sandwiches at the B&H Dairy with my poet friend Annie. No more Gem Spa egg creams. I won't run into Allen Ginsberg in his adorable Bermuda shorts at St. Mark's Bookstore, or my students in Tompkins Square Park. I'm banishing myself from my phantasmagoric, nurturing homeland full of wild, kindred spirits.

How will I survive without *tartufos* from Veniero's, cherry-filled pierogies, coconut samosas, and blueberry blintzes?

"Change involves sacrifice," Jake preaches when I whimper about going into exile in New England. I want to strangle him. After fourteen years in the East Village, I'm unequipped to survive anywhere else.

Then the real panic sets in: I'll have to become a *mother*: selfless, devoted, nurturing. My mother performed the job mostly by remote control, so I haven't inherited maternal genes. And now I'll be too far away from Rhonda to copy her.

Existential confusions like these call for my favorite distraction. I head down to Delancey Street for my final Lower East Side shopping spree and come home with a knitted black-and-red-striped designer maternity dress, silk pajamas for Jake, and a killer pair of lace-up boots. On my last stop, I stock up at the pot store.

Where will I buy the stuff in Boston? It's been my most inspiring friend ever since Tony, the surrealist painter, rolled me one of his elegant joints. I wanted to be an artist, too, and my first acrid throatful of smoke made that feel possible. I danced around his loft to Django Reinhardt more rhythmically than ever before, and could barely write down all the poetry that came to me in a midnight rush.

Smoking was inhaling self-love, balm for the wounds I never knew I had. Other sources of self-worth—jobs, accomplishments, even friendships—only lasted as long as tides. All I needed was a few deep inhalations to feel entitled to whatever I wanted: where to sit or lie, what to eat or drink. All was suddenly, utterly right in my world.

Jake isn't crazy about my indulgence, but he knows it helps me deal with him, so he doesn't interfere.

■ ■ ■

AFTER WEEKS OF arguing over every detail (which books to keep, what size boxes to pack, what moving company to hire), Jake and I follow an enormous truck five hours north in our new Honda. Our huge new apartment helps me fight back my tears. Frederick Law Olmsted's Emerald Necklace will be all around us. And everyone, even Rhonda, says Boston's a wonderful place to raise a kid.

Jake throws himself into his new job and I'm left with a home to create and utter solitude. I'm grateful for so much nature, and I love being far away from Manhattan's noise. But stranded in what feels like the provinces, with only Jake to hold onto, I'm dangerously out of orbit. Jamaica Plain's Center Street is monotonous; the café, natural food restaurant, and small bookstore are practically empty. I miss my familiar *shtetl*, my job and my friends. I feel like a refugee.

Jake has no friends to miss, so he's hardly sympathetic. "This was all *your* idea," he reminds me. "Try to develop more of a pioneer spirit."

What a brilliant idea! Why didn't I think of that?

"Maybe you should look for another job."

I ignore his suggestion. I'm six months pregnant, and someone has to cook, clean, and furnish our empty apartment. I haven't told Jake yet that my parents have offered to send me a monthly stipend so I can stay home with their grandchild for a while.

"What else is the money for?" my mother assured me. The closest she and I ever come to each other is when she makes me feel OK about my father's generosity. Even though she helped him make the money, our family resources are officially considered my father's accomplishment. But Jake considers all parents toxic resources, and doesn't want me to accept any help.

With her bottomless trust fund, Rhonda is way ahead of me when it comes to getting over cash-induced guilt. "Just because you didn't make the money doesn't mean you didn't earn it," is her theory.

         ❊   ❊   ❊

DETERMINED TO TURN our drafty flat into home, I paint the kitchen lemon-yellow and splatter-paint a secondhand crib. The baby needs clothes and I need shoes for my suddenly larger feet. I drive from one depressing mall to the next in scary traffic, always hungry and frantically lost.

"You could starve here," I tell Rhonda. "I'd give anything to meet you for a bowl of mushroom barley soup and a thick slice of *challah*." If only we could have afforded Morningside Heights or Chelsea. But Boston's beauty is comforting. I walk around and around Jamaica Pond, practically accosting women with babies in search of new friends who know the ropes.

"Reggie and I met so many couples in birthing class," Rhonda suggests. So I sign us up at a New Agey center in Cambridge where Jake and I feel old and odd among the Gen-X pairs whose lives have always been on track. Watching childbirth videos, practicing massage, and breathing on Wednesday nights are the high points of my winter weeks, and our entire social life.

There are so many alternative kinds of childbirth to learn about, I plunge into the research. Should I hire a midwife, a doula, or a birthing coach? Should we have our baby at home? What about an underwater birth, to avoid the stress of gravity? My new pregnant friends have so much information and we talk about nothing else. I follow their advice and make my obstetrician promise not to give me drugs unless I beg for them.

"I begged," says Rhonda. "And you will, too."

I read *The Power of Pregnant Sex,* which Jake always finds time for. He's as proud of my voluptuous, huge body as I am, proof we can accomplish things. I eat kale, collard greens, and calf's liver, and sing to our already-conscious child. According to *Motherhood* magazine, I should surround myself with beauty, so I walk in the brilliant fall arboretum, its trees from all over the world. Sometimes Jake comes with me and we talk a blue streak about our child. When the days get colder, I wander through the Museum of Fine Arts, staring at Gauguins, Rothkos, and bronze Buddhas.

I listen to Beethoven's *Pastoral* Symphony. And I cry a lot.

◦ ◦ ◦

I MISS MY KUNDALINI master Siv Sivaranda, who taught me the Breath of Fire. "Keep this up if you want to pull in a great soul," Siv advised me before I left. Guruless, I search for a new refuge where I can stretch, breathe, and chant my heart out.

After trying several run-of-the-mill classes, I discover Master Wah, a Korean acupuncturist, yogi, and martial artist who has quite a following. He's the most serious teacher I've ever had, small in stature, huge in strength and ego. Soon I'm a regular at his To Life! healing studio, where I contort my oddly shaped body into challenging *asanas.* When my legs feel numb, Master Wah's tiny wife, Gyonsi, massages them gently and coaxes me into strange poses.

"Hurting now so baby come out easy," she reassures me. All her childbirths were, apparently, pain-free, so I do whatever she tells me to.

* * *

JAKE PROMISED WE could go to New Hampshire for some cross-country skiing before it's too late, and now that I'm eight months pregnant, it probably is. But I still want to try. "You could fall and hurt the baby," he protests, trying to weasel out of the trip.

"The doctor said exercise is good for me," I insist, leaving out that she said it months ago.

After we rent our skis, our White Mountain innkeeper notices my state with surprise. "We're pretty far from a hospital," he says. "If you have an emergency, the veterinarian's just down the road."

"He wasn't kidding," Jakes says while I laugh. My due date isn't for another two weeks, and I'm just not the worrying type. But moving precariously over the icy snow is more terrifying than exhilarating. Jake manages better than I do, even though he's never done this before. I can't wait until we're here again with our child strapped on his back.

Back home I practice the *asanas* Master Wah says will help my baby glide effortlessly into the light. Once my due date comes and goes, it's hard to get myself out and around the pond. I have plenty of books to read about my imminent profession, and Rhonda suggests I knit a baby blanket.

"Tell Jake to stock up on food and diapers," she says. As if. My parents call from somewhere — the Seychelles? — to report on the weather and the lovely people they've met on their freighter trip.

"Do you need anything, darling?" my mother asks after she

remembers I'm with child. Since motherly advice isn't an option, I tell her I'm all set. "Isn't someone throwing you a baby shower?"

I hardly know anyone, and I'm not the shower type anyway. "I've got a crib and a changing table, and I ordered a stroller," I tell her.

"How much was it, Ruth?" my dad wants to know. "I'll send you a check."

"That's OK." I'd rather pay for it than give him sticker shock.

7.
good old william blake

SATURDAY, FEBRUARY 29, 1987. Just after Jake dashes out the door one morning, my waters finally break, but he drives off too fast to hear me calling after him.

"When are you coming home?" I ask when I reach him on the phone.

"You're not even in labor yet. Panicking will make it harder to have this baby." He sounds so well informed you'd think he'd already had a few kids himself.

"But I'm scared. Can't you work at home today?"

"Why don't you write about what you're going through?"

What a great idea—except I can't sit up without feeling nauseous. After he goes, I leave my obstetrician, Maggie, a message. Her nurse eventually calls back to say, "You have a long, *long* way to go. Just keep us posted."

I'm only a mile away, so I'm sure they'll hear me scream.

I'm eating cold vegetable soup to keep up my strength and watching *Gone With the Wind* for the third time. Just when the birth scene begins ("I don't know nuffin bout birfin babies, Miss Scarlett") I feel the terrifying cramping of an actual contraction. When Jake finally returns my hysterical call, stabbing knives of pain have thrown me to the floor and I can barely talk.

"Stay calm!" he shouts frantically. "Get the spreadsheet I printed out and start filling in how long your contractions last and how far apart they are. Did you get the stopwatch?"

Gee, honey, it slipped my mind. I'm on the floor, bicycling my legs and trying to do a shoulder stand to relieve the pressure. Each time I'm slammed, I muffle my shrieks in a pillow so the neighbors won't call the police. By late afternoon, when there's no time between attacks to recuperate, Jake's secretary promises to make him go home.

He bursts through the door like a hero, ready to take charge. I've changed out of my sopping nightgown into sweatpants and one of Jake's shirts. "Where's the spreadsheet? Did you rate the pain on a scale of one to ten?" If he'd look at me, trembling, white, and delusional with agony, instead of at the piles of paper on his desk, he could tell. "Ruth!" he shouts. "I need some data!"

If I faint, it's a ten.

"Let's see. It's four thirty-seven. I'll put this one down as a five."

I spend the next several excruciating hours running to the bathroom while Jake stares at the computer. When I wail too loudly while he's on a business call, he goes outside to continue the conversation. "What about a sandwich?" he asks, making a batch of tuna fish. The smell makes me gag.

"Things could be worse," he says. He's engrossed in a documentary about the Holocaust that he wishes I'd watch for a little perspective. Back in the bathroom again, I take a few medicinal tokes of grass. *Good for de momma . . . good for de baby, too!* as they say in Jamaica.

I open a window so Jake won't smell the pungent aroma, then spend a blissful fifteen minutes in the bathtub between contractions. *All my troubles, Lord, soon be over.* Maybe I should have checked out water births, which are so popular in France. The babies, still umbilically attached, just float gracefully to the surface and start swimming!

The next knife of pain cuts through me. I almost drown getting out of the tub mid-contraction and crawl, naked, into the hall. "Where the hell are you?" I howl. While Jake checks our to-do list, I wrestle myself into my sweats and put the joint into my toiletry bag.

Maggie calls a few times to check on me. (What would she say if she knew my self-medication strategy?) "Stay home as long as you possibly can, but don't wait too long," is her professional advice. Am I deranged or is this confusing?

"Where's your suitcase?" Jake asks. All I've packed so far is the latest *New Yorker*, a book called *Spiritual Childbirth*, and a toothbrush; I grab a pair of clean panties, flip-flops, and the soft, long t-shirt I bought ages ago on Crete, to remind me of my long-lost freedom.

Why didn't Jake give me a designer peignoir? What will my baby think when she realizes her mother's wearing a *schmatte*?

Jake helps me put on my boots and throws me a blanket since my coat doesn't fit anymore. "Sucking candies," he says. "Check. Massage oil. Mozart CD. Ruth, did you get non-slip socks? What about something for the baby to wear?"

I'm in the middle of another earthquake so I point to a bag of baby clothes in the closet. When it's over, I hobble out to the car and nose-dive into the back seat. "Open the window," I yell while he backs out of the driveway. It's zero degrees out and I'm roasting.

"Breathe. Pant. Count," Jake shouts. Each time I scream he asks me to rate the pain, but I'm too busy communicating with the baby so she'll know what's going on. Since there's hardly any traffic this time of night, we get to Beth Israel in well under the twenty-seven minutes he calculated it would take. *"I want Maggie,"* I sob. "Did you call her? Is she waiting for me?"

The parking lot must be empty. Why is Jake still circling? *"What the fuck are you doing?"* I shriek. Surely I'm entitled to loathe him at a time like this, the pinnacle of my wannabe-bitch career.

He finally stops, turns off the engine, and sits *frozen*, staring at his watch. The next bullet train slams into me. "Please, Jake," I whimper. "Help me out of here."

"Listen to me, Ruth. Your contractions are only coming every seven and a half minutes. You're nowhere *near* fully dilated. It's eleven thirty-seven. Remember what they told us on the hospital tour?"

"What are you talking about? The baby's coming *now*. Get me out of this goddamn car!"

"Our insurance will only pay for you to stay in the hospital *two full calendar days*. If you can control yourself and wait another twenty-three—no, only another twenty-two—minutes, we can check you in *after* midnight. You'll be able to stay a whole day longer!" He's excited about this brilliant way to beat the system.

My legs are numb but I'm afraid to uncross them. If our baby isn't worrying about insurance regulations, why should I? I remember how brave Maria Falconetti was in Dreyer's *Passion of Joan of Arc* after they tied her to the stake. While flames licked her legs, only a tiny tear rolled down her cheek.

"You'll be glad I made you do this, Ruthie. Only twenty-one minutes to go." When he turns on the radio, out blast the Rolling Stones' "Under My Thumb." "Would you rather hear the news?"

"A woman in labor was held hostage in the Beth Israel Hospital parking lot" is the headline I see. Let him take the rap. I'm seeing stars by the time Jake hauls me out of the car into the hospital lobby and

I fall into a wheelchair. He gallantly pushes me to the registration desk to sign a hundred forms. "See?" he points to the clock, proud of his brilliant strategy. "Was that so bad?"

When we finally get to the maternity ward, Jake's waving his flowchart and firing so many questions at the nurses they ignore me. I strip and climb up on the bed naked, which is better than wearing the ugly hospital gown.

My laid-back obstetrician is still home sleeping. Shaking, sweating, crazed, I wrap a sheet around myself and walk down the hall until I find some laboring sisters who *feel* what I'm going through. When the next contraction strikes, I lie on the floor. A woman about to have twins almost trips on me.

By the time I'm back on the bed, Maggie finally shows up, crouched ringside. Thank God I'm spared her view of ground zero. "Your baby's crowning," she shouts. She already knows our baby's sex, but she's being discreet. "Keep up the good work, Ruth." When Jake grills her about fetal monitors and intravenous drips I'm afraid she'll decide to go help someone else have a baby.

But he scores me an illegal Popsicle from the vending machine and sneaks me into the shower, where the hot spray does wonders on my back. He argues with the nurses until they let me crawl around and do *chakravakasana,* the cat and cow pose Mrs. Wah recommended. *Hurting now so baby come out quick.* The woman lied.

"Don't you worry about a *ting*," coos Gloria from Trinidad, reaching deep inside me. "Ooh, that cervix feels *lovely*." Jake massages my lower back and wipes my forehead. His t-shirt is drenched and he could use a shave, but he looks like the gorgeous, self-sacrificing guy I've always known was in there somewhere.

Things seem to be going well until, no matter how hard I toil and how much grit I summon, the baby stops dead in her tracks.

"She's a stubborn shithead, just like you," I tell Jake. Every time he orders me to take a deep breath and shove, I hate him more. "Just let me go home for a little while," I beg the nurses. "I'll come back and have the baby later, I promise."

"I've never heard that one before," Gloria laughs.

Spread-eagle, howling, I curse the medical establishment for its antiquated insistence on horizontal childbirth. Don't they know about gravity? Why can't I squat the way they do in Africa so my baby can just drop? Rushing to my rescue, Jake lifts me off the bed and helps me put my arms around his neck and hang. He coaxes me through more contractions, his voice calm, his arms strong. The gravity thing works. Rhonda warned me that the old cliché is true: it's *exactly* like shitting out a watermelon.

Our baby has dark hair; her head is tipped way back, as if she's laughing at the universe, daring us to drag her from bliss into a complicated world.

"We did it," Jake screams. "Here he is!"

My mother groaned, my father wept
Into the dangerous world I leapt.

Good old William Blake.

"Look at that head of hair!" everyone's shouting. I barely notice we have a son as he emerges in a revolting stew of vernix, blood, meconium, and placenta. Aren't we supposed to plant all that stuff under a tree? Our feisty kid wails, kicks, and punches at the doctors who are poking and probing him. Finally they place our weightless child on my belly so we're skin to skin. He tries and fails to latch onto my nipple. Gloria gives him a bottle of water, swaddles him in a teddy bear blanket, and wheels us both to a quiet room.

"Spoil that beautiful baby rotten," she tells me. If my mother were here, I'd want her to say the same thing.

"Gotta get some sleep so I can work tonight," Jake whispers. "I'll be back in the morning. By the way, is he Luke or Gabriel?"

"He's Joey," I've just decided. Our baby came with his own name. Did I hear someone call it out loud in the elevator last night? Did I dream it? Since Jake has no loyalty to his family name, he's Joey Barth Kooperman.

Jake and I don't tend to argue about what's important.

8.

baby, baby

WHEN I WAKE UP, I'm amazed to see my California cousin sitting next to me, holding Joey neatly in the crook of her arm like a pro. *"Gert?"* She bends down to embrace me and my baby at the same time. "I've been missing you so much," I say.

"I wanted to surprise you. I'd have been here earlier but Jake thought it would be too much of a shock while you were in labor. What a baby! He's got your face and Jake's curls. So gorgeous." Gert rocks Joey back to sleep every time he whimpers. *"Joey, Joey, Joey,"* she sings, reminding me of the song from *Carousel*.

"When you walk through a storm, keep your head up high, and don't be afraid of the dark." I've sung to my baby for so long, I'm sure he knows who I am.

"Too bad your mother's missing this," Gert says.

"Too bad we got gypped in the mom department." Gert's mother, Leonore, and Stella were first cousins and best friends. Neither was happily married or fulfilled by family life.

"Can you imagine our mothers actually bonding with us like this?" she asks.

"They were too drugged." Stella almost died having me, so she was heavily medicated, and Gert's mother, like most fifties women, must have been anesthetized.

Jake marches in, proudly; he's well rested and clean-shaven, wearing his loden green suit and pale pink shirt, which means he's on his way to the office. He races toward Joey, barely looking at me, not pleased he has to share his visit with my cousin.

"Your yoga teacher's wife dropped off this seaweed soup to help your milk come in. Did you see how he fought off all those doctors? That's right, Joey. Don't let anyone tell you what to do!" He holds our tiny boy aloft, then whispers to him privately.

"He's got your hair," Gert tells Jake. "I'll go do some errands. Can I get you anything?"

"Yeah, a new pair of nipples." Every time Joey tries to nurse it hurts more than the labor did. I try to stifle my screams so I don't traumatize him."

"No prob," she says.

Jake sits on my bed and hands me a box of French salt caramels. "Aren't you glad I made you stay and finish the job? You'd still be in the delivery room!" We can't take our eyes off our baby, who has his father's long legs and strong torso. "Is this what I looked like?" he asks tenderly.

We trade Joey back and forth, astonished we've borne such precious fruit. Our good moments are as deep as they are rare.

▪   ▪   ▪

GERT COMES BACK with cream for my cracked nipples and sushi for the two of us. When my luxurious almost-three-day hospital stay is over, I'm surprised they're going to let us take our baby home. I still haven't diapered him or gotten him to sleep, and I have no idea how to actually take care of him.

Strapped into the backward car seat, our tiny guy slumps over, blinking in the daylight, as confused as we are, while Jake drives slowly and triumphantly through a gentle March snowfall.

More than you know, more than you'll ever know. Man of my heart

I miss you so, Ella croons on the radio. I can't wait to play music for my baby boy, music from everywhere. And I'm so grateful Gert's waiting at home and has made us a pot of chili and some chicken soup.

"I hope it's all right, Ruth, but since your cousin's here, I decided not to take my week of paternity leave right now," Jake says. He'll take the time later on, etcetera. "You're going to be such a wonderful mother," I hear before he rushes back to work.

"He'll love our kid," I assure Gert. "Does anything else really matter?"

"You need reliable help," my cousin changes the subject. "I'll make some calls and find you someone."

My parents have sent me a generous check, some lilacs, and, most touching of all, a card for Joey which says, "Welcome to our world!"

After Gert leaves, a sweet young woman who takes her "mother care" profession very seriously comes in every afternoon for a few weeks to make us healthy meals and take care of our squalling newborn.

Despite how much it hurts to feed Joey and how brainless and exhausted I am, I'm reborn into a deep and permanent joy. Who held *me* this tightly, spun me around the room? Why is it so easy to give what I didn't get? After racing in so many false directions, I've reached my destination.

Soon I'm back in yoga class, chanting, breathing, stretching while Joey sleeps nearby. When he wakes, he flashes his Mr. Magoo smile at everyone, as if he's running for office. He looks great in red, so I drive us all over Boston looking for the right outfits. Never has shopping been more fun, although I'm not sure my boy enjoys it as much as I do.

After asking neighbors about babysitters, I find Marietta from

El Salvador who immediately loves my baby as if he were one of her many grandchildren. We communicate perfectly without knowing much of each other's languages, and I love hearing her chatter and sing to Joey in Spanish. She takes him for long walks and always returns him to me asleep so I get another precious hour or so of peace.

The rest of the time, I'm on constant call, passionately devoted to my all-consuming new work. For the first time in my free-wheeling life, I have absolutely no choice about what to do, an amazing relief. I've lost my imagination, my ability to think about anything except what's right in front of me.

Other mothers complain about sleepless nights, so for almost three months I feel incredibly blessed to have a baby who's down from midnight until five or six. But as soon as all the other babies are eating and sleeping at predictable times, mine turns into an insomniac. Marietta is the only one who can get Joey to nap for more than twenty minutes in the daytime, and he nurses every hour or two all night long. Jake, meanwhile, sleeps like a — baby! Anger wells up in me while I rock my weeping, restless child in the predawn darkness. This, too, will change — they tell me.

"Why should my child have to do anything on a schedule?" Jake says when I complain. He wouldn't last a day inexorably enslaved like this, and he'd self-destruct if he couldn't take a shower or read one paragraph or even *think* without being screamed out of it.

Rhonda suggests I hire Marietta for more hours than we can afford. After having her first child, a writer I used to know mentioned that she couldn't find a piece of paper and a pen in time to write a word down. "As far as having your own life," she told me, "you can take the entire first year of motherhood and flush it down the toilet." I assumed she was being dramatic.

Neither Rhonda nor all the books I've devoured have prepared me for the drudgery of this job and its constant emergencies: projectile vomiting, colic, diaper rash, and gas. Sometimes Joey's pain seems just from being alive, which sets off my own, and I worry we'll both drown in existential misery.

When my mother calls for news, she wants to hear that everything's wonderful. If I slip in a complaint, she stops me short. *Things will get easier, dear . . . you'll get through this. You always do . . .* Back in the country, and understandably eager to see their only grandchild, my parents decide to visit when Jake will be in Washington.

They arrive with tiny silk shoes and pajamas for Joey — my miniature Chinese emperor — and an Indonesian silver bracelet for me. They scoop up their prize with tear-inducing joy. It feels good to give them so much pleasure — and to see my boy happily perched on my mother's lap.

The day's excursion is to the museum, Joey's first cultural outing. He seems to notice the colors, but maybe that's our imagination. My dad scuffs along behind me and my mother, not exactly an art appreciator, eager for lunch. We avoid sensitive topics (my financial arrangement with Jake, my still-stalled plans to marry him). Back home, my mother doesn't rush to help me change Joey's diaper, but she's happy to feed him and read to him. My dad tries to get my four-month-old interested in the baseball game.

When I have fifteen minutes of peace, I scribble a sentence or two about the shock of motherhood for a story called "Brain Drain." I even manage to balance Joey *and* my keyboard on pillows on my lap so I can type and nurse Joey at the same time. When the phone rings for the first time all week, I almost drop Joey trying to answer it.

"Ruth? It's Riva Rosenholtz. How *are* you?"

Finally. Ever since our intoxicating rendezvous back in New York, I've been waiting for Riva's triumphant announcement that my book will be published. "I'm terribly disappointed," Riva says, as if she's a waitress telling me they're all out of the meatloaf special. "I really thought someone would snap up *Sailing Around Manhattan*, Ruth, but collections are *so* tough to sell these days."

"What about David Leavitt?" I ask. His story collection, *Family Dancing*, has just made a huge splash.

"He writes about being gay," Riva says. "That's different."

"So being gay is more interesting than being a wandering Jewish princess whose rotten relationship with her philistine father keeps her from finding love?" I blurt out.

Must be the hormones.

After a very dead silence, Riva comes up with a great suggestion. "Why don't you just turn all these terrific stories into a novel? There's more of a market for longer fiction." As if entirely rewriting five years of work will be as easy as throwing away a dozen cupcakes and baking a brand new cake.

Struck at the knees before I've had my chance to stand tall, I struggle to keep myself from pleading with her to send the book to more editors.

"*Shit.*"

"Pardon me?"

How can I tell Riva that Joey's just exploded all over me? Mustardy excrescence is sliding down my leg. "Can I call you back?"

"That's not necessary, Ruth. Just give me a call when the novel's finished, all right?"

Why don't I just get in touch when Joey's in college? For the rest of the day, I'm not crazy about my baby, and I'm sure Jake will be stingy with his sympathy. *Stop feeling sorry for yourself. Toni Morrison raised several kids and had a full-time job.* (Why did I ever tell him that?)

*   *   *

GETTING THROUGH the painfully slow minutes of each day is the hardest thing I've ever done. Our infant's primal misery sends Jake and me back to our own stormy pasts. We want Joey to know he's loved as unconditionally as we weren't, but it's a good excuse to neglect one another. I'm so enthralled with my new calling I hardly notice how little help I'm getting.

I do all our errands with Joey in his Snuggli, hauling bags from the car while he howls to be fed. If only someone would feed me, too. When Jake finds time to put the food away, or actually cook some of it, he feels virtuous for taking over my job.

"I need to wear my good dark sweater to a meeting Wednesday," he informs me as if it's a crisis. "The one Joey spit up on." Translation: *Since you're not working, you have plenty of time to wash it.*

I give him my dirtiest look.

"I dropped off the laundry yesterday, which made me late for work, but you forgot to put my sweater in the bag." I try to figure out what country he lives in, what language he's speaking. I've heard other new moms complain about their husbands, too, but mine feels worse.

I bundle Joey up in his Snuggli and rush out into the silent, frozen air to trudge around the pond. *Baby, baby, give me your answer true,* I sing at the top of my lungs to cheer both of us up. Maybe it's postpartum depression, but I want to run away. After three times around the pond, I'm calm enough to go home and try not to set off another war, even when I see Jake at the computer instead of broiling the steak he promised me.

We try to save our arguments for after Joey's asleep, but I'm sure our innocent child already feels the tautness between his parents. Thank God for yoga class.

"He has million-dollar ears," Master Wah says. Then he whispers, "When there is fighting, the mother's milk goes bad." How does he know?

I tell Jake about this later, but it doesn't faze him. I pretend to be asleep when he comes to bed. He assumes that Joey's stolen my libido, but this excuse can't last forever.

The few times he gets up in the middle of the night for baby duty, he actually manages to stare at the computer with Joey fidgeting in his lap. He walks out the door every morning looking like a *GQ* ad, while I put on whatever I can grab. Most of my sweaters are stretched out and stained; my nursing bras are so ugly I can't bear to wear them. When was the last time I got my hair cut?

While his students do pranayama by candlelight, Master Wah talks about living a balanced life. Jake used to talk about that, too, but he's given up his dance classes and hardly exercises. Once he's risen to the top of his biostatistical field, he promises, we'll take a big trip, or move to another country.

"We're out of food," I interrupt him while he's working at home on a Sunday afternoon.

"There's plenty of tuna fish. And spaghetti."

I embrace him from behind and gently massage his shoulders. "Come on, Jakey. Let's go out for Chinese food. That'll be quick, and Joey loves the fortune cookies." I don't even mention that it's Mother's Day, since Jake doesn't believe in celebrating holidays.

Already cruising from table legs to our legs, our slippery naked boy wriggles away while Jake tries to put on his diaper. We walk to the restaurant in a decent mood and I try not to notice Jake checking his watch. Joey babbles in his tabletop rocking seat, gathering compliments from the other customers. Jake likes showing him off.

Just as we're leaving, it starts to rain, hard, with thunder and lightning. I haven't brought a jacket for myself or Joey, or an umbrella, so I ask Jake to get the car and drive back to pick us up. We've waltzed into such a nice mood, but now Jake's expression darkens.

"I've already lost *two hours* and now you want me to drive *back* here, *way out of the way,* so you won't get a little wet?"

"That's what I want. Once in a while, Joey and I should matter as much as your goddamn work." He's immovable. I've never known anyone this stubborn—not even my father. "Stay here with Joey and I'll go," I snarl. "Give me the keys."

"You'll be way too slow," he snarls back, taking off.

"Daddy went to get the car," I tell Joey in a soothing voice. I'm sure he can tell there's a storm brewing.

"You always get your way," Jake says on the way home.

Out of all those lovers, how did I end up with this one?

⸬   ⸬   ⸬

BUT JAKE PLAYS with Joey so differently than I do, roughhousing, teaching him airborne tricks. And when the three of us dance to Aretha, our boy giggles like a cartoon soundtrack. He grasps us both so tightly. I could never be selfish enough to break our sacred circle.

"I'm hanging onto family life by sheer will, for Joey's sake," I confide to Gert on the phone.

She's quiet. Is she wondering if I'll have to do something drastic?

"The three of us went to the arboretum last week," I remember. It was bursting with those just-unfurling spring colors, chartreuse and pale lavenders. I took pictures of the guys playing on the lawn. "When Joey got cranky, Jake did handsprings to make him laugh. He's impossible with me," I don't have to remind my cousin. "But he sure has a gift for fatherhood, which is a killer."

"Try to remember his good side," she says. "You're stressed out and you need more support, but how many women get that from their husbands?"

Gert's married to Dave, who'll have to have his vasectomy reversed when they're ready to have a baby. Her views on child rearing are very Northern California. "We ought to live like African tribes," she says. "The women take care of each other and the children while the men go off to hunt for weeks at a time."

"Let me know when you get that tribe together," I tell her. "Joey and I want to join."

heat, water, sand

I HAVE A SNEAKING suspicion I dwell on minor difficulties because I can't admit there are major ones. On the other hand, my angelic hellion and trickster boy brings me so much joy. I've never felt so heartfully attuned to anyone, which keeps me in rhythm with myself. This is the gift that will save us both.

It's easy knowing when to hold the line and when to let Joey soar straight through the limits I've tried to set. So what if he wants to wear nothing but a diaper on his head? What's wrong with pop-corn for breakfast and no nap on too fun a day? Other moms seem to have their kids on parent-friendly schedules, but Joey's happiest when every day's different.

I ask every mom I know about how to get Joey to nap, or at least sleep a little more, but Jake mentions he was just like that, so I accept my fate: amusing a boisterous companion for hours on end. I will the clock to move more quickly toward bedtime, praying I'll have the mental energy to watch TV.

I'm constantly on alert so my kid won't hurt himself—or me. Yesterday I caught him eating mud, which could have been full of lead paint chips. After I cleaned him up, he retrieved a clump of dirt from his pocket and tried to feed me some. Last week, just as I ran to the bathroom, Jake walked in while Joey was about to yank the VCR onto his head.

As if we needed another excuse to express our displeasure with one another.

But nothing comes close to the ecstasies of hearing *Ilubyou* in his tiny voice, or watching him try to keep a bar of soap underwater by sitting on it, laughing with glee every time it slips away from him and rises to the surface. The hard-boiled egg and peanut butter sandwich he invented tastes pretty good, and his scribbling on the wall looks interesting. Our child's life force renews my own, each time I start to drown in inadmissible sorrow.

"Can you call the landlord about the leaky sink?" I ask as nicely as possible before Jake dashes out the door. When he gives me that why-can't-you-do-it look, I let it go. Since he hasn't spent more than forty-five minutes alone with Joey at a clip, he's sure I'm on a kind of vacation when he's not around.

"You have so much help," he reminds me. Marietta watches Joey three afternoons a week so I can go to the Laundromat, pay our bills, and, if I have time, take a yoga class. No point trying to convince the proud, hands-off dad that, while he spends his days contemplating higher math in a peaceful, air-conditioned office with a view of the Charles, eating catered lunches and schmoozing with his biostatistical buddies, I have to lock Joey in the bathroom with me when I need a shower. Child care is a blue collar job. No wonder so many women are secretly glad to leave it to someone else.

"By the way," Jake keeps asking, "how's the job hunting going?"

"Fine," I lie. I have no idea where my ten-year-old resume is, and when I get Joey to take a decent nap, I fall asleep, too.

"Try *networking*," Jake suggests, but the only people I know in Boston are equally quarantined mothers of newborns. I'm using my remaining neurons to read *Your Baby Can Sleep Through the Night*. Maybe some college English Department will be impressed with my literary theories about *Pat the Bunny*.

Even though Jake and I are more and more estranged, we don't have much energy for drama these days. I try to remember who Jake is, way deep down, and that we have plenty of time to work on our relationship before Joey suffers from it, too.

Despite the ice between us, it's impossible to keep cool this steamy August. "If this heat wave doesn't end soon, I'm going to lose it," I tell Rhonda. She's always the best person to complain to.

"Buy an air conditioner," is her obvious suggestion, but our apartment doesn't have the right wiring. Rhonda's on the Vineyard for the summer, but my invitation to visit her in paradise seems to have expired now that I have a cranky, sleepless kid, so I don't even ask.

The first Kooperman commandment was *Thou shalt not suffer in the heat*. If we weren't gamboling in our state-of-the-art pool, we were sailing and swimming off the boat, or visiting relatives' lakeside bungalows. My first summer in steamy Manhattan, I swam in the Carmine Street pool until I learned to buy a combination ticket from Penn Station to Bay Shore where a bus whisked me straight to Jones Beach. I'd walk to a lonely stretch of sand and spend a blissful day with the *Times*, a joint, a lukewarm beer, and a deli sandwich. Eventually I wangled invitations to Fire Island or shared beach houses with friends.

Now I'm helplessly marooned, a beached whale with my baby beluga. Ignoring the *No Swimming* sign, I dangle my sweaty kid in Jamaica Pond when no one's looking, so at least one of us can cool off; I pray his happy shrieks won't send us both to jail.

"Not only did you break the law," Jake snaps at me, "but Joey could catch something terrible from that pond. You're just not *thinking*, Ruth."

*   *   *

"WHY DON'T YOU bring Jake and Joey down here for a sail?" my mother keeps asking, even though she knows I hate being stuck on thirty-eight feet of teak and fiberglass with my father at the helm.

Jake would hate it even more. "Trapped on your father's boat?" he asks in horror. "You and Joey can go."

If I show up without Jake, I'll have to answer lots of questions.

As soon as he had the money, my dad bought his first sloop and became a Jewish Old Salt—a rare breed in those days. Afloat, his insults were even more annoying than they were on land. As a teenager I'd lash a sand chair to the foremast, as far away as I could get from my family, so I could read or take a nap. Whenever I invited a boyfriend for a sail, I felt my father's eyes darting between me and my date, taking in my bikinied body, then checking to see if his new rival was doing the same.

Irving used the same pathetic lines on every voyage: *I guess they don't teach you which way the wind is blowing (how to tie a knot, how to steer a yacht, etc.) at Yale.* If he liked the guy it was even worse: *As captain of this vessel, I can legally perform a wedding as soon as we're five miles out to sea.*

Eventually I only brought girlfriends on board.

I would never have asked Roger Linklater to join us for Manhattan's Bicentennial Tall Ships celebration, but he insisted. Roger was my parents' dream son-in-law, a successful Madison Avenue copywriter. After I published my first short story—for fifty dollars—my boyfriend informed me that that was how much he got paid *per word* for writing dog food commercials.

My talent for earning money was as good as my aptitude for long-term relationships, but things looked possible with Roger. He'd even given me a silver Bianchi bike. Loaded down with fancy provisions from Balducci's, we boarded the good ship *Pool Paradise* (named as a tax write-off) in Westport. Roger endeared himself to Irving by describing his West Village apartment as "a thousand dollars west of your daughter's." Totally smitten, my mother kept running below deck to make sandwiches for the guest of honor.

We followed the Connecticut shoreline from Long Island Sound through the perilous Hell's Gate right off Queens. While we glided royally down the East River, my father pointed with pity at "all those poor slobs in the rush hour rat race" headed to work on the FDR Drive.

We finally rounded Manhattan's southern tip to join hundreds of vessels of every nation and era, and weighed anchor between an immense Japanese destroyer and the Statue of Liberty. We were participating in history, watching the rockets' red glare, toasting our nation's birth with champagne. "This is the life," Irving announced, showing off his automatic pilot and roller reefer.

Roger was enthralled, hanging on my dad's every word, laughing heartily at his jokes, ignoring me. After I convinced him to jump ship for a while, we rowed the dinghy to the shore somewhere near Wall Street and tied it to a chain-link fence. Carrying an oar apiece on our shoulders, we found a bar where Roger drank enough beer to confess he'd postponed breaking up with me because he didn't want to miss this once-in-a-lifetime event.

Back on the boat, I faked normalcy until the worst weekend of my life so far was finally over. When Irving heard the news a few weeks later, he was stunned. "He could have had such a great deal," he said, referring to himself. "I can't believe he dumped you."

I'M USED TO terminal lovers. But that was before Joey, for whom
Jake and I will figure out how to grow up. Even happily married
Rhonda keeps reminding me that she and Reggie don't always like
each other. "Just make the best of things," she advises me when she
calls between swims in her Chilmark pond.

I drive just-walking Joey to every blue spot of water I see on the
map of greater Boston, but most of them turn out to be crowded
mud holes, shallow swamps, or private. Sometimes I end up at a
decent beach and we play in the water, but I can't let go of Joey long
enough to take a stroke on my own.

Jake says complaining about the temperature is pointless—until
Joey breaks out in a heat rash. "Let's drive to the South Shore," he
suggests heroically one Sunday. "Joey needs to catch some waves!"
During his L.A. adolescence Jake was a surfer.

I pack a cold roast chicken and plenty of treats for Joey, and we
drive past enticing stretches of exclusive shoreline until we find
a public beach in Duxbury where non-residents can pay to park.
Our boy's parents will embrace in the healing waves and all will
be well again.

Joey toddles happily down to the water and back to us a dozen
times, squealing with pleasure. We laugh proudly at his undaunted
attempts to catch the soaring seagulls. I admire Jake's body; he and
Joey look adorable digging tunnels. He'll complain later about the
time he's lost, and he won't help make dinner or put Joey to bed,
but this heavenly respite is totally worth it.

When I look up from my newspaper, Joey's watching a boy,
about twelve, who's building an elaborate castle with a moat and
turrets draped with seaweed. The thin boy wears glasses, the

serious type. Eager to help him, Joey scoops up a fistful of sand and offers it to the boy. His balance isn't great yet, so he falls — dangerously close to the castle.

Understandably afraid our little guy will wreck his precarious creation, the boy gently picks Joey up and puts him down a few yards away.

"What is his problem?" Scattering sand all over our blanket, Jake leaps to his feet and races toward the boys. I actually think he's kidding when I hear, "How *dare* you touch my child. Do you think you own this beach?" Fists clenched, he towers over the flabbergasted kid, who tries to explain he was only making sure Joey didn't wreck his sandcastle. By now Joey's happily chasing gulls again.

"*My son can play wherever he wants,*" Jake shouts. The boy holds his ground — better than I do when Jake gets this way.

I can't believe what I see next: Jake becomes a whirling dervish of arms and legs. Towers collapse, stones and seashells fly, until the castle's a pile of sand.

The boy takes off his sandy glasses and stares at Jake. He and I are watching the same scary movie. I'm as shocked as he is, even though I've seen the previews. The boy wisely joins his father, who's sitting in a beach chair holding a fishing rod.

In the movie *I* want to see, the outraged dad gets up slowly, crumples his beer can, and, like the Terminator, vaporizes Jake, teaching him a lesson he'll never forget.

But the boy's dad is more realistic than I am. *There are all kinds of nuts in this world,* he's probably telling his son. *Just ignore that asshole.*

On to the next perfect moment of his life, Joey throws pebbles into the water.

It's only five o'clock, my favorite time at the beach, but a black cloud has slid over my sun, covering it forever. I've lost the urge to take another delicious swim. Shocked into silence, I pack up the food, drinks, toys, and towels. All I want is safety from the man I thought I loved.

Probably relieved we're leaving so soon, possibly unaware that anything's happened, Jake carries Joey to the car while I take a last look at the far-too-clear horizon.

We're quiet during the long drive through traffic. When we get home I feed and bathe Joey and read him *Jack and the Beanstalk* until we both fall asleep on the futon in his room.

10.
falling

I WAKE UP IN a stupor from terrible dreams on top of worse reality, busy enough with Joey to safely ignore Jake until he leaves. Thanks to emergency cash, my survival instinct kicks in.

"Going away for a few days," I write to Jake. "We'll be fine." I pack a summer suitcase, diapers, and car snacks, and strap Joey into his crumb-coated car seat. Without even calling for a reservation, I head toward the yoga retreat center in Western Massachusetts I've heard so much about. I have no idea whether young children are allowed, but if not, we'll go someplace else.

Joey sleeps the entire trip, the most blissful and air-conditioned two hours I've spent in I have no idea how long.

The enormous building faces a lake—the biggest draw. That and being fed healthy food, as long as I can keep Joey under control while I slide my tray past all that colorful bounty. I almost weep with relief when I open our spotless, cell-like room.

Joey loves racing up and down the long carpeted hallways. Everyone smiles as if they mean it, and the place exudes such serenity I'm already considering moving in and becoming a devotee of the guru in residence. I meet a woman who does live here, and her teenage daughter is thrilled to watch Joey so I can take a yoga class.

I try to pretend I'm on a luxurious vacation with my child, but the real story aches through. When Joey and his babysitter are settled on a shady part of the beach, I force myself to jump into the icy water. Shocked smack into the present, I realize what has happened, but the choice is to drown or to swim; hot tears fill my goggles. When I flip over to backstroke, the sky's still there.

Joey's asleep on a blanket; his babysitter has drawn all over his diaper with magic markers. Later, a shiatsu therapist asks if she can borrow Joey for a baby massage demonstration. I watch my lucky little guy in the middle of a circle of students who take turns practicing their technique.

The white-robed, striking guru-in-chief drifts gracefully past us, sprinkling Joey with rose petals. *"Prasad,"* someone informs me, "a sacred offering to the gods." My charmer attracts kindness.

I never imagined such blessings, which help me come to my senses. Joey needs his devoted dad, and so do I. There must be a couples therapist in Boston who's up to this task.

* * *

AFTER AN INSINCERE attempt at make-up sex, Jake announces he's going to Washington for a meeting. "Should I wear the new pinstripe suit, or go with something more conservative?" he asks. It's a trick question. I used to like giving him fashion advice, but if I get involved I'll end up taking one of his suits to the dry cleaner.

"Wear whatever's clean."

My latest sartorial mantra elicits only his look of annoyance.

Keeping up with our insomniac little dictator is so consuming we get away with zero eye contact and minimal conversation. We only touch one another by accident: bumping heads, for instance, when we try to catch Joey diving off the couch. Neither of us sees him climb up to the kitchen table before he slips and lands, hard, on his forehead. It swells so fast he looks like a monster, and when he doesn't cry we're even more terrified. Could it be brain damage?

"Why weren't you watching him?" I spit out contemptuously. I hold a bag of frozen peas against Joey's head, which makes him howl.

"Call the doctor!" Jake bellows. He says the same thing every time Joey tumbles or coughs or has a runny nose—when he's around to notice. "*You* were in charge, Ruth. I told you I needed to finish editing this paper. He could have a *concussion*."

"I went to the bathroom, for Christ's sake. You couldn't give me two minutes to pee?"

"You're fine," I tell Joey, faking a really calm voice and holding him close to shield him from the radiation in the room. I stroke my tiny boy's back, as gently as I once stroked Jake's, until his sobs turn into hiccuppy whimpers.

"I was *concentrating*. Why didn't you say you were going off-duty?"

"From now on when I have to take a leak I'll blow a trumpet."

Does Joey notice we're not reggae-dancing him around the room together anymore? That when he crawls into our bed at dawn, we cuddle with him separately?

※　※　※

I'VE RUN OUT OF POT, and, in an emergency measure, I'm not even drinking. Life feels way too serious right now to cloud my thinking. Would I have fallen for Joey's father without being able to smoke away my reservations?

One night at an amazingly early eight o'clock, Jake bursts through the door unexpectedly with a bag of groceries. "I'm cooking dinner," he says as if he does this all the time. I want to ask if he remembered to buy toilet paper and diapers, but I hold my tongue.

Soon I smell onions burning. "Where's the garlic press?" he asks.

"I don't know. Joey plays with it sometimes."

"That's a big help. Where did you put the olive oil?"

"We've been out of it for weeks." *You could have looked at the list. Or called to ask me what we need if you were going shopping.* There are two burned pans in the sink, and the stove's a greasy mess. "That smells great," I say as politely as I can. "Sure wish I were hungry."

"Goddamn it," he mutters, "I went to all this trouble for nothing."

"A mom I met at the playground invited Joey and me for spaghetti. Why didn't you tell me you were going to make dinner? I had no idea you were even coming home this early."

He slams a cabinet door, knocking over my iced coffee.

"I ruined an expensive piece of salmon last week when you said you'd be home for dinner." I hate sinking to his tit-for-tat level, but I do it, anyway.

"I come home early to spend some time with my family and this is the thanks I get." He takes his plate into the living room to watch the news. "Hey, Joey! Come sit with Daddy."

"Please don't get him revved up, Jake. He'll never calm down and get to sleep. Besides, he's filthy." In theory, baths are Daddy's job when he's home early enough.

"All I think about is running away for good," I tell Gert, while Joey splashes in the tub. "Jake and I used to hang out together for bath time—before he decided one of us might as well be accomplishing something."

"Do you have enough money to manage on your own?" my cousin asks.

"For a while, I guess. Especially if I get a teaching job."

"Jake would have to help you."

I can't go there yet. "Joey's talking to his rubber frog," I change the subject. Later, I read Joey *Peter Rabbit* unenthusiastically while he pulls the movable tabs on the picture book. When Peter escapes underneath the garden fence before Farmer Brown can catch him, Joey laughs as hard as usual. Soon his lilac eyelids flutter and close. *Please let him not be harmed.*

At last I slide luxuriously into bed alone with a book. Sleep soon takes me, as thrilling as sex used to be.

A few nights later, after we're sure Joey can't hear us through his baby dreams, Jake and I have it out. *You lied. You promised. I'm not your father. I'm not your mother. All you had to do was let me know. That was passive-aggressive. Why didn't you just tell me the truth? You never listen. Can't you make up your mind? If I want something, you want the opposite.*

We're sitting on the living room rug, as far away from one another as possible. I pound the floor for emphasis so hard my hand will turn black and blue. Every time Jake goes to the bathroom he stops at his desk on the way back. This gives me more ammunition, but it's too late to use it.

The battle's over.

"You never wanted me. All you cared about was having a baby."

"That's a disgusting thing to say. You care more about your work than me and Joey." Our misery marathon intensifies, both of us going back and forth from mutual excommunication to terrified pleading. *Please. I can't. We can't. You have to. We've tried and tried and tried.*

Then we both apologize, but only as a prelude to more recriminations. I know I provoke him, using words like poison darts. Once, ages ago, we fought physically. He ended up pushing my face into a pillow until I apologized for what I'd said that made him do it. I have a ferocious mouth in combat. My words were all I had to protect me from my dad's putdowns; I learned to sharpen them so they'd draw blood.

We take turns breaking down and sobbing, then say more awful things. We could go on like this for years.

"We can't do this to Joey," I plead.

"I'm being fired from a job I'm no good at," Jake finally mumbles, so sorrowfully I have to resist the urge to argue.

Our heartrending decision makes itself.

II.

oh, freedom

When Joey toddles into our room at dawn, Jake and I both avoid his eager, trusting eyes. I notice Joey's leaky diaper when Jake plays with him, but hold my tongue until Jake figures it out and, martyr-like, deals with it.

"A mom at the playground mentioned that she and her husband are moving to New Hampshire. Their apartment's down the street, and it sounds really nice." I've kept this information to myself for a few weeks, and as soon as it leaves my mouth, I regret asking the woman for her phone number. As if happenstance will force us to go through with the wrong decision.

When Jake decides to move into the place, alternating currents of relief and dread course through me. *It's all my fault, it's his, we torture one another, we just need more therapy.* I can't stop backpedaling, guilt-tripping, lapsing into fake kindness, then being meaner from the strain. By the time Jake carries his still-unpacked cartons of books out the door, I'm impatient for the surgery to be over.

"Ambivalence is the worst," according to Rhonda. "It'll get better, Ruth. I promise."

Our apartment feels so empty I stay away from it as much as possible to let the place purify itself. Every time I see a couple with a baby I look the other way and wipe my tears; avoiding the few people I recognize, I push our year-and-a-half-old trouper in his stroller to a French bakery on Center Street. The first word Joey ever said—way before *dada* or *mama*—was *croissant.*

When he asks, "Where Dada?" I want to undo my reprehensible crime. Heart, stomach, wrists, every part of me aches. Neither one of us had a great childhood, and now we've ruined Joey's.

Will he forgive us?

Walking miles in the flamboyant orange, red, and magenta arboretum calms me down. "The earth is your only mother," Gert writes. "Let her heal you." Maybe this would work in Northern California. Then I notice the Great Blue Hills in the distance, and hear myself hum Odetta's version of "Oh Freedom." Maybe some courage has seeped into me.

And before I'd be a slave
I'll be buried in my grave

Jake's so busy buying furniture and a car and settling into his new place, he hardly sees Joey for the next three weeks, leaving me to deal with the fallout.

"Can't you take him shopping with you?" I plead. "He keeps asking where you are."

"I have way too much to do. Did you forget that I have to set up my apartment and work seventy hours a week?" Despite his heartfelt admission that he wasn't such a great partner, I know he also blames my unrealistic expectations.

"He has no room for grey," Gert explains. "You've betrayed him so you're the enemy. Get used to it."

Jake and I meet at a mediator's office to work on a legal agreement about custody, weekly and vacation schedules, religious education, college tuition, etc. When Jake hears that neither of us can move out of the state without the other's permission, he marches out of the office in a huff.

Jake sends me his magnum opus: he's come up with a formula

for Joey's support, which involves something he calls the Human Responsibility Factor, and when I try to figure it out I get dizzy.

According to his H.R.F. calculations, each hour he spends with Joey will decrease his monthly child support by 2.5 percent. The miscellaneous expenses he incurs during his weekly twenty-four-hour shift (diapers, scrambled eggs, babysitters, etc.) will be deducted from my monthly stipend. If I pick Joey up late from his house, I'll have to make up the time. I'm supposed to send Jake all relevant receipts, including things like wipes, animal crackers, and Joey-related mileage, excluding picking up babysitters, which is for my convenience and therefore not necessary. I guess I'm supposed to check my odometer while Joey's squirming out of his car seat, or squeezing his juice box all over himself.

"Feel free to ask me about these numbers," Jake says, proud of his computations.

I finally take Rhonda's advice and call an attorney, which enrages Jake because it costs more than mediation. But without live arguments, we soon have an actual deal: Jake will have Joey from five o'clock Friday night to the same time Saturday — unless he decides not to. I'm the custodial parent; the buck stops with me. Fortunately, Jake has no interest in spending school vacations and holidays with his son. Unlike Joey's privileged mother, he "absolutely has to work."

"What if I have to work, too?" I ask, but get no answer.

After we sign the document, his attorney admits to my attorney that his client is a beaut. I've only asked for minimum child support, just enough to keep Joey in diapers and day care so I can get a teaching job.

"I suppose you'll need more money," Irving sighs when I tell him the news.

"Whether your father helps you or not, he'll humiliate you,"

Gert says. "You might as well take him up on his backhanded offer."

At least I won't have to run interference between my father and Jake anymore.

"You sure know how to pick 'em," Irving says when I bring Joey to visit.

"Kick me when I'm down, Dad."

"Just don't listen to him," my mother says. How does she do that? My father lavishes all the praise he never gave me on his grandson. He does mention Joey's ears are a little large, but at least my kid hasn't messed up his entire life the way his mother has. Or at least not yet.

I didn't make a mistake, I remind myself. *I have Joey.*

■   ■   ■

I CAN'T LOOK FOR work until I find day care, so the playground network comes through again when I hear about a young woman named Laurie who takes care of children in her home nearby. It's not a fancy place, but she's clean and organized, and everyone says their children love going there.

Joey tunes me out when I tell him about Laurie, so I expect a scene when I drop him off for a trial run. But he races toward the toys and other children, not even frightened of Laurie's two barking poodles. I *thought* I wanted a break from my miniature, merciless boss, but as soon as I'm free I want to take him home again. I only just *had* him. Why do I have to let him go?

Out of excuses for being unemployed, I work on my resume until it's ready to send to almost every college in Boston. Without a published book, I'm a lackluster candidate. By the time I left New York I was teaching creative writing courses, but I'll be lucky to get freshman composition classes in this PhD-glutted town—and it won't be at Radcliffe or Wellesley.

After dozens of futile follow-up calls and chilly rejections, I look for full-time editorial jobs, which are scarce and pay even less than teaching. Several weeks later I land an interview for a position on the local paper. I know enough to keep my toddler's existence a secret, and they're so desperate for someone who knows what a semicolon is that they hire me. After my first day at work, I pick up Joey a half hour late; he's sitting with Laurie on her front steps looking sad.

There was no point asking Jake to make an emergency pickup.

For two weeks straight I keep up the momentum, getting up at six, making both our lunches, playing with Joey over breakfast, racing him to Laurie's, getting to work by nine. I'm brain-dead by the time Joey's asleep at eight, but it's working. After I pay for Joey's day care, I'm hardly earning anything, but I have an actual job and a reasonably happy child. Then Joey comes down with some kind of virus and can't go to day care. It takes the doctor several days to figure out what it is, and by the time he's better, I've lost my not-so-great job.

"It's the universe saying Joey needs you at home," Rhonda says.

"We might as well give you the money we saved for your wedding," my dad announces. As usual, his generosity comes with insults, but this means I can afford to take the part-time job I've been offered teaching adult English classes at a nearby women's college. Saved from copy-desk drudgery, I'll be able to laugh and be inspired by my students again, and stay home with Joey more.

Since a lot of my students barely speak English, and the native speakers hate to write, I have to rethink the curriculum I've planned. Faulkner and Joan Didion will have to wait. I'm not trained to teach English as a Foreign Language, but they never asked me, so I start with basic sentences and paragraphs. Soon my Russian student is helping a high-school dropout from Dorchester with her punctuation, and a Chinese woman bakes cookies for Joey.

It doesn't take long for my students, many in their thirties and forties, to feel like friends. Their sentences start to say things, and I'm envious of their rich experiences. Savang escaped by boat from Laos to the Philippines after watching her father and sister drown. Alex, mother of four, is tall and black, with a gap between her teeth. She has the worst skills in the class, and the deepest understanding of what everyone else is trying to say.

Miranda's best essay describes her friendship with a homeless woman: *Our conversations got us both through the worst spring of our lives. Her life was the worst of all possible nightmares. I was just a miserable, mixed-up girl in high school living in a nice house with a lot of fighting.*

Back home, my once-innocent Buddha boy has figured out how much fun it is to throw toys and food, and hide my glasses and keys. Jake brags about Joey's pitching arm. If I give him a small spoon he screams for a big one. "Not the green cup," he howls with impressive despair, "the *purple Elmo one*," which has been lost for weeks. He wants to eat his Cheerios standing up, holding the bowl by himself.

"You can put the bowl on a stool," I compromise. He dashes it into shards, dumping milk on the floor I just swabbed from an orange juice disaster. I bend down to sweep it up and cut my knee, and Joey screams for more Cheerios while I bleed all over him.

These days he hardly sleeps, and he jumps on me at five a.m. He wants to be carried even when I'm lugging heavy groceries up the stairs. One night, exhausted, I leave him flailing and crying in the entryway and run upstairs to call Rhonda the expert. "Let him scream," she says.

"But he'll never stop. What will the neighbors think?" I'm incapable of such cruelty.

"Forget about them." She keeps me on the phone for an agonizing forty-five minutes, helping me steel myself against my child's abject fit until he finally shuts up. I'm afraid he's fainted or choked until I see him clambering toward me, his wet, beet-red face now *beaming.* I hold him tight and we fall asleep without dinner. At midnight we eat applesauce in bed.

Single motherhood feels like mind-numbing bondage. Joey's tantrums set off my own, but he's only trying to find out where he stops and everything else starts, including me. He dumps over the laundry soap, loses his socks, his mittens, his favorite puppet.

The hardest job of all is constantly arguing with his dad.

Then, always by surprise, motherhood turns into art. Stuffed lions and monkeys sing in our operas. Joey makes me laugh out loud, then falls down laughing, too. How does he know I've skipped a page of his book when I'm falling asleep myself? No instrument is as sweet as his voice.

Who else will ever adore me back like this, a hundred-fold?

When Joey finally spends the night at his dad's, they both have a great time. Jake executes his weekly twenty-four-hour shifts with precision; Joey's happy to go off with him and just as happy to come home again. Maybe because Jake wasn't so nice to me, I'm surprised he's so devoted to our child, a comfort in the middle of our wreckage.

On Friday afternoons, I count the hours and minutes until my reprieve: glorious peaceful solitude. At exactly five o'clock, Jake finally appears, looking so appealing: the loving dad, whisking away our precious boy. Suddenly I have no idea what to do with myself and I want both of them back. What's wrong with me? Why did I break up our precious family?

I spend the evening drinking wine and feeling sorry for all three of us.

"I'M COMING TO TOWN to cheer you up," Rhonda says. "Reggie has a conference at MIT, so let me take you out to dinner." Lately I hardly have the energy to talk on the phone, let alone dress up and go somewhere, but I decide to rise to the occasion. After calling every sitter on my list with no success, one of them recommends her friend Kenya, who lives nearby.

"I'll make sure she's trained in CPR," I tell Jake, who expects me to get a sitter who is, or stay home. I put on a skirt that still fits and my only ironed blouse. I've had so few sitters I've never written a list of emergency phone numbers, but time's running out. I put Joey in the car to pick up the sitter. I'll have to send her home by taxi, but no matter how much it costs, I deserve a night out.

Rhonda wants to meet at a place listed in *Zagat's* near her hotel, way across the river in Cambridge. It takes me forever to find a parking space in Harvard Square. After my shoes rub my heels raw when I run six blocks to the restaurant, I wish I'd let the valet take my car no matter what they charge.

If only Rhonda had been willing to come to *my* neighborhood. But when we finally embrace and are led to a comfy, quiet booth, all the trouble feels worth it.

We catch up over braised lamb and morels, and I try not to feel out of place among all the corporate-looking, child-free diners. "Reggie can be really spaced out with the kids," Rhonda complains. "I have to remind him to put on their hats and mittens when he takes them sledding!"

I wouldn't complain about a slightly forgetful genius who can fix anything, grows pesticide-free vegetables, and goes dutifully on every family vacation Rhonda plans. She inspired me to transform my life, but hers always seems to function so much better. She takes the kids to see the dinosaurs at the Museum of Natural History and their favorite playground's right next to the Met—exotic hangouts compared to ours. Joey would love to see a real dinosaur.

But even in the mundane provinces, taking care of my child feels like a privilege. Rhonda admires my pictures of Joey and promises to come see him next time she's in town. We finish a bottle of wine and reminisce about the days when we had endless time to read and talk about books, men, and politics.

"Do you ever run into Bookstore Bert?" I ask, our ex-lover in common. He was tall, sexily literate, and an authority on the downtown artist scene. The first story I ever published was about my unrequited love for him.

"The best thing I got out of that relationship was you!" she laughs. By midnight we're punch-drunk. It's the latest I've stayed out since I had Joey.

I finally navigate my way back home across the Charles River. I remember telling Kenya to bolt the front door from inside, but I don't have the key to open it. I knock, softly at first so I won't wake Joey. Then I knock harder, but the babysitter still doesn't answer. I bang the door as loudly as I can, then run outside and around to the back door, but I don't have a key for that, either.

Back at the front door all I hear is dead silence within. I shout and pound until my fists are sore, waking the neighbors, I'm sure, and still no sound. Not even Joey crying.

There have been stories lately about abducted babies. Never far from paranoia, Jake has already warned me to only leave our child with someone I *know* is trustworthy. *Not the last one on the list.*

By now I'm sure the lovely teenager I trusted with my child is either dead drunk or has stolen my kid. Moments ago I was tossing back Pinot Noir, celebrating having survived a cataclysmic breakup, weaning, and the shock of being a single parent in a foreign-feeling town. Now I'm responsible for the greatest tragedy I can imagine.

Jake will have me incarcerated for two hundred years.

"Joey's been kidnapped!" I wake up my next-door neighbor, who says he'll call the police. I'm sure Kenya's already on a bus headed for Mexico. I promise God, out loud, that if Joey's all right I'll never leave him alone again until he's twenty-one.

"If the doors are locked from the *inside*, then someone's in there," the cop manages to tell me without making me feel even stupider than I already feel for hiring a criminal. When he and his partner pry my back door open with a crowbar, my babysitter is waking up from her sleep of the dead.

"Sorry," she says. "I guess I didn't hear you."

Joey has slept through it all, even after I've screamed at Kenya. Then I feel remorseful and pay her too much. I'm glad Joey can't tell his father.

* * *

I'M NEVER OUT OF crisis mode for long. Jake leaves me an insulting phone message accusing me of losing Joey's birth certificate, which I gave him to copy for his health insurance records. And now he wants an "invoice" for Joey's day care bills.

"I told you Laurie doesn't send out bills. What's wrong with a copy of my check?" I try not to raise my voice so Jake won't hang up on me.

"I'm not getting myself into trouble with the IRS because you flout the law."

After I put out those forest fires, the phone rings again.

"Joey says you gave him *Corn Pops*. I thought we discussed the sugar thing."

"Everyone says it's better to let him have some sweets. Otherwise kids crave sugar even more. He'll swallow everything he finds when he goes to other kids' houses." We hang up on one another yet again.

Then, on a Friday morning, he informs me he can't take Joey that weekend. He has a work crunch.

I suspect a new girlfriend.

"But I've already made plans," I plead. I'm supposed to go hiking with the Appalachian Mountain Club.

"I'm really sorry," he says without meaning it. "I have no choice." Fortunately Joey doesn't understand what I'm swearing about after I slam down the phone.

"You can't change him, so give up trying," Rhonda tells me when I call in a panic. Once I'm over my rage, I remind myself that I've never questioned Jake's devotion to his son. He makes up bedtime stories for Joey, takes him to museums; he's even figured out how to get him to take decent naps.

"I let him run up and down a big hill several times and he sleeps for three hours!" he bragged. "Works like a charm." I should count my amazing child as glory enough for one lifetime and stop complaining about his father. I guess the mountains will wait for me to climb them.

12.

grace happens

WHEN I NOTICE the only other casually dressed mom at Cedar Grove Preschool parents' night, I'm relieved. My denim overalls and wrinkled sweater echo her patchwork skirt and dark purple turtleneck. She's smiling wryly at me, as if we're amused by the same joke. We approach one another like two loose magnets. I'd been feeling crummy, an oddball single parent in a room of well-adjusted couples.

"You must be Joey's mother."

"Everyone says he looks like his dad."

"The matching denim outfits are dead giveaways."

"I know, they're ridiculous. I bought them on the Home Shopping Network after too much wine," I confess. "This seemed like the right occasion to finally wear them."

"That's how I got my bargain shower curtain, towels, and washcloths!"

"Late-night hunting and gathering. I'm Ruth Kooperman, by the way."

"Grace Stein. Louis talks about Joey nonstop. He says he's teaching him to fly. I hope that's OK."

"Sure. I'll take out flight insurance. Peter Pan's big in our house, too."

"*Who's the slimiest slime in the book? Captain Hook! Captain Hook!*" Grace belts out, right on key, and I join in.

"We have the Broadway show tape with Mary Martin," I tell Grace. "When the lost boys sing, *We have a mother, it's nice to have a mother*, it makes me cry."

"That's the best version." We're off and running. Grace is jealous when I tell her I lived in New York. "Max and I adore Manhattan. He knows the Second Avenue Deli menu by heart."

"I lived right down the street. God, do I miss the stuffed cabbage." We chat until I need to take a food break. "Who had time for dinner?" I confess.

"Try my husband's deviled eggs with Cheez Whiz," she says. "A culinary triumph. If Max didn't love to cook, we'd starve. What did you bring?"

"Orange juice. Potlucks send me into a panic."

"At least they let the kids eat what they want at this place. Our older son's preschool was so crunchy-granola they searched the lunch boxes for contraband white bread or sugar."

I don't tell her I water down Joey's fruit juice and give him tofu dogs. "Where do you stand on water pistols? Joey won't take a bath without one." I feel safe admitting to Grace that I'm worried about this.

"See the woman in the pants suit over there?" she laughs. "She *forbade* her kid from touching anything even remotely weapon-like, including sticks. Then her son chewed a piece of whole wheat toast into the shape of a gun. *Bang, bang, politically correct mom. You're dead!*"

We squeeze ourselves into small plastic chairs and eat Jell-O squares and pita with hummus while Grace fills me in about Cedar Grove. "The teachers are great, but don't let Sandy, the director, pressure you into signing Joey up for more hours. And we did have a lice epidemic this year, but only once, which is better than most places."

"Too bad I missed it."

She shouts to the balding, chubby guy who's sitting on the floor and letting kids jump all over him. "Ruth, meet Max, the human trampoline. Did I say I had two kids? Make that three. Ruth's Joey's mom."

"Superman? What a cool guy. Louis wants a cape like that." I smile at Max, the first man I've met in ages. I can't imagine Jake noticing someone else's child, or coming to a parents' night in the first place. I wonder if Joey cares that he's not here.

⸱   ⸱   ⸱

THE FOLLOWING SATURDAY, Grace and I meet at Larz Anderson Park with her two boys and mine. We zip from topic to topic: movies, restaurants, exhaustion, the books we're trying to read before we fall asleep. My favorite memoir these days is *I Dreamed of Africa*. Grace is hooked on a biography of Truman Capote.

"So what's the story with Joey's dad?" Her question doesn't surprise me, but I'm not used to answering it.

"Devoted but damaged. We've separated."

"That must have been so hard."

"I had no choice. But thank God he's a great dad."

Grace looks relieved. "I can't imagine doing this by myself," she says. "Do you at least get along with Jake?"

"He's still punishing me for ditching him, even though he sort of admitted he wasn't a good partner."

Our already-dirty boys dangle by one arm and one leg each from the top of the jungle gym, daring each other on. As soon as they're safe on the ground again, Grace and I walk quickly around the perimeter of the playground, asking and answering rapid-fire questions. She teaches elementary-school English to immigrant children from the Caribbean, Bangladesh, Haiti, Kosovo.

"Everywhere, really," she says. "My classroom is like the Tower of Babel. The kids' parents are afraid to let them out of the house except for school, so they can't practice what I teach them. I try to convince their parents to let them go to free city summer camps."

Grace seems jealous that I get to teach writing to so many foreign adults. "My Chinese and Russian students often write circles around my Americans," I tell her.

"I wasn't a serious college student," she says. "Maybe because I had to work practically full-time to pay for it. Plus, I was always wasting time with Max. What about you?"

"My father considered my college tuition an investment which would pay off when I married a brain surgeon or a real estate developer. He wanted me to go to a coed school, so I rebelled and went to a girls' school. Remember? That's what we called them in those days. Everyone else had already met their boyfriends in prep school, so I had no social life at all. Every time I went to a mixer, I struck out."

"But you were near New York!" Grace sighs.

"Not to mention Junior Year Abroad in Paris. I'm not complaining. But maybe if I'd taken my father's advice I wouldn't be a single mom."

"Oh, that's only temporary. You'll meet someone."

My conversations with Grace are uplifting. Helpful, lasting, but light as air. No psychological analyses, no deconstructing our every mood and feeling. We find common ground in almost any topic.

We both have back-to-the-earth Northern California relatives, a rich source of amusement. "Did you ever hear them call their kids in for dinner?" she asks me. "'Amerika! Che! Time to come home and eat!' And, you won't believe this, Ruth. My hippie cousin *breast-fed* her adopted son by siphoning goat's milk through plastic tubes which she taped to her nipples!"

"I'll have to recommend this to my cousin Gert when she has her kid. Gert just informed me that her West Marin town is now printing its own currency."

It's almost dark, and our boys are hungry and exhausted. Grace and I haven't stopped zooming through an unpredictable mix of subjects, from her hysterical in-law tales to some ridiculous house-keeping tip she read in a magazine at the dentist. *"Go through every drawer and closet every season to get rid of clutter. Are they kidding? How pathetic would you have to be?"*

This brand-new friend feels realer than anyone I've ever known—not counting Joey. By the time we say goodbye, I've laughed away a good amount of my recent heartache.

The evening goes downhill fast after I wrestle Joey into the car and stop for a takeout Chinese dinner. Max is home making meat-loaf and green beans for Grace and the kids. He'll probably get the boys cleaned up and ready for bed afterwards.

Dealing with Joey alone is certainly easier than dealing with Jake's infantile moods as well. But tonight Joey's overtired and obstreperous. "I hate fried rice," he announces, which he begged me to get. He throws *Horton Hears a Who* at me when I say I'm too tired to read anymore. Why did Dr. Seuss have to write such long books?

And once I leave him, sobbing dramatically in his room, I'm too wiped out to concentrate on anything except a dumb TV show.

"THE PLACE IS a mess," Grace mock-apologizes the first time I visit. "I gave my maid the year off." After that, Joey and I drop in whenever I need an anchor, tossing our coats and boots into the enormous pile. The Steins' brick Colonial is the smallest house on their Brookline street, with the only scruffy yard and broken screen door.

Even if I don't warn her, Grace is always ready for company. There's so much to look at I'll never take it all in: walls and shelves full of framed photos, art nouveau posters, unpolished silver menorahs, *shofars*, planters, dozens of miniature, unclassifiable *objets d'art*. Grace loves to give house tours and every *tchotchke* has a story.

"Aunt Sadie's candy dish!" She points to a hot-pink, rose-encrusted ceramic bowl as if it's a priceless antique.

My aesthetics are getting an overhaul. Meanwhile, Joey's totally happy hanging out with Louis and his big brother, Isaac, and lets them both boss him around. "Let's play knights," Louis says. "Who do you want to be, Joey? Except for the prince or the king." Isaac watches the little guys while Grace and I rush outside for a quick walk, even though it's cold. Then we drink tea at her kitchen table, overflowing with art projects, homework, and catalogues. The phone and the doorbell ring constantly, but Grace always returns to our conversation without skipping a beat.

While I'm on hold, I wash a few dishes, check on the boys, and take in Max's collection of presidential campaign buttons and Grace's authentically furnished Victorian dollhouse. Max comes in the door exuberant, glad to see me, arms full of groceries. An attorney at the Housing Court, he always has a story: heartless landlords, crazy tenants. He buys doughnuts for the kids whose parents are getting evicted, and pleads for the downtrodden.

He'd do anything for anyone, and I'm jealous of their comfortable marriage. But I can't imagine being in Grace's *hamisch*, homey place, a temple-going, suburban housewife who has never really spread her wings or explored other options. But why would she? She seems utterly content.

       ■   ■   ■

WHILE I'M WATCHING Grace make brownies one Friday afternoon, the gentle snowfall turns into a northeaster. "It's getting bad out there," she says. "Aren't you taking Joey to his dad's?"

It's always hard to leave the Steins. "I'd better get going or I'll never make it," I say, bundling Joey up and carrying him to the car. The snow is really coming down.

Jake opens the door, annoyed I'm there, as if I'm a Jehovah's Witness or an even worse sort of intruder. Joey's so excited to see his dad he almost leaps out of my arms.

"You're twenty minutes early," he says, tapping his watch as evidence. "I'm sorry, Ruth, but I'm in the middle of something. You'll have to come back at the right time."

Is he blind to his son's eager expression and outstretched arms? I guess Jake's paternal devotion doesn't switch on until five o'clock.

"I can see you doing this to *me*," I scream. "But Joey will totally flip out if I try to get him back in the car."

"The longer you argue with me, Ruth, the longer it will take me to finish my work." I stand there, stunned.

We'll have to send him to a shrink for such early rejection.

"The twenty minutes doesn't start until you leave."

I might as well negotiate with the Rock of Gibraltar.

"Where am I supposed to go in the middle of a blizzard?" I plead. "If I have an accident it'll be your fault." But he's unbendable. I almost slip on the ice carrying Joey down the steps. I have to force him back into his car seat, setting off his loudest wails.

"I told you to get snow tires," Jake shouts while I maneuver out of the parking spot with zero visibility. "Joey isn't safe with you."

When Grace calls to make sure I got home all right, I tell her what happened. She's silent with sadness. "I hope Joey doesn't know what *you're a total asshole* means," I say. "I couldn't help myself."

"Oh Ruth, everyone says that in front of their kids. So what did you do? You could have come back here."

"I was afraid to go too far, so I drove around and around the pond. I guess I do need snow tires. I had to drive so slowly the other drivers were flipping me off. I finally pulled over to the side of the road. By four fifty-nine Joey and I practically had frostbite."

"I was hoping you were exaggerating about him, but you have a total nutcase on your hands."

"At least he really loves Joey," I offer weakly.

"Except during inclement weather," she tries to make me laugh. When that doesn't work, she tries again. "Trust me, Ruth. King Solomon would give you the whole baby."

13.

trying to move on

WHAT I WON'T TELL Grace is that, after I got home in the blizzard, still shaking, I poured myself more vodka than orange juice. I don't think she and Max ever drink more than Manischewitz at seders. And I think they got through the sixties with only an occasional toke of pot.

While Louis and Joey run wild at Grace's place or mine, she and I regale one another with the high and low points of our very different lives. Like all the local Jews I've met, Grace grew up in Dorchester, which I've come to think of as the Brooklyn of Boston. Her family lived in a triple-decker flat, downstairs from her grandparents and her cousins.

"Just like *A Tree Grows in Brooklyn*," she says, proving my theory. "Everyone I knew belonged to our *schul*. I thought the whole world was Jewish until I found out about the Holocaust!"

"We were *sort* of Jewish," I tell her. "We went to high holiday services. Of course my father humiliated me by parking his Mercedes right in front of the synagogue." Grace loves that detail. I describe rebelling against my parents' materialism by fasting on Yom Kippur to atone for my sins, which my dad thought was stupid. Right after temple we drove to a seafood place on the shore for lobster rolls and fried clams while I self-righteously starved. "It was worth the suffering," I explain, "to feel morally superior."

"I always envied those suburban deracinated Jews," Grace says. "I'll bet you even dated *goyim*."

"*Rich* goyim would have been fine, but my boyfriends were usually poor artists. Tony, the surrealist, was a Baptist from Missouri; Alex was a German philosopher. My mother liked the fact that they were so cultured, but she wanted me to marry money."

"Your parents wouldn't have hung out with mine," Grace says. "My father's dry cleaning business hardly made a living. He wasn't the ambitious type—kind of like Max. But he was so sweet. My mother, on the other hand . . ."

It doesn't take us long to discover we each had a great tormentor: my father and her mother.

"Gladys was angry at the world. I can't really blame her," Grace says. "She was very smart, but she had to quit school and go to work at fifteen. I didn't take advantage of my opportunities, so she resented me. My teachers were witchy and high school was boring, so I played hooky a lot, which made my mother crazy. She wanted me to be brilliant and popular to make up for what she'd lost. But I didn't fit into any of the cliques: the Jewish Jappy types, the Catholic cheerleaders, or the 'rats,' the girls with teased hair, white lipstick, and fishnet stockings."

Grace's dad sounds like the gentlest soul on earth. "He thought I was perfect, beautiful, and brilliant. But I figured he just wasn't smart enough to realize my mother was right: I was a total failure. 'What do you know?' was her favorite line. 'You don't know anything.'"

"Irving and Gladys. A match made in heaven!" I tell Grace about the time my parents made me go to the neighbor's house to celebrate the pool my father sold him. "Herman Schwartz, the bagel king, had a custom-designed, bagel-shaped masterpiece, with a round island in the middle."

"Wait a minute," she stops me. "So the bagel part was water?" Grace is a glutton for details.

"Herm escaped war-torn Poland with his father's secret baking technique. He boiled the dough in his garage in Connecticut, and soon he had an empire." Grace is all ears. "Anyway, I had my period that day, so I had no intention of getting wet. I was wearing shorts, and I'd just gotten my hair done for a date that night to see *A Man and a Woman*."

"*The* film of our era," she sighs.

"'But *Ruth*,' my father announced, 'you *have* to swim. This is a *pool party*. Go home and put on that expensive bikini you just bought.' I gave him a rotten look and skulked over to a lounge chair to read the latest *Diary of Anaïs Nin*.

"'Come over here, Ruth, I want to ask you something,' my father said. Mr. Charm. I went, just to shut him up. 'What is your *problem*?' he whispered. 'If you don't swim in his new pool, Herm will take it *personally*.' My father liked displays of Kooperman togetherness. 'I guess you'd rather be swimming in *France*, is that it, Ruth?' he announced fortissimo.

"I could tell Herm had given Irving one too many Stingrays, so I decided to get out of there fast. But just as I walked by my dad, he stuck out his foot and I went flying into the water. His audience — not the most sensitive crowd — went wild with glee."

I see Grace's face turn from amused to sad. In spite of her mean mother, she somehow rests on firmer ground than I've ever felt. My shopping sprees and summer camps don't compare to that kind of gift. I've never felt my worth the way she does.

THE KID WHO USED to be mostly cute has turned obstinate. Reverse psychology—*No bath for you, Joey*—no longer works. He's onto all my tricks by now, sucking out my last breath of patience. The books say children tend to be stubborn at almost four, but what if his genes are kicking in and he'll only get worse? Will he turn into Jake?

"Please help Mommy find your other shoe," I plead. We're late getting out of the house again because I overslept after correcting midterm papers till midnight. I was supposed to write a committee report for a faculty meeting later today. And why did I volunteer to make fundraising calls for Joey's school? How foolish of me to think paying the ridiculous tuition would keep them happy.

"I *hate* those shoes." Since when does my kid care what he wears?

"Goddamn it" escapes my lips. "You begged for those shoes. I told you to get the Velcro ones but you wanted the big boy shoes and you promised to tie them."

I'm reasoning with a toddler.

"Where's my stegosaurus?" He flings his tyrannosaurus rex, which misses my right eye by a millimeter. Servile as usual, I crawl through dust bunnies, searching in vain, until I bump my head on a table leg.

Whining, clinging, screaming to get his way, my child's so fused to my body and soul I can't peel him off. And even if I could, am I still there, underneath? I've forgotten any other kind of intimacy. Joey won't even take a nap unless I'm right next to him, and as soon as I open an eye, he's onto me.

"Now I know why they have those abusive-parent hotlines," I

confide in the school parking lot to one of the more honest moms I know.

"You've never called?" she laughs.

How will I get through the next fifteen years?

Tired of being trapped with Joey in the house on another lonely Sunday, I finally drag us both out the door and drive for an hour until my nemesis falls asleep in his car seat. I park the car and stare at the trees until I love my boy again.

But it looks as if I'll be changing diapers until he's in college. Happily perched on his Barney potty seat, Joey sings to himself and stares at the pictures in *Once Upon a Potty*. It's his favorite book, but he appreciates it on a theoretical level only. I've tried every strategy in the vast, extant literature.

"Please, Ruth," Jake exhorts me, "let go of your agenda for Joey. He has his own timetable."

"You change five or six diapers a week and I change thirty-five."

"I'm tired of those bleeding-heart liberal toilet-training experts," I tell Rhonda. *The child who balks is merely expressing independence. Or he may simply be contented with his life the way it is, so don't rush him.*

Rhonda's kids were trained at two and a half. "How did you do it?" I beg her for the secret.

"God helped," she confesses. "My babysitter spent a lot of time in church."

"I'm pretty sure God didn't want women to have to deal with menopause and toilet training at the same time," I say to Grace over tea and Max's scrumptious chocolate cake.

"You're absolutely right. I saw this somewhere in the Torah."

When I come back from another false potty alarm, Grace is flipping through the *Boston Globe* personal ads. "Listen to this, Ruth.

Italian Stallion wants to take you on a wild ride. Oh, wait, here's a better one: *Academic with eclectic tastes will do almost anything within reason at least once.*"

"First you want me to join your book club and now you want me to go out with strangers?" Neither feels like the kind of life-enhancing change I yearn for, but I appreciate Grace's concern about my social life. She keeps reading ads to me, impersonating each potential lover with an amazing variety of voices and accents. *Let's walk slow in the rain and read poems in the moonlight. Do you like oysters? Are you my pearl?*

"That one flunks the grammar test." Maybe I'm being defensive. Who'd put up with a less-than-mellow mom with a bad track record—and her handful of a son?

"Watch out for guys who like to sit by the fire and walk on the beach," Max shouts from the other room. "That's code for *cheapskate.*"

It's too late in the game, I hear my parents' loud, unspoken prophecy.

⸭　⸭　⸭

"WHAT ABOUT A singles' cruise?" Rhonda suggests, even though she'd never stoop so low.

"Men in gold chains and pinkie rings who smoke cigars?"

"You're going to have to compromise a little," Cousin Gert reminds me.

Does that mean date someone whose idea of exotic travel is gambling in San Juan?

If only I had a less humiliating way to meet someone, but I'm no longer twenty-nine and invited to parties and openings. It used to be totally cool to walk into a blues bar, talk to interesting strangers, and sometimes even bring one home. Now — if there *were* a decent blues bar in Boston — I'd be a desperate cougar.

"Just ask for what you want," Gert suggests. *Yeah, right.* Even if I believed someone would come along, which I absolutely don't, I have no idea who I'd order up. "Just describe the man you could love," my cousin suggests.

"He has to have a huge heart," is what comes to mind. This time around that means adoring Joey as well as me.

"What else?" she wants to know.

"Warm, kind, smart, funny, in shape, outdoorsy? It would be nice if he liked foreign films, New York, shared my leftwing viewpoint. Jewish, but not religious." Once I get going it's hard to stop.

"You and Joey deserve someone wonderful," Gert says. "We'll just keep visualizing him until he appears."

I study the *Globe* the following Sunday and circle the prospects with Joey's green marker. After three glasses of wine, I write notes to decent prospects. Several replies arrive in the next few weeks, most of them uninteresting, or full of grammatical and spelling errors: deal breakers. I talk to two guys on the phone; the first, a real estate attorney, sounds afraid of his shadow and doesn't get my jokes, but I meet him for a walk around the pond.

As soon as we spot each other, we both know we're wasting our time but we endure the 1.6-mile circuit, making tedious small talk. He barely makes eye contact, and answers every question with data overload. "Where did you grow up?" "Well, I was born in Northern California but my father got promoted so we moved to New Jersey. I went to prep school in New Hampshire, then college and law school in Minneapolis. Then I signed on with a firm in St. Louis . . ."

All I think about is that if I get home in twenty minutes the sitter will only charge me fifteen dollars instead of twenty-two-fifty.

I meet a history professor for a drink on a Friday night in a Cambridge bar after I drop off Joey at Jake's. I'm wearing makeup for the first time in years. The guy's decent, and I'm enjoying myself, until we veer toward a dangerous subject and I have to listen to a long defense of Israel's policy toward the Palestinians. When I make the mistake of offering my opinion, he calls me a self-hating Jew and asks for the check before I've finished my drink. Dinner turns out to be a peanut butter sandwich in bed.

14.

an experiment

IT'S NEVER BEEN EASY between me and men. I take a break from blind dates until Jake mentions that he has a new girlfriend. So I drink more wine the following Sunday and study the *Globe* again.

Decent phone interviews don't prepare me for the guy who shows up in baggy sweat pants and filthy sneakers, or another's serious facial tic. Unfortunate teeth are impossible to get past. And off-putting confessions: *My wife did everything in her power to get rid of me until I finally took the hint . . .* One guy's so handsome I'm willing to overlook his over-involvement with three female Dobermans until he mentions his girlfriend in Russia.

"It's taking so long for her to get the visa," he explains, "so I thought I'd see who else is around in the meantime."

He's completely shocked that I've lost interest. "But she *might* not get it! What's wrong with a backup plan?"

Could I make this stuff up?

Most of these strangers talk about themselves nonstop; they seem either desperate to replace their last girlfriend, or utterly asexual. My only compensations for these agonizing attempts at companionship are the date deconstructions with Grace as soon as I get home.

"Everything was going great until I mentioned Joey and he

started to look around the room. He was actually cute, but I said I had to go to put us both out of our misery."

"So from now on we'll forget about the ones who haven't reproduced," she says. Grace is as involved in this project as I am. She never makes me feel like a masochist, and after each disaster she finds a way to make me laugh.

For instance, the deadly brunch with an intellectual snob. "I knew I was in trouble when he told me to look for him in the Logical Positivism section of the bookstore cafe," I report. "I couldn't get a word in edgewise and it took him three entire hours to drink a glass of orange juice. He couldn't stop spewing information at me. I kept looking at my watch while he droned on and *on* about some obscure Swiss philosopher."

"My great aunt Sadie just met her soul mate in an assisted living complex," Grace lets slip after my latest report. I know she meant to soothe my soul, but I wish she'd kept this news to herself.

I climb into bed with some chocolate kisses and read the classified ads in *Boston Magazine*. "Ready for laughter? Take a chance. It's ever after. Shall we dance?" Despite the saccharine tone, I decide to spend $2.99 to call and punch in a code number to hear the guy's actual voice.

These logistics are annoying. As I've said to every one of my friends lately, I'd rather have my teeth drilled than go on a blind date. Whatever happened to *Some enchanted evening, you will hear him laughing across a crowded room*?

This guy's recorded message sounds down-to-earth, trustable. "Never thought I'd do this, but it's spring and I'd like to meet someone special," he says matter-of-factly. "I have my own business, and enjoy varied interests. I'm honest, decent-looking, and ready for the real thing."

"Varied interests" strikes me as vague, but I like his lack of pretension. After the beep it's my turn. "I'm forty-five, attractive, lively, a college teacher with a good sense of humor. Thanks for reminding me that it's spring." I forget, accidentally on purpose, to mention Joey, and leave my number. Why scare off a good prospect?

Marty Greenberg and I banter easily on the phone, as if we already know one another. I can't hide my surprise that he's never lived anywhere but Boston. I'm disappointed when he admits he's not crazy about my beloved island of Manhattan, but I decide to invest in a babysitter so I can meet him for a drink.

"So what do you miss about New York?" he wants to know. "The crime, the noise, or the prices?"

"Mushroom barley soup for two dollars, *challah* French toast, free Shakespeare in the park. The city's full of bargains if you know where to go."

"Well, maybe you could show me around."

He seems a bit provincial and I'm a cultural snob, but we both like the Caribbean, so that's a start. As Rhonda has always said, men are fixer-uppers. So what if he doesn't read a lot and he's not athletic? There's something appealingly straightforward about him. Married unhappily for seventeen years, up front about wanting to find the right companion.

"So you're divorced, too?"

"Not exactly," I hedge. Now that the water's deep enough, I might as well jump in. "I'm a little—unconventional."

"How so?"

"I've mostly been single, in between boyfriends." *Here goes.* "I had a child with a man I never married." Marty takes his time absorbing the double shock. "Joey's almost four," I say when I can't stand his silence any longer. More silence. "So how do you feel about going out with a mom?" I ask this casually, as if I want to know how he feels about Italian food.

"I don't know how I feel about it," he finally says. "I guess I'll have to find out."

Is this a sign of openness? Of possibility?

Marty and I meet in the lobby of the Westin Hotel, just inside the revolving door. (Later, scared to admit how much we like each other, we'll joke that we should have just stayed in that door and revolved right back out to the street again.) He's paunchy and dressed too conservatively. I was more attracted to him on the phone than in the flesh.

We settle on a couch with his Scotch and my wine spritzer. I like his voice, and his thinning hair's a less-than-uptight length; at least he has a mustache. Used to interviewing clients and employees for his headhunter agency, he wants to know my story.

I tell him my students seem to appreciate my classes, and I'm glad I don't have to work full-time because I love being with my kid. I skip my East Village pothead era as well as my stalled literary career, and tell him about moving to Boston with my kid's dad.

"My marriage was dead for years before we had the courage to end it," he says without vilifying his ex. He seems kind, honest, and a little sad. He and his wife went on European vacations, a hopeful sign. After a long, slow sushi dinner, Marty walks me to my car, his arm around my shoulder. Our lingering handshake turns into a hug and a fairly serious kiss.

* * *

I HAVE JUST ENOUGH time after Jake takes Joey off my hands the following Friday to clean the apartment, cook, shower, and dress before Marty arrives with his toolbox. He rewires my favorite lamp so I can read in bed and I repay him with beef stroganoff, the first adult meal I've cooked in ages. I've stashed Joey's fleet of plastic vehicles in his room, determined to forget I have a kid for a few hours. We kiss goodbye for at least ten minutes.

Marty invites me for dinner at his place the following Friday. His small, dark apartment is tidy but depressing. His wife's still living in the house they spent the last five years renovating. "We did a great job on the kitchen but we never got around to the bedroom," he confesses.

He serves me seafood pasta and artichokes.

"Seventeen years and no kids?"

My question takes him by surprise, as if I'd asked why they never raised chinchillas.

"Guess that wasn't a priority." He puts on James Taylor and we make out on his couch. *I've seen fire and I've seen rain.* A trite choice, but I keep my mouth shut. The following Friday, at my place, I play him Karen Akers, my favorite cabaret singer: "In a Very Unusual Way, I'm Falling in Love with You," but I don't think the potential boyfriend notices the music all that much.

I bring a toothbrush and my only decent nightgown to Marty's the following week and we skip the music and undress.

"I forgot about sex," I admit when we're finally horizontal.

"Completely? Must be a girl thing."

"Or a mom thing." His pale body's large and soft compared to Jake's jazz dancer's physique, but his delight in mine's a turn-on. Each release is deeper than the last and something significant seems to be happening even though I'm not sure I want it to.

Jake used to probe the depths of my soul. Marty and I make small talk. Jake had Joey's astrological chart done and wanted us to hike through the Andes. Marty's idea of adventure is a St. Thomas beach and plenty of rum. His divorce sounds civil and he's good to his parents. Maybe, at this point, normal's the way to go.

Marty decides to stick around the following Saturday to meet Joey, who rushes right past him into the kitchen in search of cookies. I can read the look on Marty's face: my child lacks manners. He plays marbles with Joey while I make spaghetti, but then, as if he knows he has competition, Joey turns into a brat and won't go to bed.

"You go through this every night?"

"Your mother did the same thing."

We leave well enough alone and Marty goes home so I can deal with Joey.

I'VE BEEN LOOKING forward to Grace's next book club meeting because I loved *Borrowed Time*, Paul Monette's memoir about losing his partner to AIDS. Grace says Sue Ellen just got back from Greece and will be serving homemade baklava.

"Marty has volunteered to hang out with Joey while I'm out," I tell her. "What if they don't get along and it's a disaster?"

"Who gets along with their kids? It'll be baptism by fire."

"Wrong metaphor. Joey has diarrhea, so it'll be more like the shit hitting the fan."

"What's the origin of that expression, anyway?"

"Look it up in your etymological dictionary by the time I pick you up."

Monette's descriptions of his lover succumbing to disease are piercingly beautiful, and the discussion is interesting until

Raquel jumps in. "I know we chose this book to get beyond our familiar experiences," she says, "but it's so depressing. I just couldn't finish it."

"Do you have any gay friends?" someone asks her.

"Not good friends, no."

"Well maybe that's why you feel so estranged. But what if non-Jews said they felt that way reading about the Holocaust?"

"I see your point."

Grace and I talk about how illness is all around us, how we never expected so much *mortality* in our early forties. I'm not sure anyone else knows Grace's brother Jerry is gay, but she doesn't mention it. Just when we're about to probe the topic, Sue Ellen brings out *spanakopita* and *retsina* and tells us all about her cruise through the Greek isles. Paul Monette's poetic love story now tabled, we throw ourselves into travelogues and recipes.

"Max and I went to Greece on our first trip to Europe," Grace says on the way home. "We found a really cheap place to stay on Mykonos. I remember asking Max why there were so many wheelchairs parked in the lobby and then we realized we'd checked into a home for the elderly. It was in a really scenic spot, though."

"A friend and I spent a month on Crete where we both found lovers who didn't speak English. I communicated with Yannis by singing Beatles songs. Ann's friend was an adorable fireman, but I remember her complaining after they spent the night in a cave: 'Christ, Ruth, my vagina's full of sand!'" Grace is laughing uncontrollably.

Except for the rides to and from it, the book club wasn't great. And judging by the scowl on my boyfriend's face when I get home, my evening will cost me.

"Do you really let Joey have ice cream before he goes to sleep?"

"Sometimes I give him a little if he's eaten a good dinner."

"I thought he was lying. He got really upset."

Uh-oh. Joey must have turned Marty's good deed into a nightmare. "Mommy!" he blubbers, purple with self-pity, wide awake at almost midnight. *Rescue me from the enemy.* He'll be a basket case tomorrow.

By the time I've gotten Joey to sleep, Marty's absorbed in a Kojak rerun. "Maybe we should take a break," he says. After collecting his electric razor and underwear, he hugs me — insincerely — goodbye. I go to bed and whimper just like Joey when he doesn't totally mean it. My brief boyfriend's reliable kindness was rain for my parched spirit, but our growing season's over.

15.

staying safe from bears

As soon as spring turns into another beastly July, I'm too busy with a full load of summer classes and Joey — and too defeated from my last attempt — to think about men. "Some people are allergic to kids," Grace says. "Find a dad next time."

"But then I'd have to deal with *his* kids, too."

"What about a widower with grown children?" Max suggests. Cooling off at their neighborhood pool, we segue from my inactive social life to the new restaurant everyone raves about — which we probably won't get to. Max jumps into the pool, thrilled to join our screeching, splashing tadpoles while Grace and I dangle our feet in the water, too lazy to do laps in the overcrowded bathtub.

"Remember that horrible August heat wave a few years ago?" I ask her.

"God, was that awful. Don't remind me. *Augustus horribilis*, as Queen Lizzie would say. I had two kids in diapers and a sick, ungrateful mother on my hands. We spent Max's entire vacation in our backyard."

"By the time I convinced Jake we needed an air conditioner, they were all sold out. As soon as we broke up, the heat wave was over."

"Then you should have done it sooner."

"Too bad we weren't friends yet. We could have commiserated."

"That definitely would have helped." Grace tries to coax our wrinkled boys out of the water. "Most people didn't notice how bad that month was, but if you were having a terrible life anyway, it was unforgettable."

My students aren't very inspiring this term; most of them would rather be lifeguarding or waitressing than stuck in an airless classroom. I try to rouse their interest in one of my favorite essays, James Baldwin's "Stranger in the Village," which he wrote while living in Switzerland, where his dark skin and kinky hair were a curiosity. The last line, *This world is white no longer, and can never be white again*, finally generates an actual discussion.

"How does Baldwin's experience relate to yours?" I ask.

"The world never *was* white," says Marika from Dorchester, who hates to read and write. She started the course in silence, but by now she has a lot to say. If only she'd put some of it down on paper.

I lived on a dark island, but it wasn't dark enough, writes Janette from Trinidad.

"Your sentence is so interesting. Are you going to tell us more?" My job is to remind everyone that writing involves the much-dreaded task of rewriting. First drafts are letting it all pour out, murky but full of promise. "When you finally get it right," I tell them, "we'll know your real story. And so, by the way, will you."

"I totally get what Janette's saying *already*," Marika informs us. But even if she's clairvoyant, she can't seem to tell us the message, so telepathy doesn't count. Eventually, Janette explains, "I was the darkest child in my mulatto family. I was always shunned." My accomplishment of the day: uncovering how Janette was forced to hide within her own darkness.

It feels good to help others write their stories; but it doesn't feel great not to be writing my own. Maybe I need something new to write about. An ad in the Appalachian Mountain Club magazine at the dentist's catches my attention: *Women in the Wilderness*. A week-long backpacking trip in New Hampshire's White Mountains.

I'm not crazy about roughing it, but I have that week off between summer sessions, and Jake's overdue for some quality time with Joey. My only camping trip so far, with a boyfriend, was a disaster. It rained the whole time, and we both got poison ivy; he'd given me too many cans of tuna fish to carry, and whenever he wasn't looking, I tossed one into the woods. I was tempted to get rid of his heavy *Birds of North America*, too, especially after I got blisters and was blamed for forgetting to pack Band-Aids.

But life feels too tame, and I need a physical challenge, so I decide to answer this call of the wild. I'll be safe among compassionate women. I'm in decent shape from swimming and yoga, and ready to test myself in some new way.

"This is supposed to be a vacation?" Grace laughs when I read her the itinerary: five days on the march, from ten to twelve miles per day, most of them uphill. "Why don't you just stay home and clean your apartment?"

"I need to do something *daring*." But she can't relate. Neither can Rhonda, happy enough climbing Martha's Vineyard dunes with her children and her au pair from Sweden.

"I'm so jealous," is Gert's vote of confidence. "Climb those mountains for me, too."

Joey's booked into day camp with Grace's boys, and Jake says I can go, as long as Joey has sleepover plans for the weekend.

"Do you think we'll notice one more kid around here?" Max asks me, pointing to a dozen kids in his yard.

When I read the list of things to pack, I realize I have no idea what I'm getting into: water purifying tablets, rain gear, bug spray, and a trowel to dig my own latrine. I break in a serious pair of hiking boots and rent an enormous backpack, which I load up with fifty pounds of stuff and practice wearing around the pond while Joey follows on his tricycle.

Driving to the AMC Lodge in Pinkham Notch, I remember how miserable I was long ago on a Girl Scout camping trip. It poured all night and we were cold and muddy in the morning. After I was assigned to make the hot chocolate and dumped in a paper bag of powdered soap, thinking it was sugar, I was Enemy Number One for the entire weekend.

But I need to throw myself into the perilous unknown.

I join twelve experienced outdoorswomen at the lodge on a Sunday night. While they all list Presidential Range summits they've conquered, I worry about being the least in shape, and I'm not even the oldest. Our petite co-leaders, Sherry and Janine, will be carrying one hundred pounds each, so how can I complain about the weight? They prefer leading all-female groups. "Men tend to be macho and competitive," they tell us. "When the going gets rough, women know how to cooperate."

What does she mean by rough? I'm afraid to ask.

I pick tall, easygoing Claudia for my tent mate, a shrink with a Brooklyn accent and a great sense of humor. Claudia loves backpacking, but luckily she's not the bragging, four-thousand-foot-peak-bagger type.

After we slog up our first day's ten-mile trail, we have to pitch tents and cook tofu-vegetable stew in the dark. My job is cutting up onions and putting the scraps in a plastic bag so we can pack out whatever we've brought in, leaving the mountain the way we found it. After we eat, wash dishes, and put out the fire, I climb on a stronger woman's shoulders and hang our bags of food and garbage over a tree limb to keep it safe from bears.

"I couldn't wait to get away from my kid," I tell Claudia while we take out our contact lenses by flashlight. "Now I miss him like crazy."

"Oh, I know," she says. "Our whole family used to go camping and now it's just me." While we rummage through our packs and blow up our air pads, I find out that Claudia and her radiologist husband escaped New York years ago to raise their daughters on a lake in Vermont.

"Sounds wonderful," I say, envious.

"It was, for fifteen years."

Uh-oh. Is this another story about a guy having a midlife crisis and running off with a younger woman? If so, why is Claudia smiling?

"Well, a year ago—I know this sounds dramatic—that entire life was *over.*" She takes a deep breath. "Since we're going to be spending a lot of time together, you might as well know. At the ripe old age of forty-five, I figured out I'm gay."

"Really?" I ask as offhandedly as I can.

"I met an amazing woman at a conference. It was obvious something was going on between us. Amy's a sexy Jungian, black dramatic eyes and a gymnast's body. I swear, Ruth, I was clueless until she made the first move and totally seduced me."

I can't figure out what to say, but Claudia's on a roll.

"We had the weekend of our lives. We were *both* married to really good guys, but I'm talking about a different kind of attraction. It's like we're each other's other half. I highly recommend it, by the way."

"Maybe that kind of intimacy isn't even *possible* with a man."

"They're certainly a different species, but I'm prejudiced. It turns out I wasn't just going through an adolescent stage when I had those soppy high school crushes on girls. I hated field hockey, but I played for years so I could stare at all those breasts in the locker room."

"So what happened?" After the most exhausting day I've ever spent, not counting giving birth, Claudia's keeping me wide awake.

"By the end of the weekend, Amy and I had planned the rest of our lives together. I knew I'd have to leave Arnie and share custody of the girls."

"You were sure enough to give up your family?" I'm glad it's dark so Claudia can't see how incredulous I look.

"I was absolutely sure. Of course it was a horrible adjustment for Arnie and the girls. Unfortunately, Amy decided to go back to her husband and kids six months later. Arnie and I had already sold our house and bought two smaller ones in town so the girls could walk back and forth. His parents had stopped speaking to me, and my friends hardly called."

"Your female soul mate betrayed you? I thought only men did that."

"Don't be sexist, Ruth. Anyone can break your heart. Jesus. I don't usually spill my personal stuff like this, but I'm still processing. I figured being in the woods would help. I can't obsess about Amy when I'm trying not to fall off a cliff."

"I suppose it's worth the heartache to have been struck, at least once, by lightning." *Which has never happened to me.*

"Here's the latest news," she says. "I just fell in love all over again. You've got to have hope." I lie awake while jealousy overtakes me. All the other tents are silent but Claudia and I whisper back and forth until the wind blows so loudly we can't hear one another.

*   *   *

OUR GROUP IS a strange mix: a timid Japanese woman who's never been anywhere without her husband, a tattooed motorcycle buff, a type A software executive with the highest-tech gear, an older woman who sings to herself but rarely speaks. And then there's me, the one constantly scribbling in her journal while she's hiking so she doesn't forget the amusing dialogue all around her.

Drenched in sweat, we endure grueling miles on trails from steep to steeper. For relief from the heat, we skinny-dip — for a few seconds — in frigid mountain streams. When our aching limbs, sunburn, or the bugs get us down, we defiantly belt out show tunes. *Climb every mountain.* Each night we pitch our tents, make the fire, cook, and carry buckets of river water to wash our dishes in the dark.

Thank God Claudia and I have the same sense of humor. "Did someone use the latrine trowel to flip the hotdogs?" she asks while we eat around the campfire.

After six days of equal parts ecstasy and misery, we emerge from the woods and stand in a silent circle before we drive off in different directions. "By the way," I finally ask Claudia, who's sympathetic that I have no boyfriend to go home to, "what's your husband like?" I'm amazed that after all those years of marriage she's said nothing bad about the guy.

"You'd like him," she smiles. "Arnie's dating someone right now, but she won't last. I'll keep you posted."

Sore and mosquito-bitten, I'm as thrilled to get home to indoor plumbing and my bed as I am to see Joey. Climbing mountains still isn't my thing, but new courage has seeped into me, which I'm sure will come in handy.

the roaring twenties

JAKE HAS DONE Joey and me a wonderful favor and moved to Brookline so our boy can go to its excellent schools. The teachers, classrooms, and other children at the Devotion School in Coolidge Corner all seem wonderful. But when I leave Joey there it feels like I'm handing my child over to the state.

"Arnie has a meeting in Boston," Claudia says when she calls a few months later. "He wants to meet you." Her perfectly good ex-husband did break up with his girlfriend; now it's my turn.

So the upbeat, redheaded fellow takes me to a Hungarian restaurant and flirts with me over goulash.

"I'm still getting over Claudia's midlife crisis," he says as if we're old friends. "The girls keep asking me if Mommy will stop loving them, too. It was really humiliating at first. But I don't blame myself anymore."

"Kids who are loved by both parents are supposed to handle these splits well," I say. Then I tell him what a friend once told me who'd been in the Peace Corps: a study of the most successful volunteers revealed the surprising fact that many of them came from divorced families; those already used to going back and forth between parents had an easier time adjusting to different cultures.

"I think of this whenever I feel guilty," I add.

Arnie takes this in and smiles.

Our conversation zooms humorously around; he's as easy to talk to as Claudia. When he comes back the next morning for a walk around the pond, he humors Joey out of a rotten mood. "I'll bet you can't count the clouds," he says, hoisting my kid on his shoulders. Joey's eyes are glued to the sky for at least five minutes.

Grace is thrilled when I report back to her. "So you went away with a group of women and inherited someone's ex-husband? Tell me *everything.*"

"He's charming and adorable. He even likes Joey."

"A radiologist? Your parents will *plotz* from joy. Did I ever tell you what my mother told everyone at my wedding? 'It's nice that my Grace found herself a lawyer, but couldn't she find one who'll make a good living?'"

*   *   *

AFTER AN IMPROVISED Jewish Socialist *Yiddishkeit* Yom Kippur service in a neighbor's backyard (folding chairs, a guitar player, and a highly political sermon about the Middle East), Joey and I throw stones into the pond to symbolize our atonement. "Each stone stands for something we can do better. I want to be a better mom," I say as another stone radiates its perfect circles.

"I want to go to the planet with the rings so I can ride my bike all around it," Joey chimes in, tossing a fistful of pebbles toward the sky.

"Please let this boyfriend be the last so my child isn't confused," I whisper upwards.

Now that tall, adorable Arnie and I have launched our long-distance romance, one of us drives the three hours every weekend. Sometimes we drag our kids along, which is tricky. When Becca and Allie, seven and ten, tease Joey or, worse, ignore him, I have to restrain myself from giving them a lecture. I know they resent having to be nice to a kid who's too young to play Monopoly.

When we all get along I can imagine us as a real family, but those moments don't last. The kids can tell their parents are trying too hard. If it weren't for Joey, I'd be content to just date the guy and keep the future out of it. A "blended" family always sounds like a salad dressing. At least dating Arnie means that I get Claudia in the deal when I'm in Brattleboro. Sometimes she and I take the kids for short hikes while Arnie's at work; it's not as much fun as we had last summer, but I get to compare notes about my new boyfriend.

"I wish he wouldn't wake me up when he has to go to the hospital in the middle of the night," I confess.

"I hated that. Don't expect to fix it."

"Arnie is really great with Joey. My last boyfriend wasn't the dad type. But sometimes Arnie seems happier hanging out with the kids than with me."

Claudia gives me another knowing look. "What do you expect? Men can be great, Ruth, but they're *boys*."

Her apparently fickle blond paramour doesn't sound all that mature, either. Apparently Rosemary's idea of a relationship is getting together if nothing else comes up. "Sometimes I feel like her backup plan," Claudia complains.

"I thought that commitment allergy was a guy thing."

"Unfortunately not."

"What if we find a big house so we can all live together?"

"All of us?"

"Yeah, why not? Rosemary's ex-boyfriend Carl can join us, too. It'll be one big social experiment."

When she asks, "What about Jake?" I roll my eyes.

After we get back to Claudia's house, Rosemary strolls in, an hour late. "Ruth," Claudia announces proudly, "meet my *shiksa*."

Rosemary's dramatic-looking: a wild head of bright orange curls, lacey wrist tattoos. "I've heard so much about you, Ruth. I write, too, you know. Claud showed me your story about the camping trip. Was there really a Peeping Tom in the middle of the White Mountains at the exact time you guys decided to jump in that stream?"

"He was there, but I lied about the binoculars," I admit.

■   ■   ■

"LET'S TAKE THE KIDS skiing during school-vacation week." Arnie has come up with my dream plan, except for the skiing part. I told him I loved to ski, but I meant safe, cross-country skiing; Arnie is a double-black-diamond guy, and his daughters are already fearless on steep slopes. The few times I've gone downhill skiing were both terrifying and overpriced: not quite enough bang for the buck. (Or too much bang, since I ended up black and blue.) But I remember the few seconds of ecstasy. Now that I've hiked up Mount Washington, maybe it won't be so daunting.

I say, "Great!" as if I mean it. "Joey will be thrilled."

Arnie books us a mountainside condo with an outdoor heated pool, and I buy snow pants and mittens for Joey and secondhand but still expensive skis and boots for myself. The deep teal outfit I find on sale temporarily allays my anxiety; at least I'll look great until the moment of truth.

I'm a timid intermediate, as long as the mountain isn't too cold, windy, icy, or crowded. I pray I'll get myself out of the chairlift and down the easiest slope without falling, or that Arnie doesn't see me when I do. This anxiety keeps me from worrying about how the kids and Arnie and I will get along.

Suited up, lift tickets dangling off our zippers, all five of us tramp toward the mountain the next morning like the other excited families.

"I want to ski with *you*," Joey whines as soon as they run my credit card at Whiz Kids ski school. "I'm not staying here." He kicks the wall with his rented boots for emphasis.

"After they teach you how, we'll ski together," I promise. I know my kid's not the first mutineer at Whiz Kids, but Joey seemed so excited up until now I thought this part would be easy.

"You're going to have so much fun, Joey!" says the woman who takes my eighty-five dollars. "Go enjoy yourself," she waves me off. Is she kidding? I'd much rather stay here drinking hot chocolate and coloring with my kid. But I practice my first act of bravery by hugging Joey tightly and promising him a cheeseburger and fries for lunch. Then I head back out into gale-force winds.

I maneuver down the beginner slopes all morning, gaining a little speed, actually smiling to myself during the blissful lift rides far above the shining slopes. Arnie and the girls take the fast quad lift straight up into the clouds, but I like being alone, cheering myself on.

At lunch, Joey's beaming. "I catched some air!" he says. He's already advanced to the Polar Bears group, and I've managed not to fall. My feet are numb and I was almost taken out by hordes of death-defying snowboarders, but there's no reward like the outdoor heated pool. When Arnie gets back to our room he's upset that his ten-year-old went to a friend's for dinner without asking him first. I realize Joey will pull the same stunts soon enough and remind myself to enjoy my control over him while it lasts.

But even though our family trip is a big success, after we get home neither Arnie nor I feel like continuing the long weekend commute back and forth, so maybe it's geography that does us in. Or maybe we're just not in the right kind of love to throw ourselves and our kids into a salad.

⁕ ⁕ ⁕

"NO MORE ARNIE," I inform Grace. We're stamping our feet and trying not to freeze while the boys sled down the Sugar Bowl near the pond. "It was fun while it lasted. Some of the time."

"I'm so sorry, Ruthie. Did you really want it to work? Max and I were never sure, to tell you the truth. Someone better will come along. I promise."

I give her a cynical look. She has no idea how hard it is to meet a decent guy at my age, or what these late-in-life misalliances feel like when they fail. I want to quote her mother: *What do you know?*

Grace met Max when she was fifteen, which is unimaginable to me. When we get back to her place and the kids are in dry clothes and watching a video, I hear the details.

"My best friend invited me to her family place on Nantasket Beach. We called it the Jewish Riviera. Kosher living *sur la plage.* School and Hebrew classes were over, so the kids were drunk on their freedom." She and Max chased one another with water guns. "I could tell right away we had the same weird sense of humor. He pointed to a fat man with his fat dog and we both giggled uncontrollably. We'd lie on the beach making up songs for imaginary musicals. *Sea Side Story* was about a doomed romance between a Reformed girl and an Orthodox boy."

"I can't imagine falling in real love at that age."

"Who said anything about love?" she laughs. "I had zero interest in that department for a long time. Max wasn't exactly the manly James Dean type I dreamed about. But then I heard one of those cheap girls say he was cute. She was the white-lipstick type, always chewing gum, and her blouse was tied up in front so you could see her stomach. Max was so innocent, and it irritated me that she liked him, so I had to protect him from that slut.

"At first, my father liked Max more than I did," she says. "'Where's that adorable boy who's so sweet on you?' he'd ask me. The two of them really got along."

"My dad was pretty good at getting *rid* of my boyfriends," I say, feeling a pang of sweet-father envy. I tell Grace about the time I wrangled a handsome date, I don't know how, for my high school Roaring Twenties dance. "I sewed myself a black satin sheath with rows of long white fringe and a flapper headband. I was still upstairs fixing my spit curls and straightening the seams in my black mesh stockings when the doorbell rang."

Grace is all ears, so I go on.

"I race down the stairs, totally nervous, all that fringe swaying. My father was giving my date his spiel about how crummy his American car was compared to my dad's German one."

Grace has that compassionate *oh no* look on her face.

"'Well, that's some outfit you put together, Ruth,' my dad starts in. 'Doesn't she look just like a folded-up lawn umbrella?' he asks his brand new pal in the seersucker suit. My date tries not to laugh. I don't blame him. It was a killer line. 'Do you really want to go to that ridiculous dance?' my dad asks him. 'You'll have a better time here with me watching the ball game.'

"That's why I fell for guys as different from Irving as possible,"

I explain. "My college boyfriend George and I were inseparable. But by the time I got back from a year in Paris, he'd found some-one else."

"Wasn't it worth it?" Grace asks. "A year in Paris. How amazing."

"I wanted to see the world. But maybe we'd still be together, like you and Max."

Grace's father died when she was nineteen, leaving her family so poor they had to move to a smaller apartment. She had to go to a local college and live at home with her deeply unhappy mother. "Max was part of the family by then. He brought us groceries and even helped my mother cook, but she still didn't think he was good enough for me."

"So how did you end up getting her blessing?"

"Max used to stay overnight. He always slept in my brother's room, but my mother was worried about what the neighbors thought. She finally insisted we get married. 'Enough already. You've been dating for five years.' I figured the wedding would give her some *naches*. It was one of those typical gaudy affairs—stuffed capons and ugly blue carnations."

"I thought getting married meant monotony," I tell Grace. "I was afraid a husband would turn me into my mother and I'd lose my entire identity. So I slept around. I figured it would give me things to write about. I spent three years in Europe trying to be Gertrude Stein."

"Oh, she was a cousin."

"Too bad she didn't leave you any of her paintings."

"So while you were sleeping all over the Left Bank, I was on my honeymoon in Niagara Falls," she laughs. "I worked at the library to help pay for Max's law school. We never went anywhere, except to my mother's for chicken every Friday night."

"But Janis Joplin was right," I say. "I *still* have nothing left to lose." She gives me a funny look. "Not counting Joey," I amend my statement.

"Max was the only boyfriend I ever had," Grace says wistfully. "Not counting the time we had a fight and I went out with Milton Herskovitz. Milton became a great success, by the way, with a chain of carpet stores. Do you need a new rug, Ruth? I can get it for you wholesale."

17.
blancmange

"LET'S CHECK OUT this week's ads," Grace says, reading the *Globe* out loud: *"Successful software exec seeks spirited companion to scuba in the Virgins and hike in Tuscany."*

"No grouse hunting in Scotland? Don't bother."

"OK, how about, *Pagan devoted to Monty Python and Rilke loves to make home videos?"*

"What *kind* of home videos?"

"Don't be fussy, Ruth!"

"That's what my Aunt Minnie always told me! She was engaged to a Russian prince. But when he took his gloves off and she saw his dirty fingernails, she called off the deal. 'Don't make my mistake,' she always warned me. 'I was too fussy.'"

This tedious hunting for promising prospects, paying three dollars a minute to listen to them ramble on about themselves, leaving an enticing message, waiting for them to call back, then finally, maybe, having a brief phone conversation, is depressing. The exotic adventurer who lived with a tribe in New Guinea and ate grubs sounds worth checking out, so I put on a fetching outfit, find my eyeliner and lipstick, and send Joey on a play date.

At least there's the consolation prize of entertaining Grace when I get home. "He asked me if I'd pay for his coffee. Shifty eyes. And he's looking for someone to move with him to Papua."

"What about the periodontist?"

"Still in love with his ex-wife. That's all he talked about, I swear."

"Too bad. I could use some discount work on my gums."

Occasionally someone actually attracts me. The thin, dark, widowed theater professor I meet at a lecture at the college asks for my number after we chat about Chekhov. "He's the perfect combination," I tell Grace. "Half Italian, half Jewish. Smart, but not conceited. He used to live in New York. I could have talked to him all night."

"I'm throwing salt over my shoulder."

"Let's not talk about it until he calls me."

But he doesn't.

I invest twenty-five dollars in my own ad: *Spirited witwoman, mid-forties, lithe, attractive, seeks outdoorsy, irreverent counterpart for conversation, fireworks. Let's make each other laugh.*

This generates several voicemails: a religious fanatic who hopes I'm not one of those feminist types, a personal trainer who wants to meet immediately to see if we have physical chemistry, a dad of four who's looking for a substitute mom.

The fourth response I get is from Marty, but I don't tell him the next time we talk. We've stayed in touch.

"Why are all the single women I meet shrinks?" he asks. "Did I ever ask for free therapy?"

"So what does it mean when a guy hits fifty and hasn't lived with anybody since law school?"

"It means *keep away*. And I'm not saying that for personal reasons. But maybe we should see a movie."

"Maybe," is the best I can do.

"Hey Witwoman, you answered my ad!" Marty says a few weeks later.

I guess there are so few available men in Boston, I've met them all. Eternal solitude is starting to sound better than eternal dating.

*   *   *

I DON'T KNOW *where the poetry came from,* Neruda says. *From winter or a river. It touched me so I wrote the first faint line. Pure nonsense. Pure wisdom.* Then the heavens came apart for him, and he was part of the abyss. *Wheeling with the stars.*

And his heart broke loose on the wind.

Why doesn't my writing ever sound like Neruda's?

"Paper is my best friend," writes the student with a difficult story to tell about her two fathers. She never knew about the real one until recently; the pretend father treated her meanly: "Despite the meanness, he loved me anyway, as if I were his own daughter."

When I'm not taking care of Joey's multiplying needs, I'm mothering students, prodding them to figure out their best material and get the vital details down. Some are uninterested and some want me to practically write their midterm essays for them, but I usually turn around the recalcitrant and the fearful by the end of each semester.

Sometimes I'm jealous of their material: a family's exile from war-torn Algeria to France; a Vietnam vet who watched his brother die in an ambush. One of my students had an uncle who was a hit man for the Mafia; another lived with a famous tattoo artist and described his most elaborate masterpiece: the Eiffel Tower on someone's buttock.

Except for my occasional self-indulgent journal entry and endless notes to Jake, all I've written lately is another story about my tormented relationship with my father.

*　*　*

"How's Marty?" Grace asks me out of the blue. "Didn't you say you were in touch?"

"We were, until Arnie came along. But funny you should ask. We're in touch again."

I can tell Grace is glad but trying not to let on. But I've been thinking about Marty. When I call to say, "Happy belated birthday," our two-hour conversation feels as comfortable as taking a bath. "The idea of a younger woman was appealing, but the one I was seeing didn't know who the Beatles were. No kidding. And no more bitter divorcées, either."

"You don't put me in that category?"

"Not technically," he teases me. "What's going on with the long-distance doctor?"

"We're floundering," I fib.

"If neither of you wants to move," he asks so logically, "why bother?"

After a few weeks of being telephone buddies, he asks if I want to get together.

"I'm going to a Purim dance at the Jewish Center," I admit sheepishly. Going to an over-forty singles event is embarrassing.

"You're kidding."

"Would I make that up? Don't rub it in."

"How about a movie instead? There's a French one at the Coolidge."

"With subtitles?"

"A person can grow, Ruth."

"I promised to bring a case of soda to the dance."

"So we'll drop off the soda and work the room for one another. We can always leave."

Marty and I have already tried to fall in love, but it's nice to have a backup plan for the Purim party. As my escort for the Jewish Center affair, Marty gets the satisfaction of being right when he warned me against it. Mingling with a hundred unmatched remainders in garish shirts and spangled halter tops—not one kindred soul for either of us among them—is depressing. The watered-down rock and roll isn't even danceable. So we leave and drive to an Irish bar to drown our dim mating prospects in frosted mugs of Guinness.

The following week Marty asks if I'll join him for dinner with Gene and Merle, a couple he and his wife went on vacations with. I feel like a replacement wife, so I'm glad when we're alone again. After Marty drives me home, we sit in his car for several indecisive minutes, too tired for more conversation.

"The babysitter's going to cost me a fortune. I'd better go pay her."

"What if I drive her home and then come back?"

"If it doesn't work out, we can always break up again."

"We're used to that."

Joey dives onto my bed at six the next morning, not at all surprised Marty's in it. The following weekend, Marty agrees to see *Un Coeur en Hiver*, about a man who pretends to love a violinist who plays Ravel. He repairs her instrument and entices her away from a more dependable lover. But then he doesn't want her after all. Marty likes it almost as much as I do.

It takes me a few days to absorb this sea change. Marty's normal kindnesses—helping me carry groceries or Joey—still take me by surprise. We listen to music, breathing in sync. He smells like soap, and his patience with me and Joey is remarkable.

I've traded in Jake's untamable dark curls and interesting

wardrobe, his fluency with dreams, for Marty's grounded presence, his warm hands and feet. We make unhurried, unexcited love, which must be the kind that survives.

"I guess we weren't ready until now," I tell Grace.

She doesn't say she told me so.

" " "   "

NOW THAT I'VE PLANNED a gymnastics party for Joey's fifth birthday, the details are overwhelming: animal zipper pulls, tops, or trolls for party favors? What kind of cake? Space Raiders paper plates or Ninja Turtle ones? Should I invite Marty? Will Jake be rude to him?

"Just get cheap supermarket cake," Grace says. "They never eat it anyway. And if you don't give them all the same party favor, you'll have a war on your hands."

Joey gets pre-birthday jitters, unleashing his terrible temper. Marty says I should put my foot down, make him go to bed early and miss his favorite TV program. But I know Joey's only picking up my frenzy, so instead of fighting his lousy mood, I make jokes, cajoling him out of his crankiness.

If only I could manage Jake as skillfully. His anti-sugar policy is in full force these days, so now Joey doesn't want the birthday cake I've ordered. I keep it together and fume in private about my kid's fanatical dad. "The other kids will eat the cake," I tell Joey. "You can have an apple."

The party's a great success and almost worth all the misplaced anxiety. I wipe spilled juice, take pictures, talk to parents, watch the jumping, somersaulting kids. Marty picks up the pizzas and Max slices up the rock-hard ice cream cake; Jake doesn't talk to any of the parents, but I watch him do a flip on the trampoline. I finally take a break and swing on a trapeze, then jump into a pit of foam rubber blocks. It's so hard to climb out that I stay there while the kids jump in on top of me.

Joey counts his presents before going to bed: "These are the ones I really like," he explains, "and these are the ones I *said* I liked, to be nice." Marty and I sprawl on my L-shaped couch and watch snow fall through a light-pink sky. Are the clouds reflecting light from the white ground, or does the snow absorb the city's incandescence?

In his arms, I stare at the lacework of trees and hear the stillness between Miles Davis's notes. When *Kind of Blue* is over and we need a more tender mood, I put on Harry Chapin's Canadian concert tape. *Go with the wind and ride your storm. Fires in us keep us warm.* The night unfolds like a new land. I'm close to someone who only wants my laughter in return. The snow, the sounds, and then the quiet do their work on us.

The next morning I write down a persistent memory I've carried forever:

It happened last night, but I've always wanted it to, so it qualifies as memory in reverse. You imagine a night when you'll feel embraced by air. There are plagues and civil wars to get through. The peace at the end—your reward for the struggles—recedes so far into the future it's like a movie you will never get to see, but you can still imagine how it will feel.

You don't have the particulars. But somehow you're sure your child will grow up happy, and a man will keep you both in his heart.

* * *

THIS CAN'T BE LOVE *because I feel so well . . . You go to my head . . .*

There's a small hotel. I sound almost like Ella, at least in my car. This must be the real deal because I get teary when a student reads even a mediocre essay with a romantic theme. I can't concentrate on the *Times* —the Republican rage against Clinton or the world situation—and I'm even patient with Jake these days, who senses I'm in love and isn't happy about it.

I'm smart enough by now to choose Marty's constancy and readable heart. "I've freed up some time at work," he says, in frigid February. Now that we're midweek as well as weekend lovers, our next romantic step is a vacation.

After reading guidebooks and comparing notes about the islands we've already been to, Marty and I decide to go to Guadeloupe during my spring break. I want to hike through a tropical forest and write some poetry; Marty likes the idea of remote, topless beaches, and we're both up for snorkeling and Caribbean cuisine.

Jake's gone away twice this winter with his girlfriend, and after I agree to pay for the extra day care, he reluctantly says I can go. I make Joey a book with magazine pictures of beaches and palm trees so he'll know where I am, and a calendar so he can check off the days I'm gone. "You and Daddy will have so much fun together," I tell him.

When he eagerly shouts, "Margarita, too?" I'm suddenly so jealous of my kid's affection for his dad's latest Latina that I want to stay home. And learn how to curse in Spanish.

"Get over it," Marty says, tossing a snorkel mask and flippers on the couch. "I've already bought your gear."

By the time we've crammed our bags in the overhead bin on the plane, I can taste the complimentary rum drinks they'll serve us at the Point-à-Pitre airport. Our quaint *auberge* in the beach town of St. Anne seems charming until trucks and motorcycles roar past us, shining their headlights into our room and drowning out the sound of the sea.

Marty's oblivious, but I hardly sleep, obsessing about what to do, until he finally wakes up. "Let's find another hotel," I whisper.

"Can't you give this place a chance?"

"Are you kidding?" Another motorcycle revs up, as if on cue.

"We'll hardly be here," he cajoles me the next morning at a café. "The *auberge* is just our base so we can explore the whole island."

"But we'll be driving around anyway," I plead. "There's got to be something prettier and quieter." By the time we've finished our *café au lait* and croissants, Marty agrees to let me ask the *hotelier* for our week's deposit back. For the first time in years, my French comes in handy and I win the argument.

Marty's willing to drive for hours along Grand Terre's lush shoreline. We stop at every possible hotel on the southern wing of Guadeloupe's butterfly in search of the impossible: a place with both native charm and reasonable rates. Marty teases me because I want a simple place on a remote beach, but I also want a lounge chair and some shade. At least we're getting along again.

We ask everyone for leads, following dirt roads which are supposed to end at Shangri-La but don't. Each beach has a great restaurant nearby (we're in a *département* of France, after all), and our moods improve after we swim and wash *crevettes* down with *Pomerol*.

When the car won't start, we stand around in the brutal heat for two hours waiting for someone to come fix it. En route again, we take a quick, naked swim, then search the rest of the Atlantic coast for a hotel. The modest places we like are full, and the luxurious ones with vacancies are too expensive. Marty thinks we should swallow our pride and go back to the *auberge* we're now calling

"Traffic by the Sea." We're silent, too discouraged to appreciate the purple-orange sunset.

"OK," I admit. "We should have stayed where we were."

Marty doesn't answer. Why can't I accept things the way they are when they're already pretty good? We stop at a snack bar for cold drinks before turning back, and, since I need someone to talk to, I tell the owner our tale of woe.

"Well, my sister has a house," she says, naming a decent price. "It's near the sea and there's a path." Marty shoots me an *oh no* look, but it's dark already and we're exhausted.

"Let's just stay there for the night?"

He shrugs. I've already ruined his vacation, so why not. But when we finally find the small house on the top of a hill, it's where we're supposed to be. We drag our bags inside, our voices sweet again. The deck overlooks the silvery sea and the night air's pungent with jasmine. "I'll try to fix that noisy toilet if you make the bed," Marty says sweetly. By the time he succeeds, I've set out salami, melon, pâté, and crusty *pain de campagne,* but we head for the bedroom.

My sunburn hurts, especially my breasts, but as soon as our coconut-oiled bodies find a rhythm, my pain melts into hunger for his weight. Noisy lust drowns out the screeching refrigerator and all our differences until we're making slow, deep love. Wooden bed slats loosen and slam onto the tile floor. "Don't worry, babe, I can fix it," Marty says. Next, the loudest mosquitoes we've ever heard attack us like fighter jets.

"The good news is, we're armed!" Marty waves the meter-long can of bug spray he found under the bed. "The bad news is—it's empty."

We love our week at the "villa," even after someone steals three bottles of wine from our kitchen windowsill and a dog runs off with one of my sandals. Without beach chairs, we sunbathe back to back while breezes pelt us with hibiscus blossoms. We float over coral reefs, neon fish darting between our legs.

We've left our grey, cold world for iridescence, lime-green palms, and black volcanic beaches. I cajole Marty into a sweaty hike through the rain forest and later he scrubs red mud off our sneakers. How did I get so lucky?

Then luckier. "Blizzard in the Northeast!" Marty shouts after calling Air France to confirm our flight home. "All flights can-celled—for three days."

"Jake will have a shit fit."

"What can he expect you to do?"

"You *have* to get back here *immediately*," Jake commands me. "School's cancelled for the rest of the week. Who'll watch Joey?"

"I'd get there if I could." I try to sound sympathetic, but I'm giddy with satisfaction. "I'll keep trying." How many school snow days have kept me from *my* job? "Can I talk to Joey?"

Joey's on the toilet, happy to chat a blue streak until I remember how much the call is costing me. Then I call Grace for an update.

"Enjoy yourselves. You're not missing a thing. The roads aren't even plowed, but *somehow* Jake made it through four-foot snow-drifts and carried Joey to our door! The boys had a really fun day watching videos and making cookies."

Marty and I spend our windfall days drinking rum and eating at great, cheap restaurants. An alluring young woman on the beach holds a beach blanket around me while I slither into an electric blue Parisian maillot, which Marty insists on buying for me.

I've waited long enough to be so cherished. On our last tropical night we're as comfortable as old friends. We have grilled turbot and tomatoes in aspic and *blancmange de coco*—a shimmering circle of coconut custard swimming in *crème fraiche*; there are shards of fresh coconut meat in the custard and a chocolate shell balancing over this creation on sprigs of mint.

"The *blancmange*," I say, drunk on my luck, "is the point of this trip."

"Perhaps," Marty says, "of life itself."

18.
i find the catbird seat

MARTY'S BEEN DOING most of the schlepping from his place to mine, but I try to make it up to him by cooking dinners and listening to his work frustrations: broken computers, uncooperative clients, difficult employees. Since I wait to eat with him after I feed Joey, most nights I'm in the kitchen for at least four hours straight.

Sometimes the guys watch sports on television, and one blissful Sunday, Marty and Joey fix my bookcase. I try to give them equal attention, but Joey usually wins. "Do you think you can edit my newsletter tonight?" Marty asks when all I want to do is take a bath and read in bed.

"In a minute." I have to find the motor for Joey's Lego boat before he knocks over my pile of papers and Marty's as well. Even after I find it, he still won't play by himself so I can check Marty's grammar.

"Ruth, I need to talk to you about whether I have to fire someone or not." I like that Marty trusts me with his important decisions, but I'm on overload.

"Who wants ice cream?" is my escape route. A drive to the supermarket will leave me alone with my thoughts, which I hope are still there, somewhere.

"Chocolate," Joey shouts.

Marty gives me a look: your child's spoiled. I know he wants strawberry so I get Neapolitan to make everyone happy. When I get back, in a much better mood, my boyfriend's cloudy face reminds me that he's only eating fat-free these days.

"I thought you were going to help me lose a little weight."

"I'm really sorry." I try to sound apologetic but don't succeed.

"You have pretty sophisticated taste buds, Joey." Marty refuses to believe a kid can tell the difference between high-test and low-cal. But I've proven otherwise by innumerable experiments; if I water down Joey's too-sweet juice, he makes a face, and when I buy generic Cheerios, he's onto me.

"How was the checkers game?" I ask.

"Joey completely lost it when I beat him."

"He's five. Can't you let him win once in a while?" I try to say this so Joey doesn't notice.

"I'm five and a half." Ice cream drips from Joey's chin until Marty swipes him with a dishcloth just in time. Not gently enough, but I hold my tongue.

"How's he going to deal with real life if you keep catering to him?" I know I'm not great at setting limits, and I appreciate Marty's objectivity, but I don't think I'm spoiling my kid if I buy his favorite ice cream. It's already past Joey's bedtime so I forget about his bath. When I skip some pages of *The Velveteen Rabbit* to make up for lost time, my kid insists I go back and read the missing parts.

Joey's usually a good sleeper, but lately he's been waking up with bad dreams—just as Marty and I are falling asleep. *The monster's trying to eat me and you and Daddy. A snake was in my bed and he bited my eyes. I want a gun to shoot the bad monster.*

Marty carries Joey back to bed a few times and reassures him the monsters have gone away. But the following week, Joey's upset about a purple witch, so I'm distressed enough to call Jake.

"Has Joey been having bad dreams when he's with you?"

"Absolutely not," he sneers. "But I'm sure he doesn't like your boyfriend being there all the time."

"Marty's really good with him," I exaggerate. "Besides, it's none of your business."

"My child is none of my business? Joey sleeps fine over here, so I suggest you think about that."

After another week of nightly episodes I'm afraid my kid's so sleep-deprived I'll hear from his teacher.

"Tell Mommy what you're scared of," I try. When my baby boy was in trouble, I could always swoop down and comfort him, but now he pulls so far away it hurts.

The pediatrician suggests a kiddy shrink.

"Isaac was driving us crazy a few years ago," Grace says, "so we finally took him to Dr. Fish and he figured it out."

"What was going on?" I'm surprised there was ever trouble in her easygoing family.

"He was having a hard time in school. And he was jealous of his brother. Garden-variety stuff, but it was awful. As soon as Isaac opened up, he stopped acting out. You'd think we could have figured it out by ourselves."

After I talk to Dr. Fish and make an appointment, I tell Jake.

"Fine, Ruth. Just don't expect me to pay for it." He's sure it's all my fault.

"We're going to see a nice man named Dr. Fish," I mention casually to Joey after I pick him up from school. "Then we'll get cheeseburgers."

"I'm not sick," he informs me. "I'm not going."

"He wants to make your bad dreams go away."

"I don't have bad dreams," he screams. But the bribe lures him into Dr. Fish's waiting room. The psychologist smiles so warmly at my miserable child I have a crush on him.

"You must be Joey."

"I don't have bad dreams," he shouts.

"Well, I'm really glad about that. Is that a soccer shirt? What position do you play?" After a few minutes in Fish's office full of puppets and children's art, Joey's talking about his favorite, happiest dreams. A big bird takes him for a ride and teaches him to fly. "Is it OK if your mom goes outside for a little while?" Fish asks him.

Joey comes out smiling.

"I'd like to see you and Joey's dad together next time," Dr. Fish tells me on the phone.

"Sure," I say. "But we haven't spent an hour in the same room in years."

Jake agrees to go — once — for Joey's sake.

"Kids have nightmares when something feels out of control," Dr. Fish tells us. "Joey says you tell him stories about powerful monsters." He looks at Jake.

"We make up characters together. He seems to like them."

"Well, maybe he used to. But he's older now, and he takes them more seriously."

I've always been impressed with how creatively Jake plays with Joey, but this time he's gone too far in the dark direction. I know he wasn't purposely trying to terrify our kid, and I've never questioned the depth of his love, but when it comes to where he stops and Joey begins, he can be clueless. If I weren't so enraged, I'd feel compassionate.

Dr. Fish stands up, smiling at us. "You're both doing a terrific job with Joey," he reassures us.

Joey's nightmares finally stop.

     *   *   *

GRACE AND MAX are taking their boys to Washington D.C. to absorb some history.

"Our relatives sort of invited us," she laughs. "Boy, will they be sorry."

When I hear other parents discussing their family summer vacations, I'm jealous. I'd love to take Joey camping or to the beach, but it wouldn't be Marty's idea of a vacation, and I don't want to do it by myself. "Rhonda invited me to the Vineyard," I tell Grace, "but she really means without Joey."

Grace says she'll ask around, then calls me a few days later, totally excited. "My cousin Shirley stayed at a great place on the Cape. A bunch of cottages on a private beach, called—get this—Wayward Park. What could be bad?"

"We're all booked up," the rental agent tells me, bursting my bubble. He'll put me on a waiting list for next year.

A few hours later, he calls back. "You're lucky," he says. "Grey Cottage is available for the last two weeks in August." By now I'm used to Grace's amazing connections, but this time she feels like my fairy godmother.

"My neighbors Melvin and Shirley loved the place. That was before he made his millions and they bought their own house in Chatham."

"Five hundred dollars a week?" Rhonda asks, utterly sure I've rented a total dump. "Don't worry, Ruth. You'll be outside most of the time."

"What if it rains?" I ask Grace.

"It's summer. You'll dry out. You should have seen some of the places we rented. They could have been *condemned*, but we had a great time anyway. Or at least the kids did."

What else matters? I rent the bargain cottage, sight unseen. When the big day comes, I pack up the car and drive a few hours to a small group of cottages, right on Cape Cod Bay. As soon as I stop at a cottage that looks too nice to be ours, Joey runs to the playground full of barefoot kids.

I expected a shack, but the 1927 salt box is fairly clean and even charming: three bedrooms, screened-in porch, outdoor shower. It's stuffed with seventy-five years' worth of beach chairs, clamming rakes, fishing rods, and puzzles left by long-ago Grey children.

I drag our bags into the house and put away the groceries. Finally I grab a warm beer and sit in the catbird seat, an ancient, squeaky glider. I stare at trees and sky, listening to birds and wind and children, especially Joey, chattering a mile a minute on the nearby playground.

19.
sour blackberries

IN THE MORNING, Joey and I sit in a circle near the community house for story hour, and after that Coach Ted organizes a game called Cracker Dodge that Joey already knows how to play. Kids streak by on bikes, and when one of them falls, the closest adult picks him up and wipes his tears.

Wayward Park is any parent's dream, and a single mom's utopia. Joey and I take to its August ease like gulls to flight—especially when Joey chases them. I let him eat pizza for breakfast, tuna sandwiches for dinner. If my tired, sweaty boy won't take a shower, so be it. Who cares about the sand in his sheets?

"Choose your battles," is Grace's philosophy. After dinner I let Joey loose again to race around in the dark with his pack of new friends, and when he comes home, the two of us chase fireflies.

I'm definitely the outlier in Wayward Park: not only a single parent, but a Jewish one. Most "Parkies" have been coming here since childhood, and many have married one another. It's hard to be surrounded by so many intact and happy-looking families.

"You have no idea what's really going on," Rhonda reminds me. But I'm envious watching dads teach their daughters to play tennis, moms carrying huge picnics to the beach, and couples taking beach photos of their broods for their Christmas cards. Joey and I play water games and walk through the nearby cemetery where

I read him the names carved on mossy headstones. I teach him to play tennis, wishing someone would teach me.

My favorite moments are on the porch after Joey's asleep and the park's finally quiet. Sometimes I hear the intense chatter of teenagers on the swings, their lives and loves brand new.

"It's really a community," is how I describe the place to Marty, but I can't picture him at family field day, or at last night's ham and bean supper. "A swarm of kids invaded the cottage the other day, looking for Indian pennies for a scavenger hunt," I say. "You'd go nuts here."

"Sounds like you hardly miss me." He's about to leave for Nantucket, where he's sharing a "professional singles" house: flat-screen TV, dishwasher, motorboat, no kids allowed.

"Not true. But this is definitely not your scene." I've spent the morning watching Joey dig tunnels on the sandbar while the tide filled our stripe of shoreline. It was a clear enough day to see all the way across the bay to the Pilgrim Monument in Provincetown. The uncomplicated solitude feels great, but that's because I have a lover in the background.

The universe has handed me an unexpected gift, and I can't wait to tell Grace, who should be home from Washington by now. I dial her number while eating the blackberries Joey picked, their sourness a contrast to this sweet summer.

"How's by you?" I say. "You never write, you never call."

"Oh, OK. What's going on down there?" She sounds low-key, but in the mood to listen, so I go on for a while about my dream vacation with Joey. "We're invited to a progressive dinner, and I'm supposed to bring an appetizer. How does Max make those fancy deviled eggs?" There's some odd dead air between us. "Joey misses the guys. Can you come down for a visit before we have to leave? You'll love the outdoor shower."

Grace is never this quiet. Maybe her family trip wasn't so good. "It rained for two days straight down here," I fill in the empty space. Maybe a little bad news will comfort her. "Why didn't you warn me that everyone on the Cape goes to the Laundromat on rainy days? It took three hours to get out of there."

She laughs, but not as heartily as usual. We finally get around to her trip. "There was such a heat wave it was like walking around in a hair dryer. The kids fought constantly. I'm sure Max's cousins were sorry they invited us."

I wait for a punch line, some joke to keep us going. Instead, I hear, "But the real bummer is that, just before we left, I found a lump in my right breast." This doesn't register until she says, "They think it's cancer, so they're going to take it out."

Purple petunias spill out of the window boxes. I'm about to deadhead them when I hear Grace say *biopsy*. I fall back onto the glider. "You let me complain about *nothing* with news like that?"

"I'd rather hear your problems. Come on, Ruth, think up a few more for me." All I can do is ask questions, but I hate the answers. "The operating rooms were booked up before we left, so the surgeon said I might as well go to Washington."

"You were supposed to have a vacation with that to look forward to?"

"He admitted it might be a little hard, but what else could I do?"

I would have staged a hunger strike in front of the hospital until they let me in, but Grace spent a week slogging around the Smithsonian and the Holocaust Museum, trying to put the scary business out of her mind.

"I was hoping for a break after all the *tsures* we had this year." It was a tragic season for her South Brookline neighborhood. Isaac's wonderful English teacher died of lymphoma, and a sixth-grader slammed into a tree and killed himself on a school ski trip. The

Steins are connected to almost everyone in their town, so all this hit them very hard.

"The summer was supposed to be great," she continues. "Instead, I get a life-threatening illness."

I have no idea what to say. The glider makes me dizzy. I muffle a slow *Oh my God.*

"I keep thinking of that Jimmy Durante line," she rescues me. *"What a revolting development this is."*

"I can see you in a funny hat, smoking a cigar."

"I'm sorry to bum you out with all of this, Ruthela."

     "   "   "

I FIND MY SANDALS, walk out into the white noon heat, and sink down against a tree in the cemetery. I'm as terrified as if it were me. My women friends have always grounded me. Especially, these days, Grace. There's no one I want to spill these very bad beans to. Instead, I call Grace as often as I dare to bother her. She must be answering the same questions over and over, but I can't help it.

"How are things going out there?" she always asks, delaying her own dismal details.

I stretch out the local gossip as long as I can. "The couple with the biggest house is getting a divorce and fighting over their cottage."

"How was the progressive dinner?"

"One guy was actually wearing pants with lobsters on them."

"I thought those went out with Eisenhower."

"It was bad enough being the only Jew around here. Now I think I'm the only Democrat."

"But did they like your deviled eggs?"

I screw up my courage and ask for a health update. "Oh," she practically brushes off my question. "This one thinks this and that one thinks that, but no one's sure about anything. How am *I* supposed to know what to do? Too bad I forgot to go to medical school."

"You'll figure it all out," I say, having no idea what I'm talking about. *My best, most precious friend in the world could disappear.* I catch myself indulging in self-pity.

"I'm getting pretty good at denial," she says. "I'll get the lump taken out and that will be that."

When I finally reach Marty, he's very sympathetic about Grace, but busy at the moment barbecuing chicken for his housemates. "I'll call you later," he promises, tequila sunrise in his voice.

It's dead low tide in the afternoon this week. Joey walks with me all the way to the end of the flats where the tide waits to come back in again. The locals call this walking to the outer bar, or to Bermuda. Joey throws seaweed at me and crabs snap at our feet. When the tide turns, we race it back to shore.

I wake up each morning with a stone in my heart and then remember why. Now, having a good time takes a lot of effort. The bad news keeps reverberating, even when I'm swimming.

"I'm packing up," I tell Grace. "I have to spit-polish this place by eleven tomorrow morning. The least you could do is come out and help."

"Don't ruin your last weekend cleaning, Ruthie. Just sweep a little, mop a little, swish the brush around the toilet, and you're done."

"But by now I'm friends with the couple I rented the place from," I remind her.

"Oh, it's terrible when you know them," she sympathizes, always able to wear my shoes.

20.

tuna on white

ONCE WE'RE BACK in Boston I'm ready for my first break from Joey in almost three weeks. But when he jumps into Jake's arms as if I don't exist, it smarts, and I want him to jump back into mine. After they leave I have just enough time to visit Grace before Marty arrives.

Her grass needs cutting, and the impatiens I helped her plant in June haven't survived. I wonder if her rich neighbors ever complain about the bikes, helmets, and baseball bats all over her yard. I step inside the always-open door and hand Max the bag of sweet corn I bought at a Cape farm stand. "This is for my corniest friends. I think it was actually grown in New Jersey."

"She's sleeping." I've never seen him anything but jovial, but he's barely making eye contact.

"If you weren't kosher I'd have brought you lobsters."

"Lobster isn't kosher?" Max is generous enough to respond to my pathetic joke.

"What's going on?" No point stalling the inevitable. I take a deep breath and search his face for clues.

"They took out the lump yesterday and it didn't look great. They have to go in again, the doctor said. 'More seriously.'"

When I place my arms around his shoulders, Max feels so fragile I'm afraid to squeeze him too hard. We sit on the cluttered stairs where we always chat a mile a minute. I have no idea what to say. No point telling him about the Cape, or updating him about my love life. I've hardly absorbed the original awful news, and now there's more. At least the TV's blasting cartoons, so his boys don't hear us being so quiet.

Grace sounded upbeat a few days ago and I'd let her slip from my thoughts, obsessing instead about whether Marty and I are supposed to be together. Did I miss him enough and for the right reasons? Was he envious of his upscale, kidless, jet-set summer housemates? He mentioned going sailing with a few of the women. Did any of them strike? Was he tempted?

"I'll tell Gracie to call you," Max promises.

Back home, with suitcases full of dirty laundry to deal with, all I can do is take a nap, hoping I'll get a second wind before Marty gets here. I've been looking forward to shaving my legs and putting on a dress—then letting him take it off—but I may not have the energy.

Marty arrives with zinnias from his garden and a flattering tan, happy to see me. I guess I beat out the competition on Nantucket, but while we kiss I feel reticent. His aftershave smells too limey. I try not to stare at his garish Hawaiian-print shirt, obviously new.

"What do you think?"

I smile noncommittally. I did suggest he update his wardrobe, but I didn't mean orange and turquoise rayon. We listen to Jimmy Buffet in his car and catch up over popcorn shrimp and fried calamari at Legal Sea Food. I don't ask what happened to his diet. Couldn't he exercise a little?

"I almost went aground the day I took those hot babes sailing. *That* made a great impression."

"I had a *liaison dangereuse*. My eighty-year-old landlord kept dropping by for iced tea and a chat," I tell him. "What a sweet-heart." We sit in Marty's dark, wood-paneled living room and drink wine, finally quiet, which feels easiest. I try not to judge his taste in furniture, his geometric art. I need his kindness.

By the time we're in his old-fashioned bedroom I'm ready to be held and touched. Marty almost feels motherly as he strokes my hair and touches my lips when I try to talk. I let myself climax slowly. We laugh a bit before we fall asleep.

＊　＊　＊

"COMING HOME from a great vacation stinks, huh?" Grace says in her usual feisty voice, a master at faking it.

"Did I give you permission to have more trouble?"

"Oh, that last stupid tumor marker test. Not one doctor thought it would show anything. Max is falling apart big-time. He's on his third trip to Star Market to work off his nervous energy. Can he get you anything?"

"No thanks. I've been cooking for two weeks straight. Marty took me to Legal last night."

"They just redecorated," she says. "Is it gorgeous? I hope you ordered the trout amandine. By the way, are you bringing Marty to our party?" I'd assumed she and Max would cancel their twenty-fifth anniversary bash, but it's probably a good distraction. "Max has been shopping and cooking for weeks," Grace laughs. "He should have been a chef."

I'm in luck, Grace tells me. They're having one of their popular "tacky" parties I've heard so much about.

"You've never been to one before? I guess they're not so big in the East Village."

"What am I supposed to wear?"

"It's kind of a fifties thing. Just go to the thrift shop. And bring whatever dish your mother used to make for parties. Try to have bad taste for once, Ruth. It'll be educational."

I find neon-pink clam diggers, a sheer lime-green blouse, platform sandals, and pearlized pop-it beads at the Hadassah Thrift Shop. Marty has a sky-blue polyester leisure suit in his closet from the seventies.

"Good thing I didn't take your advice," he says because I suggested he get rid of whatever he hasn't worn in decades.

"Love the threads!" Max greets us, hardly an Elvis lookalike, although he has the right wig. He's sticking blowup flamingos all over the lawn and wearing a truly awful double-breasted suit and a Betty Boop tie. "I hope you and Marty are going to enter the Twister competition."

You'd think his world was perfect.

I put my lemon Jell-O mold with pineapple and cottage cheese on the table with all the other unappealing delicacies: Velveeta and olive sandwiches, sloppy Joes, tuna casseroles. Good thing I have no appetite.

"That looks fabulous," Grace says. "My mother made *her* molds with orange Jell-O and brown bananas. I can still taste it—what a Proustian memory!" She's wearing a chartreuse and white polka-dotted sailor dress and cat's-eye glasses. The star of the evening—despite the sadness in her eyes.

"Love the mules!" I tell her.

"Pig in a blanket?" She's surrounded by a gaggle of her garishly dressed girlfriends all talking at once. Who else knows the news? Who else is faking a party mood?

"Twenty-five years is a quarter of a century!" someone announces when Grace and Max kiss and blow out the candles on a heart-shaped cake decorated with a couple in a red hot rod. Grace looks exactly like Lucille Ball tonight, her gestures and singsong voice adorably wacky.

"And it feels," Max says, "like only twenty-four!"

Marty's in better spirits than I am, maybe because he's passing out the mai tais. "Three kinds of cheap rum," he says. "Not bad." Some couples are doing the cha-cha á la Xavier Cugat. I notice Grace's boys spying on all the ridiculous-looking adults from the top of the stairs, and remember doing the same thing when my parents and their friends took dancing lessons in our living room.

Marty and I gyrate to "Rock Around the Clock" and "Maybellene," then pretend we're adolescents in lust to "Over the Mountain, Across the Sea." *Tell all the sands and every blade of gra-ass. Please tell the wind to let my love pa-ass.* When he dips me, I'm thirteen again.

"Amazing party," I tell Grace the following day.

"Good news!" she announces. "I passed the blood count test. Now I can get the poison." She's seen several more specialists, read six books and dozens of articles, and talked to every breast cancer patient she could track down. Fortunately, her oldest friend, whom she still calls Baby B for some reason, is married to an oncologist.

With nothing but abysmal options, Grace has chosen Plan A: partial mastectomy (one day in the hospital), then chemo and radiation, depending on what they find. Her glands don't feel swollen, a good sign they'll get "clean margins" the next time they go in.

My friend has moved to another country, and I'm trying to learn the language she's already fluent in.

"By the way," she says, thrilled to change the topic. "I ran into Eleanor." One of the book club doyennes, Eleanor would win the Self-Absorbed Olympics. "She went on for at least a half hour about having ordered the wrong couch. '*Why does everything bad always happen to me?*' she actually whined. If I'd thought it would shut her up, I'd have filled her in a little."

"Want some company for chemo day?" I ask, as if Grace has front row tickets for a great concert.

"You're the best, Ruth. Are you free tomorrow afternoon?"

"My last class is over at two. There's an English Department meeting after that, but no one cares what I have to say anyway."

As soon as we enter the Faulkner Hospital parking lot, I'm assaulted by the real deal. I pass the building all the time without noticing it or caring what goes on inside, but now I have to find out. Does Grace know I'm relying on her for courage?

Fortunately, we're alone in the infusion room, on a high floor with a wonderful view of the still-emerald Great Blue Hills in the distance. Sun streams through the windows. Grace keeps up a lively repartee to charm the staff, especially a young black nurse who seems to genuinely like her.

"So they finally awarded you the magic bullet?" the nurse asks with obvious sarcasm.

My friend rolls her eyes, then fills me in. "The last chemo made me *miserable*. I vomited for hours. *Then* I find out there's a pill that totally takes away the nausea. But they don't give it to you the first time because it costs three hundred dollars."

The nurse shakes her head sympathetically. "Probably only ninety-five percent of chemo patients end up needing it, so I guess they figure, Why not wait and see?"

I absorb each heartrending blow, trying to hide my distress while Grace seems almost adjusted to the terror and indignity. And when Dr. Cynthia Weiss finally makes her grand entrance, only forty-five minutes late, add annoyance to the list.

"Oh goody," Grace whispers. "Time for our pre-chemo literary chat. All she wants to talk about is books. *What did you think of Homesick Restaurant? Well, that's interesting! By the way, your prognosis looks so-so."*

Breast oncologist Weiss, looking perky in her red, size-two DKNY suit and tasteful diamond studs, is the spitting image of Grace's imitation of her.

"You were so right about *The Accidental Tourist!"* she tells Grace. "I couldn't put it down." Just as she's about to get to the cancer part of the conversation, her phone rings and she spins around on her designer heels and rushes out to take the call.

"She gets smaller every time I see her," Grace says while the nurse hooks her up for the three-hour drip. I pull out cheese Danishes and coffee, pencils, and the *Times* crossword puzzle.

"This will feel cool," the nurse says. I watch the venomous needle drain into a vein on the back of my friend's hand and feel an icy, mainline twinge go through me, too.

Grace doesn't look like Lucy anymore. I read about the Middle East while she dozes. But as soon as she's awake again, she fills me in on how the Palestinians ended up as refugees in Gaza. We study the newspaper maps of Israel in 1,000 B.C., in 1967 after the Six Day War, and today, October 17, 1993.

When it's time for her second plastic bag of fluid, my friend sits totally abandoned, hooked to an empty IV, with a sadly resigned look on her face. I can hear Dr. Weiss chatting in her office across the hall.

When I walk by, I realize she's talking to her au pair.

"Well, if they don't eat the soup, just give them the crackers and milk. You don't have to call me about every decision!"

"I think she's having a terrible, no-good, very bad day," I tell Grace. "Child-care problems." We look at one another, thinking the same murderous thoughts, so I go out again and stand in front of Weiss's open door to catch her eye. "Grace is waiting," I whisper, motioning.

"I'll tell the nurse you're ready in there," she waves me away.

"So how's your practically live-in boyfriend?" I knew Grace would ask sooner or later.

"Well?"

I know what she's thinking: *Isn't it time to move this thing along?*

The truth is I need the breathing space between our romantic visits, sliding into an empty bed and not having to be a compassionate companion, or even to talk. Is it because Grace has never lived alone that she doesn't seem to crave the pleasure of solitude?

"I kind of like things the way they are."

"That's because Marty's doing most of the *schlepping.*"

Maybe I'm supposed to feel guilty, but Dr. Weiss breezes back just in time to save me from that conversation.

"So we're giving you the sandwich plan," she says as if it really has to do with lunch: "Chemo, radiation, then chemo again." She rushes through the clinical part of the conversation so she can ask her patient what to read next.

I draw a blank. Thank God for Grace's amazingly retentive bookish brain. "*The Kitchen God's Wife* is much better than *Joy Luck Club*. The mother-daughter conflict is believably intense, and it's so rich with details about those poor women in nineteenth-century China," she fires off so we can get out of there and complain about Weiss all the way home.

21.
laundry

JUST AS GRACE predicted, Marty's tired of going back and forth from his place to mine. I'm sympathetic, just not ready — or guilty enough? — to change our routine. Joey's a good excuse. Plus, full-time life with Marty feels risky. "Let's think about it," I stall.

Then, a few days later, he mentions, nonchalantly after pouring us both a glass of Scotch, that he put his house on the market. Joey's jumping back and forth from my lap to Marty's, not even close to winding down for the night.

Marty smiles at me warily. "Are you kidding?" is the best I can come up with.

He stares back, defiant. *Fait accompli.* I'm too surprised to catch Joey before he bangs his chin on the coffee table. I drag my screaming kid to his room and calm him down enough to put on a story tape and turn out his light.

Now I'm the one who feels like screaming. "I assumed you'd let me know before you made that decision," is the most polite response I can come up with.

"What's the big deal, Ruth?" He's watching television to avoid eye contact.

I'm in self-righteous mode. "Where you live kind of in-volves me."

"This doesn't mean I have to live *here*." Marty's mesmerized by a commercial for pantyhose.

If he doesn't want to live with Joey and me, I'm devastated. But if he *assumes* he can move in with us without discussing it, I'm bullshit. "You just spring this on me?" Our first real storm, which I hope Joey's *Phantom Tollbooth* tape will drown out.

"Business is awful. I guess I've been feeling so upset I couldn't level with you. The mortgage is too much. But if you want me to, I'll rent someplace cheaper."

I finally stop listening to my story and hear his. Marty's the kindest man I've ever known. He adores me and my kid, and I can't imagine losing my chance to have an actual, more or less normal family.

"I know we're kind of messy and way too noisy," I hear myself say, my eyes now full of tears. "But if you can deal with the chaos around here . . ."

If the right thing happens, does it matter if it's for the wrong reason?

        ▪   ▪   ▪

"MY HAIR'S STARTING to fall out," Grace mumbles in an unguarded moment. "It was all over my pillow this morning. I'm glad Max didn't notice."

I stifle a gasp.

"Do you think the hair fairy will take it away and leave me a quarter?"

All I can do is change the subject. "Any ideas for a writing assignment based on Alice Walker's essay about Zora Neal Hurston?"

"I'll have to reread the essay. Bring it over and we can figure something out. You can be the first to see my new wig if you get here tonight. Alice is taking me shopping."

When I drop in later, a shockingly well-coiffed Grace comes down the stairs singing "Here She Comes, Miss America." Alice (not exactly a fashion maven) convinced her to spend the extra money for real hair, but it looks totally fake.

"Let's go to the mall before the boys come home!" I hope my enthusiasm comes across as real, but I'm a lousy actress.

Never one to turn down an excursion, Grace jumps into my car as excited as if we were taking off for the airport to fly to Tahiti. A Bloomingdale's saleslady in the hat department helps Grace try on cloches, head scarves, and velvet headbands.

"I always feel so inadequate when it comes to accessories," she mock-sighs. It's a toss-up between a purple silk combination head-band/scarf and a Black Watch plaid beret, so I buy Grace both.

￭   ￭   ￭

WHEN I GET HOME, Marty's knee-deep in pots, pans, dishes, and bowls. "I thought I'd sort through what we both have so we can organize the kitchen a little better," he says. Can he tell I cried all the way home in the car over Grace's lost curls? I drag him to the couch to tell him the latest sorrow.

After all the men who painted, made music, or traveled the globe, I'm in thrall to a man who spent a Saturday afternoon cleaning out my cabinets and throwing away boxes of rice full of grain moths. His clothes hardly take up any space in my closet, his music system sounds better than mine, and he's resuscitating my houseplants.

Better yet, I can meet a friend for a movie while he and Joey watch baseball. Now that we're sharing the bills, I buy oysters, brandied chestnuts, a case of designer beer. I've bought celadon-colored sheets and let Marty put a lock on the bedroom door.

"The clean and neat issue's going to be a little tricky," I tell Grace, whose house makes mine look orderly.

"Get someone to clean. It'll be one less thing to fight about."

"There's only one problem."

"Only one is amazing."

"I can live with the antique oak ice chest he uses for a liquor cabinet. But you should see his Art Deco dresser. I think that's why it took me so long to let him move in."

"How bad can it be?"

"Words are inadequate."

"Try, Ruthie."

"Dark ugly swirly mahogany with atrocious Bakelite and silver handles." I hear her groan. "It looks like a super-gaudy coffin. And it's his prize possession!"

"You'll have to train yourself not to look at it."

"I was hoping his ex-wife would take it since she has the matching bed and night table, but no such luck. 'My bedroom's spare and Japanesey,' I told him. 'I didn't notice an actual *décor* in here,' he said. OK, so maybe my patchwork quilt and velvet curtains don't exactly go together, but now the room looks like a bad yard sale."

"You're going to have to get over it."

"Tact is not a Kooperman trait."

When Grace finally sees the dresser, she actually shrieks. "You weren't exaggerating, Ruth. It's hideous. But eventually you'll redecorate together. Wait, I have an idea. When Marty goes out of town you can give it away and say it was stolen. *Honey, I can't believe it. They must have known how valuable that dresser was because it was all they took!*"

When I come home from work one night, Marty's rubbing Joey's legs to take away his growing pains. The man who never wanted kids is definitely stretching. During a gospel concert in a Baptist church, Marty and I hold hands while Joey runs around amusing strangers. *Lean on me when you fall, hold on tight, I am all.*

And we'll rise. And we'll rise. And be free. I feel something akin to spiritual. Have I ever felt this way in a synagogue?

*   *   *

A FEW DAYS AFTER Grace's last—we hope—chemo and literary session, a market researcher calls to ask her if she wants to join a focus group. "It's about washing machines and dryers," she announces cheerily. "I signed us both up. They'll pay us seventy-five dollars each, so we'll have a fancy lunch afterwards."

"How about a movie or a facial instead?" I try. Why, in the middle of fighting cancer, does she want to discuss *laundry*?

Will it help life feel more normal?

"It'll be fun, Ruth. Max will pick up Joey and feed him at our house." Of course I agree. "Oh, by the way, Ruth. We have to pretend we don't know each other."

"That will be the hard part."

Later that week, we take the subway downtown and sit at a large round table in a windowless room with seven other women. Grace sits directly opposite me, which could be a problem.

"I do ten loads a week," the chatty young blond with four kids says, "and I adjust the settings on both machines for every single load."

I chime in to complain about lint collectors and unpleasant-sounding timer buzzers. I learn a great deal about detergent developments, sorting whites and colors, stain removal, spin and soak cycles.

"Would you like a machine that actually talks to you?" we're asked. Grace says yes and I say no. "To work by remote control, even from your car?" Everyone loves that.

"Can you tell me why my dryer does the cha-cha-cha?" asks the woman who looks much too old to be pregnant. This cracks Grace and me up, and we almost blow our cover.

Several times during the passionate discussion we roll our eyes at each other. You couldn't make this material up.

"Why can't they invent a machine that shoots the clean wet clothes straight into the dryer?" someone suggests, and the group goes wild with enthusiasm. When the cha-cha lady brings up her terrible problem again, Grace and I almost slide under the table in hysterics. I finally escape to the ladies' room before I lose it altogether.

"You were right. This was the perfect outing," I tell Grace after we grab our checks and get in the elevator.

*   *   *

THE SANDWICH PLAN is moving along. Grace's hair has grown back even curlier than before, and we've banished illness from our minds. We ceremoniously throw out both her wigs.

"*Oy*, if my mother could see me now. *My daughter the big spender. One expensive wig wasn't enough—she needed two.* Want to come to my mapping session tomorrow?"

"Sounds exotic." If only she were talking about going to a travel agency.

"They have to mark me up before I get the radiation. I'm thinking of it as getting a cool tattoo."

The next morning, late as usual, we race through the Dana-Farber marble and chrome lobby. Hospitals feel like hotels these days, if you block out a few details. When a friendly volunteer offers us doughnuts, Grace tells me to take one. "They're stale, but it makes the candy stripers happy."

Way down in the sub-basement, we follow the signs to Nuclear

Medicine where I sit in the corner of a cell-like room while my friend lies bare-breasted on a cold table. Doctors confer over her as if she's not here. Everything's grey, no windows to stare out of, and the magazines are two years old.

"You never know what will be the worst part of a procedure," Grace says while holding onto a bar behind her head. She looks like she's stretched out on a medieval rack, but I spare her the image. "In this case, my arms are being pulled out of their sockets. They made me do the same thing last week. Then I lost my car in the garage and it took me forever to find it. That was even worse than the arms."

Time to distract her. Thank goodness we have the last book club session, at my house, to deconstruct. "I promised the women they wouldn't get mugged in your neighborhood," Grace confesses.

"And my East Village poet friends would consider me a bourgeois sellout!" I remember making fun of suburban women's book clubs, which I don't confess to Grace.

"Did you see the funny look I got from Claire when I served the cake on *dinner* plates?"

"You were taking a huge risk."

"I had no choice. My dessert plates are plastic. But according to Claire, I was totally in style. *It's fine*, she informed me. *They're using large dessert plates now.* Boy, did I breathe a sigh of relief when I heard *that*."

We call Claire "the Authority," and quote her often. "Claire's probably bragging to all her Newton friends about her daring excursion to the Boston slums," Grace says.

"It took me two days to clean my apartment. Thank God we actually talked about the book."

"That hardly ever happens! You achieved a miracle."

Why do I always believe Grace's hyperboles?

The book we discussed, *When Heaven and Earth Changed Places*, tells how a young Vietnamese woman survived the war both as a member of the Viet Cong and a friend of the American GIs. Only forgiveness can heal the horrors we inflict on one another, according to author Le Ly Hayslip. I started thinking about who I need to forgive.

While a scary, loud machine charts Grace's lymph nodes, I watch flashing dots on a screen: stars in a clear night sky. The radiologists have to calculate where to shoot their invisible arrows so they don't strike Grace's heart or lungs.

"I used to ask questions," she says, "but who cares what the answers are. Now I prefer to be an uninformed consumer."

"Princess Di is so anorexic they make each of her gowns in several sizes so she always has one small enough!" I paraphrase the article I'm reading in *People* to change the subject.

"I always order multiple gown sizes. Don't you?"

After Grace's constellations have been charted, we wait forever for the nurse to tell her she can put her clothes back on. Grace shows off the dozen permanent blue dots across her chest, so no one in the future will radiate the same spot.

"Just think. Even if I'm in Cairo they'll understand the international sign language on my boobs."

"You and Max have to plan a trip to celebrate once this is all over. What about a safari, or a cruise down the Nile?" I'm ready to start researching the trip and tap out my savings to buy them the tickets until Grace brings me back to reality.

"I'd take a week at home — cancer-free."

It's raining when we get outside, so I walk to the garage to get the car, thankful for some time alone. I feel like I've been irradiated, too.

22.

been there, done that

MARTY AND I USED to spend Sundays in bed, our one precious day when Joey's with his dad now that Jake has agreed to change our schedule. Now we get up early and write to-do lists. Our aimless country drives and romantic dinners have turned into Home Depot runs to look at flooring and soundproofing options.

"Once we organize this place, things will run more smoothly," he says optimistically.

"I thought things ran pretty smoothly already," I tell Grace.

"Just pretend you have a housekeeper. Maybe he can work for us if he has a free day."

"Let's keep the condiments in the same general area," Marty suggests, in the endearing tone I used to hear in bed.

"The cinnamon's with the baking stuff." I wish we could discuss current events, which concert to go to, *anything* but domestic efficiency. "Am I supposed to alphabetize the spice jars?" I ask with a soupçon of snootiness.

"You're not the *only* one who cooks around here." Marty was married for seventeen years, so he's used to thinking in terms of *us*. When I say *I* instead of *we*, he notices. Our differences seem to multiply. I don't mind walking around toys in the hallway, but Marty's sure he's going to trip on them and break his neck. His whole family seems to worry about unlikely disasters.

[173]

I finally appreciate my parents' much more carefree attitude about life.

"Put those cars and trucks in your room," Marty orders Joey after a bad day at work. I slip my kid a cookie to sweeten the deal.

"You're ruining his appetite for dinner." Marty's making shrimp, which Joey won't eat anyway.

I found a book for Joey called *Mom's New Friend*. Now I need to find a movie for Marty about dealing with your girlfriend's kid. Sometimes I'm understanding. "I know stepparenting is a thankless job," I tell him. "You put up with all the crap, but you don't really get a vote when it comes to policy."

I read Joey a very short book and enjoy Marty's shrimp, focusing on him for a change, pushing away all the Gracie troubles, at least during dinner.

*   *   *

I'VE STOPPED ASKING Grace how she feels in every conversation. We're out of the woods, so why discuss lab results, nodes, margins, and the odds about more scary news? I steer our conversations toward the past, the safety of nostalgia. When Grace reminisces about anything at all pre-cancer, her delight in existence itself is still impermeable, as well as her remarkable ability to ignore the downers.

I've never known anyone so comfortably ensconced in her own life. Grace never wondered who she was, a gift I can't imagine. Until Joey, I had no clue. The more countries I visited, the more things I accomplished, the less I felt entitled to happiness. I had to *do* things, be things, prove I deserved all that freedom.

Following a more usual road map, Grace traveled more

smoothly than I could ever imagine, the wind at her back and Max at her side. Her eyes widen when I tell her about living with an Irish boyfriend in southern Spain, and working for the famous feminist in London. But I assure her my exploits sound a lot better than they were. The lover and I fought constantly all over Europe, and the politically correct feminist treated me like a servant.

"Grace has always looked exclusively at the bright side of life," her cousin Roz once told me. "Her glass is always overflowing!" We were trying to figure out how some people never set foot in a therapist's office while the rest of us are lifers. "How many people find their soul mate at fourteen?" Roz exclaims. "Grace's father adored her, so she knew what to expect."

"What's up with you today?" Grace asks when she detects I'm holding back something important. "Are you and Marty getting along?"

I nod.

"So *nu*?"

"I think I'm starting to want to"—I lower my voice—"get *married.*"

"It took you long enough," she says, as if I've just decided to come in out of a raging blizzard.

"Marty says he's been there and done that."

"Just give him time so he can think it's his idea."

As if I could follow her advice.

"Believe me, Marty's over the marriage thing. Way over it. And I was fine with that, Grace. But for some weird reason, I think I'm changing my mind."

"No big deal. So will he."

My friend the eternal optimist.

The following week, Marty and I see a therapist—my solution

to everything. (I can't imagine Grace and Max even having a serious issue, let alone outsourcing it.)

"What happened to unconventional?" my boyfriend wants to know. "Remember when you told me Marx's theory about marriage and capitalism?"

"I know," I admit. "I'm confused, too."

"There are a lot of people in this room," the shrink finally says. It seems that Marty's mother persuaded him to get married the last time, so now he's afraid I want to control him the way she did. But as soon as he says this, he realizes it's an unfounded fear. His other issue is harder to refute:

"Do you really want to marry me, or are you just trying to prove something to your parents?"

Nothing gets resolved.

The following Saturday, in the hardware store, Marty proposes.

"Which aisle were you in?" Grace wants to know. "Plumbing or electrical?"

"Marty said he had a wedding already, but that I should have one, too."

"What a sweet guy." Grace waltzes me around her kitchen. "I'm ordering blue-tinted carnations," she threatens, just like her own glitzy 1968 wedding.

Let her be there, I ask God, who must be surprised to hear from me.

*   *   *

THEN, AFTER A FEW months, just when everything seems fine with Grace, another crummy surprise. "Max's doctor calls out of the blue," she reports, more down than I've ever heard her. Apparently, Max was told many years ago to have yearly colon scans, because of some pre-cancerous condition. "Every year he has the test," she explains, "and every year they send a postcard saying he's fine."

I try, and fail, to brace myself. "So he went for the test?"

"The kids were still in school, thank God. I'd just come back from grocery shopping—I had to make macaroni salad for a pot-luck dinner. When the phone rang, I thought it was someone call-ing to tell me to pick up more paper plates. But no such luck."

I hear her take a deep breath—or is she crying? I pace in anxious circles, stalling Joey, who needs dinner. My day had been crappy. I'd gotten into an argument at a department meeting, Joey came home with a sore throat, and then Marty was annoyed because I didn't have a plan for dinner. I was counting on Grace to smooth over my troubles, but she has a whopper of her own.

"'This sounds like bad news,' I told the doctor, praying it wasn't true. But a doctor, calling in person, can never be good. 'I'm afraid so,' he said. Don't you hate that expression?"

Another atypical long pause. "Did you notice what a gorgeous day it was, Ruth? Bright sun was streaming in the kitchen win-dow. Then all of a sudden the light made me dizzy. I felt so faint I had to sit down. Then Max walks in, with that big smile he has whenever he sneaks out of work early. 'Max just got home. Maybe you should talk to *him*,' I tell the doctor, and hand over the phone. Then I see him slump to the floor, just listening, not making eye contact with me. After he hangs up, he mumbles something about how they suspect colon cancer. We just stare at each other until the kids burst in and we have to get it together and feed them."

"Fifteen minutes after I get better, Max gets sick," she tells me later. "I thought nothing bad could happen to us anymore. That we paid our dues. Remember Art Spiegelman's first volume of

Maus? His father endures the Holocaust, so of course the guy can't imagine anything *worse.* Then the second volume comes out, *A Survivor's Tale: And Here My Troubles Begin!*"

I hardly have the strength to kick Joey's toys out of the way before Marty gets home. "Mom doesn't feel good," I say, microwaving some noodles for Joey before I collapse on the couch and close my eyes.

I remember the Steins' photo album: Max and the two baby boys, Max and Grace cutting their wedding cake, Max graduating law school, Max in his Darth Vader outfit one Halloween.

23.
darkness

I STILL WAKE UP surprised I'm finally *with* someone. My heart feels full and safe, and I catch myself singing, "I'm not at all in love, not at all in love am I," from *The Pajama Game*. My fiancé's weekly supermarket flowers trump orchids once a decade. (Someone once gave me orchids, but I can't remember who.) The hardest part of all this normalcy so far is making dinner for Marty's parents, but Grace and Rhonda both advise me to think of this as playing the role of a dutiful daughter-in-law but not having to be one.

When Marty and Joey spend a spring afternoon watching television, I manage to keep my disapproval to myself. Joey has Jake for intellectual stimulation; Marty will teach him kindness.

Suddenly, it's almost summer. Max and Grace are sending Louis and Isaac to an expensive overnight camp, the only one that had room for them at the last minute. Max calls it Camp It'll Costya. For thousands of dollars, your child can live like a Native American.

The boys are leaving right before Max's surgery.

"I hear that camp has gourmet food and sailing lessons," I tell Louis, who gives me a blank look. Isaac says he hates sailing.

"Last year they both begged to go to that camp," Grace says. "I thought it'd be an easy sell, but they're acting like we're sending them into the Army."

"Maybe you and I should go to the camp instead."

"What a great idea! As long as they don't make us play sports."

Last summer was ruined because Grace got sick, but this one is in the nightmare category. I try to distract her with my latest problem: one of my female students is in the process of changing her gender. "She accuses me of being prejudiced because I keep using the wrong pronouns."

This gets a tiny laugh out of Grace, who's stumped for advice for the first time since I've known her. For more diversion, I tell her the latest issue with Jake. "He thinks it's dangerous that I let Joey talk to strangers." No suggestions about this from Grace, either. I sweep her kitchen floor and do the laundry while she takes a nap.

"Did my dryer do the cha-cha-cha?" she wants to know later.

Max's parents drive the boys to camp, which must make the kids even more nervous about their dad's "minor" operation. "We'll come up for Parents' Weekend," Grace and Max promise the boys.

After his surgery, Max is actually able to make the trip. "We practiced all the way up telling the kids Dad is going to be fine," Grace reports. "But he looks so thin, and he has to sit down every five minutes, so I don't think we fooled them."

I don't say it, of course, but maybe the truth would be less scary.

"Max cried on the way home," Grace continues. Then she wants to get off the phone because she's running out of things to say.

Another first.

"I can mow your lawn," I volunteer the next time she calls. "Or I can make you dinner tonight. Your choice."

"Who cares what the neighbors think. Just don't forget dessert."

Even though I should be packing for our Cape vacation, I'd rather hang around at Grace's. I bring takeout roast chicken and potato salad, a chocolate cake, and even have time to mow part of her backyard. "I can't believe this is our life," she says, serving the food on paper plates.

I want to change the subject, but I'm out of topics, too.

* * *

AFTER THE BOYS are home from camp, the Steins visit us at the Cape cottage. Max looks years older than he did last month, but he's as cheerful as usual. Not even Grace knows how he manages to stay in such high spirits, and she's a master at that sort of thing. I try to keep my mood above water by making sandwiches and setting up the badminton net. When the kids want to play miniature golf, Max takes them. Marty stays home to try to fix an old fishing rod.

All of us, not counting Marty, pile into Max's van one night and head for the Wellfleet drive-in to see *Babe*. Grace and Max love anything retro, so it's the perfect thing to do. "This reminds me of those necking-in-the-car days," I whisper to Grace. Joey turns into a total wild man with Louis and Isaac, who seem to have permission to throw popcorn all over the car. I'd rather be walking on the moonlit low-tide flats with Grace all to myself, but how can I miss a chance to share the Steins' good times?

* * *

A MONTH LATER, back home, on a perfect September morning, I call Grace from the gym to see if I should stop by for our usual visit. When I hear her friend Alice's dire whisper I know why she's answering Grace's phone before she tells me.

Max died last night. Gone, at five a.m., a silent heart attack. Even if he'd been in the hospital, they couldn't have saved him. "It was merciful," Alice mumbles. "The doctor said the cancer would have gotten him and it would have been worse."

The sky darkens for everyone in their world, for that home of boys and boisterousness. My huge-hearted Gracie, left with a fatal gash through the middle of her life.

When Marty, Joey, and I walk in that evening, Louis grabs Joey and they race off together as if things are normal. Hidden behind the crowd in her kitchen, Grace sits at the table, her head in her hands, legs shaking. Marty stays silent because he knows the limitation of words.

"He was talking about your wedding yesterday," Grace says when she sees us. "He had some suggestions for the menu."

I'd been praying Max would be there. No one loved a party more. He was the king of abundance. His kids' parties were neighborhood celebrations. He'd turn the backyard into an amusement park, music blasting, and make trip after trip for more pizza and soda.

I hold my friend as she tries to make sense of what's senseless. How did she fall out of her already-not-so-normal life into this horror film? "He woke me up at two a.m. with an aching shoulder. I rubbed it and rubbed it. Then he got so quiet." Her trembling slows, then quickens. "I should have called the ambulance sooner. I kept asking Max what to do and he kept saying wait until morning. Why did I listen to him?"

"Eat," someone says. "Max would have made three runs for bagels by now."

"You couldn't have known," I say. "He didn't *have* a heart condition." She looks up at me as if she's really listening. "Please don't blame yourself," I say, over and over, but I know it's all she can do.

That night Joey wants me to read to him as if it's a normal night, and I'm relieved he's not ready to ask any questions. I get into bed too numb to talk to Marty. This death is worse than any I've ever been close to, a father snatched from his family. How dare tragedy enter that house of mirth?

Grace and Max. Who will she be without him? His disappearance is inconceivable.

Enraged and despairing, I sped to their house one night after arguing with Marty. They were full of silly lines to help me remember the light. "Find someone else," Max told me. "There are at least two other available men in New England you haven't met."

When Joey finally talks about Max, his first death, I want my answers to be wise enough to comfort us both. "Some people believe our spirits come back to the world," I explain.

"That's what I think."

"How's Louis? Did you tell him how sorry you are?"

"He didn't want to talk about it, but I know what he's feeling." My smart-aleck six-year-old, so keen. Kids devise their own ways to deal with crisis, and rise to the occasion.

* * *

"OUR MAX IS GONE," the rabbi intones, forcing us to believe it. The modest temple in the woods is full to the rafters with mourners from all of Max's worlds: his fellow actors from the temple production of *Fiddler on the Roof*, his court friends, Max and Grace's enormous, extended family, their neighborhood, and almost the entire town.

A dozen men and women speak from the *bimah* about Max's selflessness, the way he lived for others, for the kids. Always the kids. His cousin remembers the two crazy teenagers who met on Nantasket Beach. "And that was it, for the next forty years."

Grace was protected and loved for most of her life. I've been mostly alone for that same long time. Now we've changed places.

I hear how Max saved poor tenants from being evicted and about his knack for helping people resolve the bitterest disputes. "He can't stand conflicts," Grace once explained. He'd get angry landlords, pressured by banks, to give tenants one more chance. He passed out candy to crying kids, cracked silly jokes, and did *Three Stooges* routines to relax the anxious plaintiffs. When he walked into that courtroom, the tension evaporated.

Someone speaks about the secret thirty-six souls in every generation who watch over the rest of us. The pure ones, the *Last of the Just* in the Schwarz-Bart novel. We know Max was one. Another friend reads the letters Max wrote to the boys before his surgery, when things looked so bleak.

Isaac, I've always been so proud of you. We took you home from the hospital and realized we had no idea what to do with you! Louis, your brother wanted a friend, so we promised him we'd have you.

When the boys read the letters they wrote to their father, all the sobbing releases my own. Marty gives me his handkerchief and puts his arm around me. "I keep thinking how few people will be at *my* funeral," he says.

"There are other ways to measure our worth besides a packed synagogue," I tell him, though I'm thinking the same thing about myself. We drive to the cemetery without speaking while Joey and a friend of his from Louis's neighborhood tell jokes in the back seat.

The boys push through the crowd to get close to the grave. "That was pretty cool the way they lowered him into the ground," Joey says on the way home. I wanted to pull my little boy away from the coffin, as if to protect him from what absolutely happens.

How can we have our wedding without Max?

24.
faking it

MAXLESS, GRACE CARRIES on without bitterness. "I always knew where he was," she tells me. "I'd wonder, *Where's Max?* Then realize he probably stopped at Aunt Joanie's for some kugel, or he was doing something for his mother. Now I can't figure it out. That's the weirdest part."

But my friend has never been a *dweller*, so every firefly idea that pops into her head distracts her: a neighbor's trip to Hawaii, the rabbi's Peruvian mask collection. "How many rabbis do you know, Ruth, who are into the Incas?"

"Let's start with how many rabbis do I know, period." I'm too ambushed by mortality to keep up with Grace's multiple trains of thought. I can't handle Joey's moodiness, or avoid bickering with Jake even though I know better. I barely notice Marty, which isn't fair, and it makes me feel even worse.

When Grace picks up my blueness, she's all heart. "If you *know* why you feel so down, it's better than feeling rotten for no reason."

"There's always an upside with you. Can't we just wallow in a little misery once in a while?"

"Try me at three a.m. Tears on my pillow."

"Thank God for fifties lyrics."

"Wordsworth and Homer would be jealous."

IT'S EASIER THAN I thought to get through Shabbos dinner at Grace's. Her brother Jerry and his partner, Sam, give us their latest Manhattan theater reviews, and the boys have a contest to see who can bite his challah into the best shape. After Marty and I do the dishes, he retreats to the den to watch the news. The kids shoot baskets in the driveway; Max would have been out there with them.

I hear Isaac teasing the two little guys. I wonder if Grace is concerned about him; he's prone to outbursts, and now, of course, he has good cause. "It's a good thing my attention span is so short," she says. "I keep forgetting what I'm supposed to be worried about."

"Maybe you have too many choices."

Her latest catastrophe is financial, no laughing matter, which means she's determined to laugh anyway. Max loaned money to total strangers; he was too busy helping anyone who asked for anything—going on the eighth-grade trip to Washington, for instance—to get his own affairs in order. He had no life insurance, and no mortgage insurance, either. Grace could actually lose her home.

"Neither of us was such a good bookkeeper, I guess," my friend mutters after admitting this bad news. "Max said things were under control, so I believed him."

"Didn't Cousin Nathan give him good advice?" *Talk to Nathan,* Max told Marty and me. *He's a financial wizard.*

"We were always going to ask Nathan over for dinner so he could take a look at things. So now he'll get his chance."

"What if I come over and help you do a little spring cleaning? Maybe that'll cheer you up."

"Great idea! Maybe we'll find a Rembrandt in the attic."

After tea and scones the next Saturday morning, she reluctantly takes me down to her basement to face mountains of toys, clothes, books, furniture, bedding, magazines, dishes, suitcases. "We were saving stuff for the temple yard sale," she shrugs. "Unfortunately, we've missed a few decades. Let's just get Clinton to send in the National Guard. Take his mind off his troubles."

Then I notice the rusted magenta Taurus sitting in the driveway. "Let's clean out Max's car," I suggest.

"What about taking a walk? I want to see the house they're renovating down the street." Grace looks longingly at me, like a dog that needs to go out. "They're building a *gazebo!*"

"That'll be our reward," I promise. Tough love. I don't know if Grace will feel better if we accomplish something, but I will.

"I'm warning you, Ruth. I'm afraid to look. Max was kind of a pack rat."

The trunk is full of Steiniana: an aquarium, a hamster cage, clothes for Goodwill, and Isaac's science fair electricity-from-potatoes project. I pick up what looks like an authentic Kewpie doll. "We should take this to the Antiques Roadshow."

"That's what Max said. Did you see the farmer who found a pitchfork in his barn worth a thousand dollars? I thought he was going to have a heart attack."

Ignoring her slip, we throw shoes and newspapers into trash bags. Grace takes a shopping bag of what we think is junk mail into the house and dumps out what looks like a year's worth of unopened bills.

I stifle a gasp, and even she looks stunned. "These are the times I wish I were Catholic so I could cross myself," she says. "*Oy veh* doesn't quite cut it."

"Just take it to Cousin Nathan." I help her stuff all the scary-looking envelopes back into the bag. "The financial genius."

*   *   *

ISN'T IT IRONIC? asks the op-ed piece about Max in the *Boston Globe. Max Stein spent his life keeping people from being chased out of their homes. Now his family is in that same jeopardy.*

I'm upset at such a public humiliation. Grace spent a few hours with the columnist who, she said, seemed compassionate, but isn't this a betrayal of confidence? As a result of the article, however, a large number of the Steins' friends raise enough money to pay down Grace's mortgage so she and the kids can stay put. Deep-hearted Marty contributes as much as I do, without my asking.

The winter has been mild, without the drama of serious weather and the beauty of snow. At least Grace doesn't have to drive on treacherous roads, which Max could do so fearlessly. Then a surprise Easter blizzard buries the purple crocuses poking through the ground.

Others grumble, but I feel a reprieve. Spring can't make anything better for Grace, so I want the winter gloom to last until the bad news goes away. Then she calls to report that the snow melted through her roof, her ceiling is buckling, and there's a leak in the den.

"Now I can literally say the roof is caving in." Grace's dark wit to the rescue. "But thank God it happened *this* week, when I can sort of handle it. And guess what, Ruth? The rabbi knows someone who can fix it, cheap."

"So that temple membership is really paying off."

The earth still shakes but our jokes are back. My best friend is a widow, not a word I ever imagined using for someone my age, but Grace would rather discuss anything other than her sorrow.

I never call without some news or hearsay to feed my gossip-hungry friend. "Did I tell you about the new English Department hire?"

"You didn't get the job *again*?"

"Of course not. Being Jewish doesn't count as a minority."

"What's he like?"

"An arrogant Hispanic Melvillean. Can you believe it? When I told him I went on a whale watch last summer, he confessed he's never seen a whale because he gets seasick."

"He should have specialized in a landlubber like Thoreau. Or Emily."

Then, beneath her drollery, disappointment shows. "Isaac wouldn't go on his science class field trip to the Peabody Museum. He said he didn't want to look at all those dead animals. And Louis is acting supernormal, as if nothing has happened. He won't mention Max, and pretends to be deaf when we talk about him. He can't say 'Dad.' If he has to refer to him, it's 'you know who I'm talking about.' His shrink says he hates being different from his friends who have fathers."

And mothers who might get sick again.

"But in the middle of the night, just as I'm falling asleep, Louis comes into my room. 'Are you breathing?' he asks. 'Mom, I can't hear you breathing.' Here's the awful part." We both laugh: as if there were only an awful *part*. "The kids are driving me so crazy I keep screaming at them. I'm afraid I'm turning into my mother."

After Grace's father died, she and Max had dinner with her mother every Friday. *How was your day?* they'd ask Gladys.

What kind of day could I possibly have? she'd answer. *Don't ask, because my life is over.*

"Slide yourself a break. You're not the bitter type." I can't imagine Grace taking her misery out on the boys any more than I can imagine her not eating chocolate, even though it's not good for her immune system.

But she surprises me when, for the first time in her life, she goes to a therapist. "She says I'm holding back my anger at Max for leaving me in the lurch. What am I supposed to do, have a total nervous breakdown?" I'll bet Grace cleverly changed the subject to make the shrink feel better about whatever *she's* dealing with.

Grace has also joined a bereavement group, and tells me the horrific details after every session. One man's wife died on a river-rafting trip. Someone's husband fell out of a tree. A young black woman lost *two* husbands.

"I know it sounds awful," Grace confesses during one of our midnight calls. "But I walk out of there feeling lucky my story isn't worse. One woman's rotten ex-husband dragged her back into his life when he got sick. Then there's John the widower, our star. His wife got cancer right after they adopted a baby girl from Honduras. His big complaint is that too many women invite him to dinner. Can you imagine a single guy asking me over for lasagna and apple brown betty?"

I wake up dreading each day, imagining more bad news. When Marty wants to know what we should cook for his parents, or when we can clean out the coat closet, I'm annoyed at him for being predictably pedestrian—hardly a capital offense.

Even Joey, my once-reliable source of delight, won't let me read him a story on a night when I especially need to. Does he think I'm too distracted and don't deserve to be his mom anymore?

And I still don't have enough publications to apply for tenure at the college, which means I'm a failure.

"We're *all* failures," my therapist reminds me.

I spare Grace my bad moods. She's back to teaching four days a week, and she's even planning an anniversary party for her in-laws.

(Will Marty expect the same of me?) Every Friday she takes the boys to temple. Meanwhile, I can barely manage to bring home groceries and make dinner.

* * *

BUT WE HAVE a wedding to plan, which is sometimes hard to remember. Marty and I spend our precious Joey-free Sundays visiting venues on the Cape until we find a lovely inn, right on a lake. Then, on a day without sun, we drive to Falmouth to meet our prospective wedding ceremony rabbi. Our charted course still doesn't feel like destiny, but maybe that's too much to ask.

The Kabbalah rabbi we've already interviewed suggested we swim naked at dawn on our wedding day with all our friends. I'd go in that direction, but it's not what Marty has in mind.

Was Joey supposed to join us?

Rabbi Gottlieb strikes the right balance: he wears a Mexican vest, and I notice a guitar in the corner of his study. He wants to get to know us.

"I answered Marty's ad in *Boston Magazine*," I begin. Rabbi Gottlieb must have met his wife in a temple youth group, or while working on a kibbutz, so I wonder if he's a bit surprised by our desperate midlife dating strategies. I study his bookshelves and look out at the winter Cape Cod fields. I want to be here and I want to marry Marty. But maybe it's too late for such a U-turn.

"Ruth gives me excitement," Marty says. "And I think I calm her down. I like the way we talk to one another, which I couldn't do in my first marriage."

"I never felt so trusting or so trusted," I tell them both. *My dearest friend has lost her husband so is it OK if I don't feel the appropriate joy right now?*

When I tune back in, Marty's telling the rabbi how he almost sold his company last year because business was so bad. "I guess I was having some kind of midlife crisis," he says. "But I didn't know what else to do, so I borrowed money and kept going."

The rabbi thinks about this. "It would be hard to decide not to be a rabbi anymore," he says empathically. Then we talk about my work, and I become tearful about having more success teaching others to write than as a real writer myself.

"The last time I heard," the rabbi smiles, "writers publish books when they're eighty and ninety years old, so you still have time."

I reach for the Kleenex and joke about paying the rabbi at the end of the session, as if he's our shrink.

The rabbi suggests we have our ceremony in his synagogue, just down the road from the inn on the lake.

The day picks up speed. We stop at Wayward Park to see how the unheated cottage looks this time of year. Not even the thought of renting it next summer cheers me up. "I'm afraid I'll be sad forever," I tell Marty.

"That wouldn't be a great idea." I'm glad he's willing to ignore my sadness.

Then we meet my friend Sara, who lives on the Cape by herself, for a bang-up lunch at Off the Bay in Orleans. She and Marty are jovial, and they can tell I'm faking it.

"I've forgotten how she laughs," Marty tells Sara.

I wonder how long he'll wait around for me to be normal again.

25.
halley's comet

THE MAGNOLIAS ARE OUT for their five minutes of glory and the smell is sweet and acrid and romantic. I want not only a perfect wedding, but a splendid life to go with it. I obsess over every detail. Will anyone know my Italian cream silk wedding dress is secondhand? Is red meat a good idea? Who's going to hold up our *chupah*? Will twenty-three children ruin the event?

We decide we'll *both* crush the wine glass to reinvent the ritual, but do we want to have the pieces of glass encased in plastic as a memento? How about a hand-painted *ketubah* from Israel? There are so many new wedding developments to choose from!

What about Marty and I stealing a few moments to be alone after the ceremony for the ritual *yehud* seclusion, originally meant for the consummation of the marriage? This would save us from the dreaded receiving line, but Marty's mother insists on it.

"You can handle an hour of kissing and hugging," Marty reasons with me.

It's hard not discussing the wedding with Grace, but I know it wouldn't be fair. So who can I turn to when my queenly mother-in-law says she hates buffets. "Can't we be *served*?" she wants to know.

Eventually, Grace and I will have a field day with this.

Another hurdle: even though Marty says it's "overkill," I want an engagement ring. My conservative partner accuses *me*, the unconventional one, of utter conformism. It finally comes out in therapy that Marty lost the engagement ring argument with his *first* wife, so he can't give in this time around.

"One ring is enough," I say, magnanimously. Then I find a jeweler who'll make me a wonderful Byzantine-looking wedding ring with a pink cabochon sapphire in twenty-karat, peach-colored gold.

Marty finds his white gold band in fifteen minutes at the mall. "I've done this before," he reminds me.

"Let's not get the actual license," I hear myself suggest. "Why involve the state in our intimate life?"

"Great, Ruth. Let's not pay our taxes either." My rebellious rhetoric clashes with my rapidly growing wedding wish list. I hire a friend to take candid shots of Joey, Marty, and me in the arboretum for our invitations. I order a whipped-cream and fresh-strawberry cake, and after our "tasting appointment," we come up with a wonderful menu of swordfish and teriyaki chicken.

Do I really want ivy wrapped around the tent poles? Two separate wedding dresses? What's wrong with me? Why can't we just elope and go hiking in the Pyrenees?

Marty's not much of a hiker, a voice answers me.

"Now that you're into this, you're really into this," he teases me.

Am I trying to please my parents? By the time I hit thirty-five, they were so eager for someone to "take me off their hands" I subconsciously made sure that didn't happen. Isn't it a little late to prove to my dad that I'm lovable?

I want Joey and me to *belong* somewhere.

I want to gather every bit of joy while there's still some left.

How will we dance and laugh and eat without Max?

*　*　*

WHY CAN'T YOU GET *married?* my father yelled at me in disgust when I was thirty and about to live in Spain with yet another boyfriend. *Why can't you get married since you're having a baby?* he shouted years later, even though he couldn't stand Jake.

Now my parents are getting to invite their friends from far and wide—whose offspring's and *their* offspring's weddings and bar mitzvahs, in several countries, they've enviously described to me. But as my own thrilling nuptials approach, all my dad can say is: *"I can't believe you're going to spend so much money on a wedding. You could take a trip around the world instead."*

"If you try to get over your father, I'll try to get over my mother," my fiancé says. Such a reasonable request. This makes me teary, always a good time to make love.

*　*　*

JOEY LEANS OUT his car window on the way to soccer practice, letting the air whip into his mouth because, he says, "it tastes good." He stares unashamedly into the rearview mirror, struck with his own beauty. "Oh my god, Mom, my hair looks so awesome, it's sticking straight up."

Was I ever so thrilled with myself?

My boy has let his hair grow to his shoulders and ties it at the nape of his neck. When strangers mistake him for a girl, he thinks it's funny. Marty thinks I should make Joey get a haircut, which makes me more determined not to.

Maybe Joey and I have been put on this earth to shake Marty up. When we visit his parents, I make Joey tuck in his shirt, but he can tell my heart's not in it and pulls it out again.

It is a shock to lose control of your kid. "Why do you *care* if there's a hole in my pants?" my no-longer-sweet child wants to know. "It's so phony." I have no answer. I could do without the black marker on his fingernails, the snotty attitude, the mud he tracks through the just-cleaned house. And I hate that look of persecution when I make him clean it up.

"I'm not your slave," I say, hoping Marty can hear me sounding so parental. But compared to the complaints I hear from other moms, Joey's an easygoing guy.

"First you worry about safety," my wisest friends remind me, so I try to limit what I hound my kid about.

* * *

"WHY DO YOU HAVE to get *married*, anyway?" Joey wants to know, even though we've been through this a dozen times. He got over Marty's moving in after they built a skateboard ramp together, so I'm hoping he'll deal with this, too.

"I'm bored," he whines one Saturday when all I want to do is take a nap. Jake won't pick him up for his overnight for another four hours and I'm desperate for a reprieve. I could start an art project, but Marty just scrubbed the kitchen table. I suggest every solo activity I can think of: marbles, Legos, computer solitaire, but Joey makes a face at every one. "Can't you use your inner resources?" I actually suggest, a really important concept to an eight-year-old.

We'd both feel better outside, but I'm too resentful that Marty has the right to fall asleep on the couch, oblivious. I call every kid we know until one of them agrees to come over.

"Andre?" Joey sneers. "I'm not in the mood to play with Andre."

My fiftieth birthday is on its way, a deadline by which I have to feel wonderful, and lately I'm far from it. In my childless, single days it didn't matter how I felt because no one was around to be affected by my bad mood.

"I got your present," my boy announces, waking me up too early one grey morning, two weeks before the right day. "I want to give it to you now." I bite my tongue and don't tell him he's ruining the surprise. "Grace took me and Louis to a store so I could pick it out. It cost a *lot*."

"Let's wait until my real birthday." Maybe I'll feel worthy by then.

"How come you don't want it *now*?"

When there's only a week to go, Joey wraps his gift, leaving paper, scissors, and ribbon all over the kitchen floor.

"Can't we just ignore the occasion?" I ask Marty when my day finally dawns. Then Joey bounds into our bed with his box, wrapped in four colors of tissue paper. The kid has style. I unwrap each layer and come to the prize: a golden ceramic plaque of the sun, its shining face mocking my spoiled discontent. "A sun from your son," says the handmade card.

As Grace would say, *Again with the unbidden tears of joy.*

      ＊   ＊   ＊

WEDDING ANXIETY dreams: The rabbi tells an X-rated story to try to be hip. The glass won't break no matter how hard Marty and I stomp on it. Joey giggles uncontrollably, then so does everyone else in the beautiful Quaker meeting house-turned-synagogue. The band gets lost, and when they get there late, the caterer won't let us dance because the food will get cold. What am I doing here? I panic, sweat ruining my dress. I don't recognize any of the guests, and all I want to do is take a walk for some fresh air, to figure out my next move.

As our wedding day approaches, I feel so close to Marty I want him to know everything about me, even if it's hard to confess: "I don't plan on being a perfect daughter-in-law," I begin.

"What a surprise," he groans.

"If we can ever afford it, I'd like my own bedroom."

"That could be sexy."

"OK. There's someone I would probably still run away with," I blurt. "It will never happen, of course."

"Oh yeah?" he asks. "Who's my rival?"

"It doesn't matter. It was always unrequited love. He was never serious about me. He's married and he lives in Switzerland. Besides, he has no idea I moved to Boston. And he never liked kids."

It's like saying, *I'll leave you if a comet lands in our backyard.* My fiancé just figures I'm showing off, or drunk. "I have a crush on Raquel Welch," he says.

I give him a massage to reward his sweetness, and get one back.

Then, as if I've put in a cosmic suggestion to the universe, the phone rings one night when Marty is working late.

"Aha! I've tracked you down!" That familiar, adorably high, sharp voice; that trickster earnestness.

"Harris." I try to ignore my pounding heart, to sound blasé. We haven't seen each other since he stayed with me on Second Avenue at least ten years ago. Between his divorce and his second marriage. "What are you doing in *Boston?*"

"Doing what I always do." Harris scours the globe for Asian antiquities—bronzes and thangkas, porcelain and textiles—and sells them to museums and prominent collectors. Besides being smitten with him, I wanted to live his life. Nepal, Shanghai, Tibet, London. Whenever he was in New York, for years on end, no matter what else was going on, I'd jump. (Once I left a boyfriend's bed to race uptown to his hotel.)

But I've wised up. I'm beyond all that pointless pining.

"I'm in town to show a few paintings to the Fogg," he announces breezily, as if we still get together every so often. As if he's certain I've been waiting for his call. "I've wondered about you."

"I'm engaged," I brag. "I'm getting married in two weeks."

"I always had great timing." *What does that mean?* "What are you doing tomorrow?"

I consider playing hard-to-get, but he's flying back to Geneva in twenty-four hours. Par for his course. Maybe his marriage is rocky. *Will I toss the man and wedding of my dreams for a streak in the sky?*

"How did you find me?"

"You forget I make my living knowing things like that."

I agree to meet Harris in Cambridge the next day. As soon as we hang up, I calculate how I'm going to rearrange my already-full schedule and get to Mass Ave by nine in the morning.

I have a hard time explaining my hysterical state to Grace. "I guess we'll chalk this up to pre-commitment jitters," she says.

Harris. I'm dying to know why *now*, but vow I won't ask. I should have pretended not to recognize his voice so quickly, but I could never play coy within his force field. His self-deprecating jokes; his charming banter about missing me, as if I hadn't been waiting for months—or years—for his next card or call; his modesty about his latest coup in the rarified world of high-stakes antiquities; his stories about detecting real from fake, or flogging high-stakes treasures to wealthy collectors with utter *sangfroid*. His stutter is still endearing. You can get away with a lot if you sound insecure.

"By the way," I tell Marty before he turns out the light that night, "an old friend's in town, so I'm meeting him for breakfast." He hardly hears me. "The one I said I'd run away with if I got the chance."

"Am I supposed to worry?" he mutters with utter confidence.

I toss and turn all night while my well-adjusted fiancé enjoys the sleep of the faithful. When he wants high-risk adventure, he drags me to a Hollywood movie. I get up at dawn to take a long, lilac-scented bath. I tell Joey to get his own cereal while I try on several outfits. I want a refined, but arty, look. I decide on my V-neck chartreuse silk shirt over lime-green leggings with the purple blazer for self-defense. My best gold earrings with hieroglyphics, to catch Harris's eye for detail. I stop at every mirror on my way out the door.

I drop Joey off at school early to beat the rush-hour traffic over the B.U. Bridge. "Why do you smell so bad?" he asks, whiffing my *Je Reviens* as I kiss him goodbye. My romantic past awaits me at Starbucks. I pinch myself at red lights to make sure this is the live-fiction present.

I never had a clue when Harris would surface next, or how many others were waiting for him in other time zones. I wish I'd been able to get a haircut. Harris once stayed at my apartment on Second Avenue for a few glorious weeks. We roamed the city, money no object. I watched him in action at Sotheby's, cunning and graceful until his statue of Buddha had changed hands for many times what he'd paid in Kathmandu. Later we took a carriage ride through Central Park and toasted his success at the Oak Room.

I remember playing Harris my new Joseph Spence album, the Bahamian old-time guitarist who sang earthy, scratchy music. "Let's go down there and meet him," said the casual globetrotter. We never got around to it, but the point was, we *could* have.

We had drinks at a collector's apartment that was decorated like a Hindu temple. We danced at reggae clubs and watched the sleeping, entwined sea lions at the Central Park Zoo.

Then my enticing explorer was always off again. I'd get cryptic, infrequent postcards: "Good idea to visit Nepal during wedding season when families let go of priceless treasures to raise money to marry off their daughters." Harris broke my heart on an irregular basis.

My dear abstract expressionist neighbor, Ed, consoled me. "Don't cry your heart out over someone who buys and sells dead art. That parasite never *created* anything. He isn't worth your tears."

⁂

I GET TO CAMBRIDGE on time, still in a dream, and we spend a typical Harris day, thrilling as always, except for the lack of sex. He tells me how, with split-second timing, he detected the forgery of a Third Dynasty Cambodian bowl. I'm supposed to be grading final essays, looking for wedding shoes, meeting with the florist, and arranging hotel rooms for out-of-town guests.

"So besides getting married, what are you up to?" he asks, in a how-could-you-have-left-New-York tone of voice. All I can think of, besides my non-tenured teaching job, is Joey's starring role in the dragon dance for his class's upcoming Chinese New Year celebration.

"My marriage is fine," he says. "But I don't recommend it." Did I blurt out my big news too early, missing my chance for a big confession?

"So this is the last time I'll see you as a single woman?" We're having a rushed late lunch at an unworthy Chinese restaurant.

I have time to change my mind. If it weren't for Joey, I'd actually trade the life I've put together for another ill-fated try with the one who got away.

Harris drives off toward the airport before I find out why I never made the grade.

        *   *   *

I HAVE TO FIGHT another traffic jam to get to Joey's school on time. "You promised we could have pizza tonight," my little dragon dancer says, jumping into the car.

"How was school?" The question that never gets an answer.

"Did you remember to get a room for my cousins from Pasadena?" my intended asks me later over barely-warm pizza and wilted salad. "Did you call about the tent in case it rains?"

In my former, more passion-driven life I'd have wanted my lover to grill me jealously for details about my daring day with an old flame. It's great that we trust one another, but I'm disappointed anyway.

26.

ten seconds

JUNE, 1996. EVEN though I've been warned that something always goes wrong, our wedding happens without the slightest hitch. There's a bit of suspense while Joey struggles to take our rings out of his pocket while holding up his corner of the *chupah*, but he does it, to an audible sigh of relief. After the ceremony, he flings off his jacket, tie, and *yarmulke* and dashes away to join his friends.

My cousin Gert calmed me down and helped me get the flowers to stay in my hair after everyone else failed. My friend Martha's infant, Ale, is here. Every wedding needs a baby. For comic relief, her three-year-old Sammy puts his chubby fist into the wedding cake before we cut it.

It feels wonderful to be surrounded by all our friends and family, to feel their genuine wishes for our happiness. But it's an impossible day for Grace, and I see her trying so hard to smile. She and Max loved nothing more than *simchas*. We hold each other, missing him together.

The caterers keep everyone happy and even get me to eat. The band plays Dixieland for my parents, reggae for Marty and me; I dance with aunts and uncles, Joey, my father, even the sixties renegade cousin I hardly speak to who thinks I'm selling out by marrying a businessman.

Just before I throw gardenias to my single women friends, I remember my father's classic, mortifying line, at every family wedding since my adolescence. "Ruth! Put on your sneakers," he'd announce before the bride tossed her bouquet. "Don't forget to jump." Then his aside to the crowd: "She needs all the help she can get."

Is this why I'm getting married?

But it's the best party I've ever been to. When Marty and I have to leave too soon to catch the ferry to Martha's Vineyard, I wish we could change our plans and spend the night carousing with the far-flung friends I rarely see. The entire production felt like the best ten seconds of my life.

"You're *glowing*," Marty tells me.

"Your suit was *not* too baggy." We stand on the breezy ferry deck as the night Vineyard comes into view. I've stashed two bottles of champagne in my suitcase, and my cousin Naomi packed us up plates of swordfish and wild rice that will taste great at midnight, in bed, at the Duck Inn.

We're too tired to make love until the following afternoon. When we finally do, I wear the classy French nightgown Grace insisted I let her buy for me. For the next few days, we roam the Gay Head bluffs, and find a rich lode of sea glass on the beach. We skinny-dip in a Chappaquiddick pond, and hear Richie Havens sing in the old Whaler's Church in Edgartown.

We do the dance. We dangle on a string. And make believe that everything is real. Lost in a trance.

When I call Grace from the Vineyard, we discuss the latest J.D. Salinger gossip, her in-law problems, her neighbor's over-the-top renovation. "Come home before they move back in," she says. "So we can snoop."

• • •

MAX DIED A YEAR AGO, but Grace hasn't mustered the courage to have an unveiling of his gravestone, or even light a *yahrtzeit* candle in the house. After confessing she's not much of a Jew after all, she adds, "Except in one respect. We're going to Florida!"

In an unprecedented show of generosity, Max's parents have sent plane tickets for her and the kids. "They live in Jupiter! As if I didn't already know it was another planet."

"May I ask why this is so terrible?"

"If only I could stay home alone for a few days. But I can't insult my bereaved in-laws."

After she's back, her Florida stories crack me up, the theme being Sadie's and Myron's unbelievable cheapness. "The *restaurants* they took us to for early-bird specials. Both of them raved about the *fabulous* meals, with those *gigantic* portions. 'Can you believe it? All this food for only $4.95?' Of course I believed it, it was *awful*. Jell-O molds with little marshmallows, stringy chicken, and soggy French fries. And there was so much of it, we had to take it home in doggy bags and eat it the following night."

The real problem with the trip was the pain in Grace's neck and shoulders, which bothered her the whole time. "I'm sure it's nothing," she says. "Probably a pinched nerve from carrying the suitcases. But you know worrywart Alice. She's dragging me to the doctor."

I don't see Grace until later that week, when Joey and I go to the Brookline Eighth Grade Speech Contest to watch Isaac perform. She and Alice arrive suspiciously late after Grace's appointment with a bone specialist, so they've missed the beginning of Isaac's speech about wanting to be Louis XIV.

When I finally make eye contact with Alice, I know something's wrong. I have to deal with dreaded thoughts for two more hours of speeches about homework, divorced parents, and lost pets. When we finally all rush out into the refreshing cold, Grace is in a hurry to get home.

"I'll call you later," Alice says. Meaning: *Don't call Grace, so she won't have to tell you.*

"I held her feet while she was in the tube," Alice says later, "and we both chanted, 'Make this be a pinched nerve,' but the machine let us down. They're pretty sure it's a metastasized tumor near her upper spine."

Grace calls me the next morning from the teachers' lounge at her school. "When they sent me back to my oncologist, and my therapist was there, too, I knew it was trouble."

"But here's the good news," she reports the next day—never leaving me standing in total darkness. "I found out about a service called HomeRuns, which delivers groceries right to my door. The prices are great. No tipping allowed! And Ruth, wait till you hear the rest. My shower drain was clogged up again and my brother came over with some industrial-strength Drano and, voilà, it works fine. *Another* free house call. My life is too blessed for words."

❋   ❋   ❋

Two long weeks after this crummy, unfathomable update, I still alternate between thinking life is normal and realizing, several times a day, that it isn't. "What if I head to the airport and we jump on a plane?" I ask Grace while we drive to another hospital. We toss around Bali, Venice, Morocco.

"It's tempting, Ruth. But if I stay here, I may win the prize for visiting the most hospitals in Boston."

"The prize is a tour of the hospitals of France," I tell her.

Grace wants the news kept quiet, so I try to act cheerful around Joey and my friends. In the dark safety of our bed, Marty and I ask the unspeakable question: *Who'd take the kids?*

* * *

BOSTON WINTERS ARE interminable compared to those in New York. Then, suddenly, when you've totally given up all hope, the dismal brown world turns into an impressionist canvas of chartreuse buds and hot-pink azaleas. Did Grace even notice the onslaught of so much beauty this year?

Our repartee skirts around the bleakness. As droll as ever, she keeps coming up with ironies: "Isn't it too bad there's no more *Queen for a Day*? I could win a new refrigerator."

"I'd rather not bother with the doctors and just try to enjoy whatever life I have left," she mumbles in a weak, sad moment. We both fill in the rest of that thought: *the kids deserve every hour they can have with their only parent.*

"If I could just stop screaming at them," she adds.

After Grace's next appointment, we decide to drive downtown to buy discount tickets for *West Side Story*. We need some normalcy. When Grace spots a priceless parking space, she gets out of the car to shoo away other drivers while I back in.

"Wouldn't it be weird if an irate driver ran you over?" I ask. I guess I have my own hysteria to discharge.

The show's all right, pale in comparison to the original Broadway version we both saw. Joey, Louis, and Isaac hang over the balcony, dangerously close to the action; the rumble scene is too much like ballet, but the kids like it more than they admit.

I invite six of Grace's closest friends over the following Sunday morning to figure out how we can help her bear the new, unbearable weight. We could have gathered dozens, but Grace has only told certain people she's sick again. She helps me decide the cast of characters.

Marty makes us coffee and brings home bagels. I have to remind myself it isn't a *klatsch,* and that Grace can't come. But she calls me to check in. "Did you get half-and-half?"

The women commiserate for a while, then we divide the tasks. Marion is a darling, one of my favorites, a school nurse and the president of Grace's temple sisterhood. Concerned, but calm and practical, she'll deal with the boys' summer plans.

Besides figuring out what camps to send her own kids to, Grace has always helped the rest of us sort through the options, as well as finding city-run camping programs for her students. If it weren't for her efforts, a lot of these kids would have nothing to do all summer. Now someone has to do this for her kids.

Marion thinks she can get Louis a scholarship to the sports camp his friends are going to. Isaac is going on a youth group tour to Israel. Alice will coordinate doctors' appointments and take copious notes at each one. The take-charge type, she's already done extensive research on Grace's kind of cancer and made dozens of calls to experts. Alice has a law practice, three kids, a sick father, and she's on a dozen committees. Grace can never understand how she does it all.

"I love the little book Alice gave me to organize my appointments," Grace once marveled. "Except now that I'm writing everything down, I don't remember a thing."

"I'll tell the family," Alice says. "Some of them are going to freak out." She's been bringing Grace casseroles and soups, and has taken the boys to the dentist and to get haircuts.

I have the best job: keeping Grace distracted, which she's always done for me. My friend's unimaginable agenda for the day is to tell her kids what's going on, which they must have figured out by now.

"I told them to come into the living room," she tells me later. "'Oh great,' Louis groaned, 'now we'll hear more bad news,' which broke my heart. After we sat down, Isaac suddenly remembered something he had to do for school and left the room."

"Oh, Gracie," I say. Sorrow is swallowing my friend and her children whole.

"I don't expect my life to be perfect. I just want to get back to status quo."

27.

it never rains
in sunny california

"WHAT IF WE VISIT California with Joey for the holidays?" I ask
Marty, after promising myself I won't get mad if he says no. Now
that I have a family, I can't let go of my dream of a family vacation.
Since I ask him during a week when his company is actually making a profit, he lets me book the flights.

Gert and her husband, Dave, drive us from their place in
West Marin toward Lake Tahoe, but a huge storm moves in near
Sacramento. After we rent tire chains, we find out the Pass is
closed until the next day, so we spend our first night in a rip-off
hotel where the pool we promised Joey is closed.

After sliding for hours on blizzardy mountain passes with
whited-out road signs, we arrive at our snowed-in ski house where
Jane, my other California cousin, her husband, and two kids are
waiting. We take turns shoveling while the kids sled down the side
of the house. As soon as we get the driveway somewhat cleared, a
gargantuan Sierra snowplow comes by and barricades us in again.

"Let me get this straight," Marty complains. "I'm on a vacation
from winter in Massachusetts, and I'm drenched in sweat, shoveling snow."

We spend the week cooped up, dealing with kids and watching

the weather channel. I've wanted Joey to know his cousins, but Marty would rather be somewhere else. At least, as the newly-weds, we get the master bedroom, but I'm torn between joining the others and hiding out there with my husband.

We see a chilling documentary at the Donner Party Memorial Museum, which inspires jokes about eating the kids if we run out of food. Once the blizzard stops, Marty agrees to join us all for some High Sierra ski runs on endless, powdery trails, which he won't admit he enjoys.

My cousins and I cross-country ski for miles one stormy after-noon while the dads and Marty stay home with the kids — the high point of my trip. And one night Marty and I go to a bar in Truckee where I get drunk enough to join the pianist for "Lady Be Good." I can tell Marty thinks I'm making a spectacle of myself.

After Lake Tahoe, we stay with my friend Marylou, who has a Victorian dream house in San Francisco. Marty has a great time fixing her stubborn bathroom fan, probably his favorite part of the vacation. Joey plays with Marylou's infirm cat, now nicknamed "Barf Boy." And he loves getting a haircut in a salon where the flamboyant, overweight stylist entertains us with his stand-up rou-tine about dieting.

The three of us spend an afternoon in Golden Gate Park while Joey whines that he's bored. We see people buying turtles, frogs, and live chickens in Chinatown, which amuses him for a while, and then spend a good hour at the Cliff House, overlooking the wild Pacific where Joey's transfixed by a long line of surfers in wet-suits catching waves. Marty and I drink wine and watch the sun sink too quickly behind the World's Largest Camera.

It rains almost every day, but we walk around Point Lobos among the redwoods on our way south. There are mudslides on the coastal highway, so we have to turn back just before Big Sur and take the freeway. I cajole Marty into stopping for a short hike. He stays in the car to nap while Joey and I climb up to a magnificent view of the crashing ocean. I try not to dwell on Marty's disinterest in nature, letting the beauty fill the distance between us.

It's so foggy for three days in Los Angeles that we never see the Hollywood sign. But we like our seedy hotel, where the manager lets Joey walk his Great Dane around the block, past Grauman's Chinese Theatre. I'd planned to take Joey to the Museum of Tolerance while Marty went to a business meeting. Then I see a minivan advertising *Tour the Homes of the Stars*.

We cruise slowly through lushly landscaped Bel Air, trying to use our imagination about what goes on behind high stone walls and thick hedges. Our Hungarian tour guide searches hard for any movie star evidence to point out, but the glamorous enclaves are too well hidden.

"Notice the extra-large garbage cans for those beeg Beverly Hills parties," he says. "On your right, Michael Jackson's high school. Take a gooood looook. I drive reeeeeeel slow."

The tour's more promise than delivery, but we see the house poor Dustin Hoffman can't seem to sell for twenty million, Julio Iglesias's Mercedes, George Burns's barely visible portico. The Christmas decorations on Hugh Hefner's castle are a big hit with our fellow passengers, who snap pictures and take notes.

Joey doesn't care where celebrities live, but he likes the Hungarian's funny accent. Cruising around in that minivan, searching for what we never really find, ends up being the most memorable moment of our trip. "I drive reeeeeel slow," Joey says for weeks afterwards. "Take a gooooood loooook."

On our last day in L.A. we visit Universal Studios, where I love the E.T. ride, floating gently through the sky on a magic bicycle with that adorable little alien in my basket. And we see how they orchestrate movie disaster scenes: flash floods topple bridges, subway cars collide, and the shark from *Jaws* devours a fisherman's leg. Just when everything seems doomed, someone pushes a button and the calamity is magically undone.

If only Grace could push that button.

28.
a medical breakthrough

WHAT DO YOU DO if your best friend is gravely ill? If you're beyond the dreading stage, even though it's too awful to be possible? What do you do if something just as unspeakable has already happened to her husband?

When things were normal, Grace and I could always *kvetch* to one another for laughs. Now I let her grumble without waiting for the punch line. Her oncologist seems more interested in improving his golf score than her blood count.

"Would you believe an enormous photograph of a *golf course*? I don't expect Picassos in every office, but an aerial view of his country club?"

"Maybe bad taste in art isn't the same as bad medicine?"

And the mother of a kid in Louis's class keeps calling to complain that Louis is being mean to her son, Ryan."

"You're kidding!" I hope this mother is in the dark about the Steins, but, even so, this sounds preposterous.

"Louis says the boy is very annoying and no one likes him, so he's always trying to get kids in trouble. I told Louis he has to be nice to him anyway. Guess why he was mad at Ryan? Because, get this, Ruth: Ryan told Louis, 'You must be jealous of me because I have a dad.'"

The meanness of a ten-year-old makes me feel faint.

"The guidance counselor came to the rescue and read Ryan the riot act. She confided to me that she'd like to follow the kid home and let his parents have it. The principal said that would be fine with him."

Grace has stopped going to her breast cancer support group. "Too many people moaning, *Why me?* What a ridiculous thing to say. What about the Holocaust and the terrible things people endure? The real question should be, Why *not* me?"

I have a strong suspicion that if I were afflicted with some far less horrible fate than Grace's, *I'd* be one of those pathetic whiners. But at least I'm good at complaining about minor details so she doesn't feel like the only one with bad news. Another battle with Jake, a student who got indignant when I asked her to turn off the music blasting through her earbuds during a writing conference.

"I wouldn't have the guts to flunk her either," Grace admits.

*   *   *

AFTER THE TEACHERS at Grace's school raised money so she could hire a housekeeper, Grace found a wonderful Irish lass named Angela. But now Angela has to go home to Dublin for a few weeks. *"Oh, Mrs. Stein, I think I'm going to have another accidental baby,"* Grace, a talented impersonator, mimics Angela's brogue.

"Don't even look," she says when I come over to clean up a bit. "Things are too far gone around here." Today's big excursion is to see another specialist, this time at Mass General.

"How did I ever have time to work?" she wonders. "The job I've been waiting years to retire from now feels like total fun compared to the rest of my life."

By now we have a favorite restaurant on the way to every

hospital, so we stop for cream-cheese-stuffed French toast at Zaftig's in Brookline. Grace keeps apologizing for using up my free time, but the truth is that even our hardest dates are easier than being around Marty, who seems gloomy.

"But aren't you glad he's researching new storm windows?"

"You're right," I agree. "Focus on the positive."

Then I hear all the news in Grace's social network. Baby B and her husband are on an opera trip in Vienna and Arlene just got back from a mystery weekend in Savannah based on *Midnight in the Garden of Good and Evil*. There's a storm brewing at Temple B'nai David: Should men have to wear *kippahs* in the sanctuary? Not to mention the morbid scandal about someone being buried in the wrong grave.

"I kid you not, Ruth. The rabbi confided in me. He knew I was that desperate for a laugh."

Once we finish the news bulletins, we deconstruct the last book club, at which we "discussed" Wallace Stegner's *Angle of Repose* chez Claire the Authority.

"I loved the house tour. Remember when she assured us that window treatments don't have to be intimidating?"

"Not if you're spending a thousand dollars a window," Grace reminds me. *"The secret, girls, is to trust your decorator."* Her imitation of Claire is cutthroat. "Every time we tried to discuss the book, she changed the topic back to valances."

"That's because she hadn't read it."

"Right. She went into a major pout after we picked such a long book. You know, light diets, light novels."

▪ ▪ ▪

GRACE DOESN'T SLEEP the following night. "Maybe it was an anxiety attack," she admits.

"Put the kettle on. I have an hour before I have to pick up Joey from karate. I'm coming over for tea."

"Now what in the world could you possibly be anxious about?" is my feeble joke when I get there.

"*I broke a nail*," she says without missing a beat. "And I just had that expensive manicure." There's a pause while I switch from serious gear into the more familiar absurd one. And that's when she finally tells me that, two years ago this week, they told Max the terrible news.

We're never this quiet. I take her hands in mine.

*   *   *

I DON'T TELL GRACE that Marty and I aren't exactly copacetic these days. I suggest films and concerts for the nights Joey's at his dad's, but my husband would usually rather stay home. It's too cold out, or he has a cold, or he has to get up early to take the car in. When he asks if I want to meet his friends at a noisy neighborhood bar, I turn him down without admitting their conversation isn't exactly scintillating.

Now I know why they call marriage an institution. Did I just want to join a club I felt excluded from? We used to take baths together by candlelight; now we'd rather soak in solitude.

"If you'd covered the pot, the sauce wouldn't have spattered all over the wall," I remind him while we make lasagna.

"So you had a crappy day?" he asks, handing me a glass of Chianti. That must be it. How can I be angry at the sweet, helpful guy who drives Joey's friends home from soccer games? Am I just too miserable about Grace to let myself feel good about anything?

Joey kicks off his shoes, aiming them at the closet door instead of putting them inside it. The black streak on the wall doesn't come off when I scrub it.

"Go to your room," Marty bellows.

Does my son need three parents?

I suggest they both go outside for a little while, but after five minutes, they're back.

"Joey says his stomach hurts, so I made him come in," Marty says.

"*I didn't say it hurts that bad!*" Joey screams. "I *still* want to play basketball! You're just lazy."

Fighting words, not to mention unacceptable insolence, but, I confess, I'm on my kid's side. Marty's whole family makes a big deal out of the tiniest symptom. The moment you sniffle you're supposed to cancel your plans and call the doctor.

"Apologize to Marty," I say, praying for a miracle. He's a good kid most of the time, and I'm definitely not prejudiced.

"OK," he mumbles toward Marty. "What she said."

Wedlock feels like gridlock. Everything the other person does that you can't stand makes you react as if you were three years old. You're doomed to suffer one another's lifetimes of annoyances, prejudices, slights, and unhealable parental wounds. It's not just you versus him, but the Montagues versus the Capulets. The odd thing is, now that I'm sort of part of Marty's annoying family, I'm starting to appreciate my own.

Eventually I get Joey to bed, glad the buck stops with me. I make myself a cup of tea, ready to stare into space. Then Joey calls me again. "Who do you love more, me or Marty?"

"How can I answer that? What if I asked you who *you* loved more, me or dad?"

"Oh, I could answer that," he says. "I won't tell you, but I know."

This mystery will drive me crazy forever.

I retreat to the bedroom to read, then stomp back into the living room. "We have to talk about what's going on around here," I fume.

"You're too crazy to talk rationally right now." Marty's evidence is that I'm naked. He's probably right, but does he have to be so unbearably calm about everything? I refuse to give him the satisfaction of laughing at myself. I'm stubborn, I'm selfish, and I side with my kid no matter what.

"Why did you and dad get divorced, anyway?" Joey asks me the next day, even though he knows Jake and I weren't married.

"Because we couldn't get along." *I didn't want to bring you up in a house full of fighting,* I want to add, but I know this could make him feel responsible.

"But you and Marty fight all the time."

He's got me there.

＊　＊　＊

THE SADDEST I'VE EVER seen Grace is on Mother's Day morning, when she appears by surprise at my door. "Forget breakfast in bed," she mutters. "The kids left cereal all over the floor, and there are candy wrappers and dirty dishes everywhere." *How can they absorb all that pain?* I don't ask her. *Who else can they take things out on?*

I remember how jealous I was a few Mother's Days ago, when Max took the boys to get flowers and presents for Grace. Jake's oblivious of what he calls Hallmark holidays, so I was glad Marty told Joey to make me a card this year.

Grace cheers up a little while we take a short walk around my block. "Remember what Mrs. Portnoy said when her son wasn't treating her right?"

"Remind me." When it comes to literary references, I'm no match for Grace.

"I know my problem, she said. *I'm too good. I'm just too good."*

Philip Roth to the rescue.

I elaborate on the boring lunch we have to go to later for Marty's mother. "It's one of those terrible restaurants on the highway, so everyone can get there easily," I tell her.

"I hate those places."

"Marty's sister will sprinkle confetti on the table and tie balloons to everyone's chair, and the waiter will have to take pictures of the event. After that we all schlep back to his parents' house so Marty can plant the rose bush he got for Rosalyn."

"Forget it, Ruth. His mother got there first. But don't worry. Someday your son will plant a rosebush for you, too."

"I never thought of that."

⠿　⠿　⠿

A BEAUTIFUL BLACK nurse, her hair woven into intricate corn rows, ushers us toward yet another upscale hospital conference room. After interviewing the nurse about how she does her hair, we discuss the mauve and aqua décor until a bevy of docs file in. (Grace and I enjoy deciding what to call each group of physicians: a gaggle of gerontologists, an entourage of endocrinologists.)

"A posse of proctologists!" Grace shouts and we both crack up. We could keep this game up for hours.

Enter a snaggle of surgeons, each specialist with a different view about the tumor on Grace's spine. Two of them actually argue about it, right in front of us. Surgeon One says she'll lose mobility unless he operates. Surgeon Two says to postpone the surgery until she's worse.

"Well, *that* gives me a lot of confidence," Grace shrugs.

"I saw them flipping a quarter after we left," I tell her. On the way home, we sing twisted Broadway show tunes to drown out the experience.

There's no business like sick business, like no business I know . . . Everything about it is confusing. Who knows what your policy allows . . . The funnier Grace is these days, the surer I am that my emotional fortress of a friend is oh so secretly falling apart. Not the way I'd do it—sobbing into the phone at all hours, mumbling awful predictions.

I bring Louis and Isaac to our house as often as they'll come so Grace can fall apart in private. The boys like pretending to be characters in stories I can never quite follow, and turn our living room into a haunted house, a fort, or a stage. They ask me to videotape them giving a karate lesson. Bare-chested in their boxer shorts, they stare ferociously into the camera, flexing their miniature biceps. "If you're ever in trouble, remember your *moves*. And don't forget to watch the Barefoot Duckies!"

I've volunteered to go on Joey's fourth-grade camping trip and am looking forward to getting away, even if it's only fifteen miles. As I'm rushing out the door with our sleeping bags, Grace calls from Beth Israel, where she's having more tests to determine if they can do a bone graft. "Bring me a s'more," she says. "And Ruth—there's a good Motel Six about a mile from the campsite, in case there are mosquitoes."

Watching frisky fourth-graders climb ropes and bury one another in the sand, I feel a universe away from Boston hospitals. I take a long hike with the other moms, my favorite part of the trip. The kids cook hotdogs and Joey toasts me a marshmallow. In the middle of the night, a few kids wake me up because they want to change tents. I'm annoyed until I see the enormous moon, then fall back asleep, glad to have my own tent. It's the first night I've slept alone in months. I have my first erotic dream in ages.

The next day I strike up a new friendship with the raven-haired mom of a girl in Joey's class. Leslie, the image of vitality, loves to ski, hike, and bike; she has a South American boyfriend, and a good sense of irony.

Am I casting around for a new companion?

We emerge from the woods and get ready to leave just as the kids have started to calm down and really be here. Someone sprained their finger, and one kid disappeared for a while, but there were no disasters. "We've created a harmonious new world," Joey's teacher says at the last campfire.

When I get back to town, I can't wait to give Grace the details: food sprinkled with dirt and hardly any sleep. She's never been the outdoors type. "I always made Max go on those nature trips," she laughs. "I did the museums."

They want to schedule her neck surgery for Tuesday (the knives always win), but Isaac will be graduating from eighth grade that night, so Grace gets a brief reprieve.

"I'm not supposed to worry," she reports. "'This stuff is my *specialty*,' the surgeon assured me. And get this. He's going to consult his buddies before he makes the final decision." Whatever he does, Grace will have to wear an upper-body brace for weeks, and she won't be able to drive.

"Each kind of neck collar is named after a city," she tells me. "Miami, Trenton, Saratoga. I'm wearing an Aspen. They're doing them in white this year." She turns serious: "Another summer gone again before it starts."

"You'll have chauffeurs. You'll swim from your neck down."

Then her mood lightens again. "But Ruth, I forgot to tell you what Estelle said last night." Grace's ditsy neighbor who has a heart of gold. *"Why don't you ask the doctors to just* take out *the tumor?* 'Estelle!' I said. 'You've come up with a brilliant medical breakthrough! What a *great* idea. I'll tell my surgeon.'"

29.

jews on the bluff

I KEEP FINDING excuses to go shopping. If I have an hour to spare, I figure out what store I'm near and roam the soothing aisles searching for something someone needs: soccer shorts for Joey, undershirts for Marty. A consignment shop surprises me with a perfect scarf for Grace decorated with flying books and Emily Dickinson's *There is no frigate like a book to take us lands away.*

Grace's portable phone is broken, so she can only talk on the one tethered to the kitchen wall. Thank God for a vital mission, and that Marty's happy to stay home with Joey. Any excuse to get out of the house while the television's on. Rhonda suggested I get Marty earphones, but he says he won't use them.

When I first moved to Boston, I swore I'd never enter a mall, and now I enjoy strolling around in them. Especially after I find the perfect phone for Grace, bright red with huge numbers so she won't have to look for her reading glasses when she wants to make a call.

"Maybe that old phone was my whole problem!" she says after we plug in the new one. "All I ever heard on it was bad news. I'll only hear good things on this one."

We decide to walk, far more slowly than we used to, and head toward the woods near Louis's school, where our boys are playing. She's wearing a foam rubber collar to support her neck, which I pretend is hardly noticeable, even though it's summer. We spot our little Tarzans, swinging from branches, and I hear about Grace's upcoming surgery and the bone marrow protocols.

"The lawyer wants to know my plans for the boys." She drops the unthinkable into our conversation so deftly it takes me a moment to understand. It's the first time I've heard her mention what really could happen, so I'm both relieved and terrified at the same time.

Some tennis players who know Grace approach us. "Is that a fashion statement?" the woman asks about Grace's turtleneck.

"Just a little neck problem," my friend smiles, then artfully changes the subject until we escape.

     "   "   "

WE'RE MARCHING DEEPER into the jungle of all that's wrong with my dear Gracie. The orthopedic surgeon, top-of-the-line but uncommunicative, hasn't called to explain exactly what he plans to do to her. "'If you don't call me back,' I told him, 'I won't show up for the party.'"

The surgeons work on her upper spine for eight hours, putting in some kind of pin as well as bone grafts. Except for the brace, only a few staples in the back of her neck tell the tale. I go to Mass General after her surgery with a doll from Peru, three pairs of flowery underpants, and a fruit-juice-and-sorbet concoction. I don't tell Grace about the lecithin and spirulina I asked them to throw into it. And I try very hard not to show my surprise that she looks older than she did last week, and her skin seems even paler.

After she moves to the Spaulding Rehabilitation Hospital, I bring Joey for a visit. His hair is braided Rasta-style into little snakes, which cheers Grace up.

"He marches to his own drummer, doesn't he?" his teacher said.

"I figure I've saved enough money on haircuts for the last six months, so I treated Joey to the dollar-a-braid special," I tell Grace. Joey finishes her hospital apple pie and tries not to show he can't wait to leave. He doesn't say anything to me about Grace, and I don't ask, but I realize he's never been to a hospital before, or seen anyone as sick as my friend looks these days.

By my next visit, Grace is learning to navigate with her more serious neck brace. They've given her a grabbing tool, like the ones they used in old-fashioned grocery stores to get jars from high shelves. She snatches a bunch of flowers out of my hand to demonstrate.

"When I woke up after the surgery, all I could think about was Kafka's Gregor Samsa, lying there on his back wiggling his pathetic legs." Then she's serious for a moment. "I was really a mess this morning."

"Why?" I ask, before we both laugh at such a ridiculous question. *Why, among the hundreds of reasons?*

"It's Isaac's birthday. And it's also the day I was first diagnosed four years ago." She sits on her bed, waiting for someone to arrive with her Percocets, which she should have taken two hours earlier. "You have to ask for them, and I forgot." She interrupts her story about Isaac's birth thirteen years ago to mutter, "Who knew pain could be this bad?" before continuing. "I was in a hospital then, and here I am in another hospital. I remember Max lying on the bed with our baby and me talking about what our life would be like in a year, which seemed forever. We tried to imagine Isaac going on dates, and leaving for college." I water the plants and straighten up her room. "Now I'm trying to visualize happy times again, but the truth is, they may not come."

The room full of beeping machines and darting orderlies is suddenly too quiet. I hold Gracie's icy feet in my sweating hands and force a smile for her. I'm relieved she's sharing her sorrow, but I can't bear its weight. When the nurse finally brings in the pain-killers, I want one, too.

The main event of my visit is helping Grace take off her lying-down, minimal neck brace and putting on the medieval torture model so we can stroll down the corridor. I can't figure out where all the Velcro tapes attach, and at one point she winces when I pull too hard. "I guess I'm not cut out for a nursing career," I apologize.

She takes me on a tour of the rehab unit, making amusing comments about the terrible paintings and the personalities of the various doctors and patients she already knows. We visit the solarium, where they're going to have Isaac's party when Max's parents get here with the boys in a little while.

Grace shows me the hospital roof terrace, which has a wonderful view of Boston Harbor. "I'll have a first-class view of the fireworks," she brags. "Max would have loved this location. Come on, Ruth, admit it. You're jealous."

■　■　■

I WOULD RATHER stay in town, near where Grace lies captive, but we've paid for a month at the cottage this summer, so I'll have to come in for visits. Wayward Park already feels like a community Joey and I actually belong to. It's always been kept somewhat secret—a treasure so glorious the regulars want to save it for themselves.

The bayfront property cost six hundred dollars in 1906, when the plan to build a hotel fortunately fell through. The early vacationers lived in large tents, then in structures called Hodgson

Portables, which look quite lavish in old photographs; most of them were destroyed by hurricanes. Cows grazed among wild summer children, and many families had victory gardens. In the fall and winter men would come to hunt fowl and deer.

Hardly improved since the twenties, our cottage has a small living room and a narrow screened-in front porch; the kitchen incorporates the original back porch. The place is a putterer's dream—lots of junk to sort through and fix, which Marty's so good at. Our landlord is thrilled about these improvements.

Even though we're in a heat wave this year, Marty insists we clean out the attic, which is crammed with fishing rods, horse-shoes, old beds, and mattresses. He squeezes oil on the old rusty glider where I love to sit at dawn, listening to the bird orchestra. We have a noisy view of the tennis courts, the playground, and the basketball court where Coach Ted runs the kids ragged. Joey's the smallest kid playing rough German dodgeball, which I can barely watch, but when he's knocked down, he refuses to cry.

Compared to our fifth- and sixth-generation summer neigh-bors, we'll always be newcomers, lowly wash-ashores. I want to bake peach pies for Joey's children in this kitchen and tell them stories of our first two weeks here when their father was three.

"Maybe Joey could go to overnight camp next summer," Marty has mentioned. "We can rent a place on Nantucket." He takes his small Sunfish out on the bay to get away from everyone, while I talk to as many people as I can. When we ride our bikes past remote houses in the woods, Marty gives them longing looks. In the meantime, he insists we put a telephone in the cottage, which I admit is a lot more convenient than bothering my neighbors.

"Tell Marty if you improve the place too much, your rent will go up," Grace warns me.

I paint some of the furniture and Marty puts a door on the bedroom. He even goes, reluctantly, to a cocktail party. "I draw the line at progressive dinners and sing-a-longs," he's warned me. Other parents and I read stories to one another's kids after moonlit picnics on the beach, and I love the community ham and bean suppers. On family field day, we run three-legged races and toss water balloons. Coach Ted gives each family paper, sticks, and tape to construct small sailboats. My competent husband designs a vessel which goes fastest and farthest, winning us our first Park trophy.

My car is always full of the bounty of the land and sea: sweet-smelling basil, just-picked corn, and mussels. Except for worrying about Grace and feeling the sad difference in our lives these days, I'm determined to have a good summer with Marty, even though he recedes into the background. Is this my fault?

"You just can't expect me to love living at a children's camp," he says. I hide my disappointment.

You can't change him, I remember Rhonda saying about Jake. I teach Joey to play tennis, which he doesn't enjoy because I'm better. Marty isn't crazy about the game, so I join a group of octogenarians whose tricky alley shots and curve balls more than make up for their lack of speed. If getting old means more victories with less running, I'm all for it.

       »   »   »

JOEY JOINS ME for a walk on the beach one morning. He's been feeling his oats with all this freedom, and today he's sweet company. "The kids are building a clubhouse in the woods," he tells me. He clams up when I ask where it is, and I can tell he's sorry he told me about it. *He's already leaving me.*

He climbs onto the jetty to fish for crabs, tying reeds around smashed periwinkles for bait. I want to keep walking, but since he won't follow me, I crouch next to him on the boulders and dangle a baited reed while he shouts excitedly each time he feels a nibble.

I think about Grace constantly: when I wake up and when I go to sleep, when I read a story to Joey or go out to eat with Marty. When I see Canada geese overhead, because she corrected me once when I called them Canadian geese.

Marty and I aren't spending much time together, which I don't mention to Grace. "When do you want company?" I ask her.

"Wait until I'm feeling better. All I do is sleep right now, so it would be a waste." Her brother Jerry and his partner, Sam, are in charge at her house these days. Sam, the ultimate organizer, finally puts me on the Grace-sitting schedule for the following week. "Watch out, Ruth," she warns me. "He'll make you polish the silver."

The air conditioned car feels like a respite on the humid day I drive to Brookline. I've gotten Grace a buckwheat hull pillow, a Japanese invention which is a big hit. "It's just what I've been looking for to relieve the pain in Grace's neck," Jerry tells me. The house is sparkling clean and quiet, except for the sound of the vacuum cleaner. I notice Sam's *Instructions for Life Enhancements* posted on the bulletin board: *She likes flowers in every room. The kids should not eat too much junk or watch too much TV. Don't let them inflict their bad feelings on their mother. Make sure Grace doesn't hear the phone ring, and screen all phone calls.*

"You left paradise for me?" she greets me.

"Things look under control around here."

"For the first time ever! Sam gives me backrubs and plays Mozart tapes to help me relax. Now he wants to clean out the attic, but I told him to call the Smithsonian first. Oh, and get this. He's trying to make the boys answer, 'Yes, Sam,' instead of grunting."

Sam met Jerry through Evelyn, Jerry's girlfriend at the time. "He dragged my brother out of the closet," Grace told me once. "If my mother only knew how well Jerry married."

Grace wants some Wayward Park gossip. She's on top of the various story lines, even though she hasn't met anyone in person.

"Remember that really nice dentist I told you about last year, who comes to the Cape from Houston every August with his Southern belle wife?"

"The ones who brought a black nanny in a uniform with them?" Her memory is amazing.

"Well now they have *six* kids. And they just bought a piece of land on the bluff. I hear they're going to build a palace and put his childhood Park rivals to shame."

"What about all those environmental protection laws?"

"Their lawyers will find loopholes. Why let a few piping plovers stand in the way of progress?"

"Isn't that the property *you* were going to buy, Ruth? It's about time there were some Jews on that bluff."

She's referring to the funny Park story my landlord, Bob, told me. I'd asked him if we were the first Jews to rent a cottage in the Park. Maybe we were trailblazers!

Bob smiled at my question. "As a matter of fact, my great-grandfather Amos was Jewish," he said. "Not that he was proud of it." Amos had married a *shiksa* and built her a cottage in the Park to blend into her world.

"You'll enjoy this," Bob continued. "Amos was up on the bluff one day, with an old-guard Episcopalian who was complaining that the Irish Catholics were moving in. Someone named Mulligan had bought land all the way down near the main road. 'Well,' said the snooty Episcopalian, 'as long as we keep the Irish off the bluff, we'll be all right.'"

Amos, the secret Jew, didn't say a word.

" " "

I HUG GRACE GENTLY. She was so nauseous after her last chemotherapy treatment, a nurse had to come and give her a shot of Compazine. "If I'd had a gun, I would have used it," she confesses. "The worst part was that the kids woke up; Louis freaked out and started screaming that he hates living in this house and wants to be an orphan. I never should have taken him to see *Oliver*, I guess."

We go outside to eat the sandwiches I've brought. Sam has put out the table, chairs, and umbrella Max bought, on sale, just before he got sick. "He was so proud of his latest bargain," Grace says.

Sam wants me to screen Grace's calls, but she grabs the phone every time it rings. Just as I'm getting her to rest, Alice shows up with her son Billy, who's about to leave for camp. Grace insists we go up to the attic to find some of her kids' outgrown shorts and bathing trunks for Billy.

"What are you doing?" we keep asking her, but with so much empty time going by, she wants to accomplish something.

"Did you get a plumber yet?" Grace asks Alice, whose bathroom sink hasn't worked for weeks. Alice the hotshot lawyer is so brilliant and efficient that Grace's doctors want to borrow the notes she takes during Grace's medical appointments. But Alice's own life is always a little out of control. Her house is so messy it's almost uninhabitable, and she can't decide what to throw away or even hire someone to help.

"He came," Alice says. "But the sink's broken, so we have to pick out a new one, plus a faucet and vanity." This is apparently way too much for Alice and her husband to deal with.

"You're in over your head," Grace says as Alice is leaving. "Maybe Ruth can help you make some bathroom decisions." I volunteer to take Alice to Home Depot on my way out of town, but she's too busy getting Billy ready for camp.

"Pretend *Grace* needs a new bathroom sink," I suggest to Alice. If that were true, Alice would have helped Grace get one by this afternoon.

Then the plumber arrives to fix the washing machine. "I never took care of anything before I got sick," Grace tells me. The plumber comes up from her basement with the four dollars' worth of change he found stuck in the drain pipe.

"What can I say?" Grace smiles. "I have to launder my money."

By the time the new housekeeper arrives, a woman from Poland, I feel superfluous. I've driven all the way in from the Cape hoping for a deep connection with my besieged friend. Whether we laugh or cry wouldn't matter. I want to ask her what to do when Marty's too hard on Joey. I want to discuss Claire Bloom's memoir about her difficult life with Philip Roth. And I want some wisdom from Grace to savor on the long drive home.

But what was I thinking? I leave reluctantly, hoping to beat the rush hour traffic, but I get stuck in it instead.

30.
starfish

Back home in Boston, I'm joyless, which I can't blame on the predictable shock of facing the reality of September. I have a full load of classes to teach and a kid who'd rather be outside and barefoot than at a desk in school. And now Marty thinks we should renovate the apartment.

"If we had more places to put things," he says, "I could walk around without almost killing myself." We used to enjoy joint projects, but even though we discuss traffic flow and clutter in great detail, grand improvements feel beside the point.

Three different architects walk around the apartment with us, analyzing what's wrong with every room. We need built-in shelves, more closets, soundproofing, a more functional kitchen. The most promising scheme will cost more than I'd ever spend.

"It's such a good investment," Marty says, disappointed with my lack of enthusiasm.

"More counter space is a great idea." After I say this I realize my favorite word in that sentence is space.

*   *   *

Joey's playing the pirate Smee in a lavish school production of *Peter Pan*, and Jake has signed him up for tap dancing lessons. My kid is so happy doing new things, I don't mind all the driving. And the time with him in the car is often conversational. Who knew he was tapping to "Take the A Train"? Or that his class had dim sum in Chinatown?

But at home Joey swallows up my energy and I have to wait until he's finally asleep to read students' essays and prepare classes. This is the semester I planned on applying for tenure, but without any recent publications, that's a hopeless plan. And, as I moan often to Marty and Grace and anyone else who'll listen, I'm not very popular with the PhD-types in the English Department who consider me an academic flake. Someone's article in *The American Scholar* twenty-five years ago about some obscure Elizabethan poet seems to trump my stories about love in the East Village.

      ❊   ❊   ❊

"YOU DON'T LOOK as good as the last time I saw you," Grace's clueless British oncologist remarks. She may be a suitable candidate for some hard-to-get-into bone marrow protocol and he's the gloomy gatekeeper. According to Grace, it would be easier to get into Harvard Medical School.

"*Of course* I looked great last spring," she says after we're a safe distance away. "That was before three rounds of chemo—and the spine surgery *he* told me to have. So now I'm not the radiantly beautiful candidate he wants for his precious experiment. Just because I've lost my hair, my color, my strength, and I'm in a neck brace. Is this a beauty pageant?"

I wake up in the middle of every night, trying not to hear the traffic so I can pretend I'm still at the beach. I keep flashing on that sublime moment when we first arrive at the cottage. To save precious seconds, before I even slow down, Joey wants to jump out of the car so he can find his friends. When I shout at him to help empty the car, he's beyond earshot. I love watching my kid race into each blissful August. All that summer promise. The oasis of bay waiting to cool my overheated body and spirit, and the dream of family harmony.

Here at home, a volcano erupts without warning. Joey left his backpack at his friend's house and someone has to drive to the other side of town to get it.

"He's so inconsiderate of others," Marty grumbles.

"You want him to be an *adult*," I counterattack. Marty had to toe the line when he was a kid, no chaos or untidiness allowed. Is he jealous of Joey's shocking amount of freedom? I know when to bear down on my kid and when to lighten up, so I ignore him.

"You're giving him mixed messages."

We pull out the big guns and insult one another's families: the everyone-should-be-perfect-like-us Greenbergs versus the inconsistent, do-whatever-you-want Koopermans. I know it's hard to be a stepparent, and somewhere deep down I have compassion for Marty's frustration. But I have no control over where my loyalty resides. Instead of staying up late to make things better with my husband, I fall asleep crying.

Grace's latest family drama: "Louis said I was mean because I wouldn't let him watch TV. 'I'm going to get even and flunk out of school,' he threatened, 'and everyone will know it's because my mother is such a witch. No one will want to be your friend anymore.'"

To make her feel better, I fill her in on last night's War of the Forgotten Backpack. "Marty will get used to a little chaos," my friend the optimist promises me. "Oh, now I remember why I called. Want to come with me to the Wellness Center tomorrow night? They're having a special beauty session about how to look gorgeous when you have cancer." I agree to take her, even before she mentions they'll be giving away free cosmetics.

Thrilled to be going somewhere new, we join a few dozen women, some young and beautiful, most ravaged by illness. We watch a film of inspiring success stories: *At this crucial time, you need to look wonderful on the outside so you can heal on the inside.* We learn makeup techniques to highlight our best features: cheek-bones, eyes, lips, brows, and how to work with artificial hair and wear scarves dramatically.

The high point of the evening is when they pass out mascara, lipstick, foundation, moisturizers, the works: Lancôme, Clinique, Elizabeth Arden. Grace tells them to give me a bag, too, "for your sick mother," she announces loudly. There's a lot of trading and excitement; I give away most of my stuff and feel guilty about taking the rest, but there *is* a truckload. "No matter what you're going through, free makeup cheers you up," someone tells us as we leave.

When I come in the door, Marty and Joey are under a blanket on the couch reading a book called *Oddballs*. Joey's eating his nightly apple, and Marty looks at me as if I shouldn't be surprised they've reached a truce.

Now it's our turn, which will be harder.

        ▪   ▪   ▪

WHEN ISAAC PICKS up the phone, I ask him how his mom's doing. Wrong question. Instead of answering, he talks in a funny accent and tells jokes, but I don't have the heart to join in. Louis is probably outside, playing imaginary football games by himself, wearing the helmet Max had bought for his birthday and hidden in the closet, where Grace found it just in time.

When Alice, in a rage, finally fills me in, I find out the real deal. "Dr. Weiss actually told us that the next round of chemo won't put Grace into remission. So I asked her, 'If it *definitely* won't do anything, why the hell are you giving it to her?' She looked at me as if that was a totally dumb question. Does a medical degree come with a degree in arrogance as well? Who do these doctors think they are?"

I'm glad Alice has the job of being Grace's bulldog.

"'Believe me,' Weiss said, *bristling*, 'I'll be the first to cheer if we get any kind of change from this new drug. It's a stopgap measure. She really doesn't have remission in her future.'" Alice looks like a defeated warrior.

"Well," Grace says, actually trying to sound upbeat a few hours later, "at least she used the word 'future' in the discussion. I hate to say it, Ruth, but I don't get involved in the decisions anymore. Get this," she laughs. "A secretary calls this afternoon and says she has great news for me: 'Your ovarian cancer numbers look better this week!'

"'I don't *have* ovarian cancer,' I tell her. 'So I guess it isn't such great news.'"

When the cutting-edge Taxol gives Grace a temperature of 104 and sends her back to the hospital, I'm recruited to spend time with her boys, who are understandably off the wall. They've eaten Rice Crispy squares for breakfast. Isaac teases his brother and Louis won't say much to anyone, including the shrink I sometimes drive him to.

"Grace hides the junk where they can find it," Jerry tells me.

"Isaac was so obnoxious last night, I locked him out of the house for a few minutes," Sam the disciplinarian reports. "I turned off the outdoor lights and told him, *I hope the skunks get you.*"

ON YOM KIPPUR, the Day of Atonement, Joey and I try out a secular Jewish congregation, this time in a rented church. I want him to know something about being Jewish. Grace and most of her friends are attending real synagogues for the High Holidays, services one has to buy tickets and dress up for, but I prefer our countercultural gathering.

The sermon is about trying, yet again, to hit the mark: to hold back the jibe, to honor those around us, to be gentle with ourselves. The God part is optional.

We sing "In every season, turn, turn, turn," and Phil Ochs's "When I'm Gone," instead of chanting responsively about the Almighty and listening to a droning organ. "This is boring," Joey moans. When I stand up to mention Max, a loved one we've lost this year, I notice Joey looking sad.

Marty's unhappy I'm not sending my kid to Hebrew School so he can study for a bar mitzvah, but neither Jake nor I have that in mind.

"You *work* on the High Holy Days," I remind Marty when he lectures me about Joey's lack of Jewish education. Marty has complained bitterly about being forced to spend so many of his childhood afternoons learning prayers in a language he'd never speak.

"It's the principle," he says.

"Joey will have so many Jewish friends, he'll spend every Saturday of eighth grade in temple anyway," Grace informs me.

I'M HAVING ESCAPE fantasies, yearning for the intoxication of great distances, and find myself looking desirously at suitcases when I buy sheets and towels at Marshall's. Going away was my remedy for depression in the old days, until Joey banished my wanderlust. Now, wherever I read about sounds appealing: T.E. Lawrence's Arabia, Paul Bowles's sun-blinding Tangier. The two years I lived in Paris have turned to fiction.

Harris the globetrotter and I had a list of future destinations, most of which I'm sure he's visited by now: the Cheops Pyramid, the Forbidden City, New Orleans for the Jazz Festival.

"Remember when you said you love to travel?" I ask Marty. "I mean, more than a week in the Caribbean?"

The strange look he gives me belies his answer. "Maybe. Someday."

"What if I went away alone?"

"I'd miss you," he says. "In case you forgot, I love you."

"I'd miss you, too," I say, and absolutely mean it.

"I'm so sorry about Grace."

*　*　*

MY STILL-HUMOROUS friend has a new installment about her California cousins. I used to think she embroidered her family's eccentricities to make me laugh. There's news about her cousin Annie's ex-husband, who had so many affairs she finally dumped him. "He comes over one day, just like that, with an *emu*. On a *leash*. He thought it would be fun for the kids. Annie screamed at him, but he told her it *followed him down the street*. He said he was going out of town and had no choice. She had to take it, at least for the weekend. Then she found a receipt for the huge bird in the bag of emu food he gave her."

"Not even you could have made this up," I say.

"And then there's Max's family. His cousin Carmen hired a limo on her wedding anniversary to take her husband and kids to the jewelry district so they could help her pick out a diamond tennis bracelet. Now isn't that your idea of the perfect anniversary?"

"What else is going on?"

"One more dose of the Taxol, and then I get to go back for the really serious discussion."

I know it's cowardly, but all I can think about is getting out of town.

"Joey doesn't have a soccer game this weekend," I tell Marty when he comes home from his miserable Friday at work. "Maybe Bob would let us stay at the cottage for a few nights before he closes it up."

Marty's business is slow again, so all he expects from the weekend is to not be at work. I go in the other room and call our summer landlord, who says he'd be happy if we used the cottage. We can rake some leaves instead of paying. My enthusiasm for the escape trumps Marty's apathy. As we cross the Sagamore Bridge, Satchmo croons "What a Wonderful World," piercing my heavy heart with a tiny shard of joy. I've only been gone for a month, but I feel like Odysseus returning after years of tribulations. The cottage waits patiently, petunias still colorful in the window boxes.

I fall into the comforting off-season silence. Squirrels scrabble on the porch roof, the wind howls, and crows squawk. I imagine wintering alone so close to nature. In the Russian-Japanese film *Derszu Uzala*, a woodcutter lives happily in a lean-to in the forest. Once he becomes very old, his concerned daughter insists he move into her home in Moscow to live out his days. But condemned to the "comfort" of a room with a real bed and a wood-burning stove, the old man is miserable. He finally pitches his tent in the backyard and dwells there happily, even in the snows of a bitter Russian winter.

While Joey and Marty play Monopoly, I go down to the desolate beach, the horizon an invisible blend of water and sky. I walk until the rocks hurt my feet, then turn back toward the huge red sun slipping into the water. A man wearing a hat full of colorful lures is fishing for blues.

"See all the bait fish? They're out there." He points to dark shadows on the water, then excuses himself and runs up the beach, casting his line toward the disappearing light. On my way home I chat with Ursula and Betty, two of my favorite older Park women, rare year-rounders. They've been friends since they were sixteen.

"Isn't it wonderful to be down here alone?" they ask me. Even though I'm not, I feel that way.

I broil sea scallops and toss them into spaghetti for dinner, listening to *Lush Life*, my favorite jazz program on WOMR, Provincetown's Outermost Community Radio station. Being in my favorite place doesn't keep me from lying awake for hours. I remember finding this cottage, sitting on the porch that first summer feeling so joyous.

The next morning I walk to the graveyard, the best of all resting places. The earliest stones are from the 1600s; many husbands had two or more wives, often sisters, who died in childbirth. The men succumbed to wars, the flu epidemic of 1918, Vietnam.

This is where Joey's crew plays Manhunt and Kick the Can. When I asked him the rules of these games, he referred to several of the main headstones and monuments as different bases. "You start at Thornton," he explained. "You have to get to Taylor without being tagged. Or else you're dead."

The next night Marty and I hold each other quietly for a long time, then make silent love. "I'm sorry I'm so drained and useless," I say. "But have you ever felt you have no right to happiness because others are in trouble?" He says he hasn't. "How can you put up with me these days?"

"I agreed to put up with occasional bad moods," he says. "It's on page six of the contract."

Why do I find so much fault with such a good guy?

On Sunday morning Marty wants to rake leaves, so Joey and I drive all the way to where Cape Cod ends at Race Point in Provincetown and climb the moonscape of high dunes. Rolling and yelping with pleasure, Joey pretends he's snowboarding down the gullies, which are like half-pipes. We pass the historic dune shacks where Eugene O'Neill, Edward Hopper, and their bohemian ilk retreated from the madding crowd.

We spot a couple on the deck of one of the shacks. Their radio is blasting rock and roll, and they're waving their arms at the surf, dancing out the very end of summer. I expect the ecstatic dune dwellers to shoo us away like pesky tourists, but it seems they're hard-up for company, so they talk to us for a few minutes.

We finally get to the water. "You can try to see across the ocean to Europe," I tell Joey.

"I'm going to meditate," he says. My little Buddha takes me by surprise. I walk along the shoreline while he sits, in his ten-year-old version of peace. When I come back, he's on his back, eyes wide, arms flung out. We've each picked up a tiny starfish, softly alive. Joey throws them both back into the sea.

31.

touring the orient

MARTY AND I INVITE our parents and his brother's family for Thanksgiving at our place, as silently expected. No one will know we're not getting along. My father will complain about the two flights of stairs, and Marty's mother, Rosalyn, will notice I haven't ironed the napkins. Joey will be miserable without any other kids around.

I've never cooked a turkey. During my unending single era, I avoided family holidays. Irving and Stella were often safely steaming off on freighters, so I was spared the guilt. I'd meet friends in Chinatown for Peking duck, all of us thankful about our jailbreaks from family folds.

This is a labor- and psyche-intensive occasion, but Marty and I are a good team in a crisis. He borrows a long table, and we buy extra glasses, silverware, and plates. I make lists and drive all over town for organic vegetables and an exorbitant free-range bird.

Did that turkey go to prep school? my father will say, or something like it.

I've decorated our curtainless windows with crepe paper and painted a Japanese lantern with watercolors to cover the bare bulb in the dining room. Joey draws a picture of a turkey raising a white flag for the front door.

"Amazing! You're still hanging in there!" My father slaps Marty sympathetically on the back. "I can't believe you've lasted this long." Marty lets him get away with it instead of coming to my defense.

"Show Grandma and Grandpa the mural you painted on your wall," I tell Joey. My parents adore their grandson, no matter how he behaves. I like their visits, at least for the first twenty-four hours, before I lose my cool with my dad's inevitable pot shots.

"That fireplace looks dangerous," he says, just because a few bricks are loose. It's all he says about the apartment I'm so proud of—except for asking me (again) how much I paid for the place and reminding me it was too much. I look at Marty for support, but his silence is hard to decipher.

Eventually we hear, practically verbatim, most of the wise-cracks I predicted my dad would make. "It's a good thing we live so long in our family. I could have been dead before Ruth ever cooked me a turkey," Irving says while Marty carves.

"Keep it up, Dad, and you won't live long enough to be invited back," I say when we're beyond earshot.

My parents and Marty's are about as different as two sets of Jewish in-laws can be, but money is always common ground; they discuss how much houses, shoes, electricity, and, of course, turkeys cost and used to cost. Joey wolfs down his meal and races to a friend's house until I call him back in for dessert.

"*Oy*, look at him," Rosalyn gasps. He's a little sweaty, and his pants are grass-stained.

"Go wash up," I whisper. "Joey gave his allowance to a friend to help him pay for the baseball glove they lost," I say, changing the subject. I'm proud my kid knew enough to do the right thing without my asking him to.

"Did you ever find that jacket Joey lost last winter?" Rosalyn asks. What a memory for mishaps. Grace has warned me how the in-law situation takes its toll on matrimony. She spent the first five years of her marriage haranguing Max after every family visit about the way his father ignored her. "Don't make my mistake," she says. "Just ignore the insults, drink a lot of wine, and smile."

"I'm bored," Joey whispers, too loudly, during our post-pie small talk. He's read my mind. I let him turn on the television.

"How about a quick walk around the block?" I ask Marty when we're alone in the kitchen.

"That would be rude."

Since he doesn't feel my need for fresh air or togetherness, I excuse myself and go alone.

"I can't believe you let my father get away with those remarks," I tell him after everyone's finally gone.

"Why do you let it bother you, Ruth?" We argue for as long as it takes to wash the dishes, sweep the floors, and rearrange the furniture, then call a kind of truce.

"HAVE A NICE weekend if you can," I told my students before Thanksgiving break. "Come back with an idea for your final paper. Being with your family will definitely give you material, so take notes." We'd finished discussing someone's story about a love affair on Mars, and another's nineteenth-century tale about a mother dying and leaving her two daughters in the care of a wicked nanny. It was time to give them that final push toward truth-telling.

My own story of this November's feast would include my long deliberations over stuffing recipes and which flowers to get for the centerpiece. Underneath the effort would be the dreaded point-lessness of the ordeal. Once we were finally seated, what did we actually have to say to one another? Was it supposed to be enough that we were all just *there*?

⁕ ⁕ ⁕

"I HAVE A NEW way of getting rid of telemarketers," Grace announces. "I just tell them I'm waiting to hear about a heart transplant, so I can't tie up my phone."

The next time we get together, I notice pauses in our conversations when she's trying not to complain about the pain—in her hip, in her ribs, in her neck. Despite several rounds of chemo, blood tests for tumor markers, bone scans, bone-strengthening injections, and a dressing table full of luridly colored pills, Western medicine seems to be failing her.

I've started wondering *(is Grace?)* what it would take for her doctors to simply admit defeat and bow out. I wish she'd go AWOL and plan a vacation with her kids instead of showing up for all these futile—once you read between the lines—appointments.

The goal was to get her white cell count low enough for that cutting-edge bone marrow transplant. I both hope she can have it and pray she can't.

"Maybe there's some mistake. Let's do the tests over before we panic," Weiss said after the last disappointing results.

"The bone scan is kind of relaxing," Grace tells me. "You just lie there and sleep while a machine hums slowly over you. If I forget what they're actually doing, I can enjoy it."

In the middle of what we now think of as Grace's oncology residency ("if they'd only give me the appropriate salary when I finish," she says), I keep thinking about pushing my friend toward more holistic terrain. My first try failed miserably last spring, when I sent Grace to Eric, the brilliant homeopath I'd heard about. Good friends raved about his curative powers, so I hoped Eric could at least counteract all those toxins the doctors were doling out.

"He's not a very normal person, is he?" Grace reported after Eric's house call.

"Oh no. What happened?"

"He asked me about my relationship with my mother."

I wanted to strangle the guy, but Grace just laughed.

Then, during one of Joey's soccer games, one of the moms mentions her brother's bout with cancer. While our team suffers a bitter defeat, the woman and I talk nonstop, not even watching the game. The truth is, I hardly ever watch the games, as there's too much to talk about with the other parents. In fact, after how many years of Joey's growing skills on the field, I don't really understand all the rules.

"Kevin was diagnosed with terminal lymphoma a year ago," she tells me. "But a Chinese acupuncturist seems to have gotten him into remission!"

When it comes to holistic matters, I'm a believer—not that I've ever put my own struggling body to the test. I wait until the right moment to spring this idea on my less alternatively-inclined friend, telling her the whole story: how three other guys on Kevin's high school football team also contracted cancer, possibly from pesticides used on the field.

"What do you think about visiting Dr. Lee?" I slip into our conversation. "Apparently Kevin's Mass General medical team are flabbergasted about his improvement." I wait for Grace to change the subject to Louis wanting to be Catholic, or Isaac's high SAT scores, but she's quiet for a few seconds.

"So book me in." I don't tell her that the miracle worker isn't officially taking any new patients. But after I make some calls, it seems that Kevin is doing so well he'll let Grace have his next appointment with the Chinese wizard.

A few weeks later we slowly thread our way toward Dr. Lee's Chinatown office. Thanks to Grace's new handicap card, we park right in front.

"You just hang out with me for my special privileges," she says.

Dr. Lee is in his forties, full of fiery vigor. After Grace follows him into a small room, I talk to people in the waiting room so I'll have stories to tell my friend. I hear about Lee's great successes with carpal tunnel syndrome, leukemia, and macular degeneration. One man has driven his wife in from Pennsylvania. The doctor hasn't cured her rheumatoid arthritis so far, but they're hopeful. "Besides, what choice do we have?" the husband asks me.

A stooped-over young Russian with a cane arrives, who also sings Dr. Lee's praises. "The physical therapists at the hospital were working on the wrong side of my body!" he tells me.

"You will go home without your cane today," Lee says to him when he appears.

I join Grace for the consultation part of her appointment. Lee talks about guns and enemies. He isn't easy to understand, but later we figure out he meant that cancer cells aren't like bad armies you can kill with weapons.

"You don't come to me soon enough," he tells her, shaking his head. But then he smiles and says, "Not a worry. I can help." He tells Grace to lie face down so he can insert his magic needles into all the right meridians. I say a few prayers in the waiting room.

We never find out if the Russian guy left without his cane. "It's like Lourdes in there," I say during our Szechuan lunch. Grace is making a face while eating the broccoli Dr. Lee ordered her to eat three times a day.

"Remind me to look for the pile of crutches," she says. Then, "Did I ever tell you I can't stand broccoli?"

But I've got our biweekly trips to "Needle Man" all worked out. I drop Joey off at school, then stop for two hot chocolates and cinnamon buns before picking Grace up. I can get her home in time to get to work. I've scheduled my student conferences for Fridays when Grace stays home, not a popular move.

No matter how many times we drive to Chinatown, my navigational skills don't improve, so it's touch and go. Grace is too busy telling me neighborhood and town news to catch my wrong turns before I make them, so our routes are always circuitous, each trip different but never quicker than the last.

Before he inserts his needles, Dr. Lee performs qigong on Grace, moving his hands mysteriously through the air around her, I assume to break up bad energy patterns. "Diabetes," he says, "I cure it. Parkinson's, I know how to treat that very well. Doctors tell my patients, *You have one month to live*, and I make them go back to work."

My friend and I try not to look at each other so we don't make skeptical faces.

While Grace lies in the dark, her body a landscape of needles, I read Dr. Lee's self-published pamphlets and books about the immune system and ridding the body of impurities by redirecting the *chi*. During one visit, he spends a long time shouting into a speaker phone in the waiting room. Then I notice that while he's talking, he's putting pins into tiny holes representing acupuncture points on a white plastic human figure.

"I fix my patient in California long distance," he explains later. Everyone else in the waiting room seems nonchalant about this. "Some people, they think I do voodoo," Dr. Lee laughs. "And *joke* is, I *do* do voodoo. Why? Because voodoo works."

I wasn't going to tell Grace about this aspect of Dr. Lee's practice, but she notices the plastic voodoo doll full of pins while she's writing out her check. We have a field day on the way home.

"Didn't Beckett write a play about a Chinese doctor?" I ask.

"The weird thing is," she says, "I always feel *better* after Needle Man. He's the only specialist I see who looks *happy*. Maybe that's his secret—he's an optimist."

On our next visit, I'm the one who's feeling awful. Marty and I have had a hard weekend, and I'm weepy and anxious, hardly sleeping or eating these days.

I don't go into it with Grace, wanting to spare her my worries, but when she's in the other room, I ask Dr. Lee's assistant, whom I know quite well by now, if he treats depression. She mumbles something to the master, and during his next break, the doctor approaches me, moving his hands over my chest and throat. He looks like he's shadowboxing and doesn't say a word. Then he rushes off to put needles into someone and take them out of someone else.

"You may feel worse for a few days," the assistant warns me. "But then you'll notice a big change."

Two days later I feel mysteriously uplifted, even loving toward my husband. We've started touching again. Is there a reason why everything can't turn out all right, at least for a while?

⸪

DR. MILLER, A NEW and unusually compassionate oncologist, has taken over Grace's case since Weiss's time was definitely up. "The hospital lured him from North Carolina," Grace reports on our way to her appointment. "New man in town." I'm impressed with Dr. Miller because he wants to know about my friend's life, not just her illness.

By the time Grace finishes her story there are tears in the doc's eyes. He even books her in with a nutritionist. "Will I have to mention my chocolate-cake diet?" Grace asks me with that adorable, naughty look. Dr. Miller apparently pays less attention to blood tests, and watches patients instead to see how they *feel*. He even approves of Grace's extracurricular visits to Chinatown.

"Needle Man said the same thing about not paying attention to the blood tests," I remind her after our visit. "Remember? He said your elevated white blood cell count could mean your body is just behaving like a rich country. It doesn't necessarily have more *crime*, just lots of money to hire more policemen."

The other good news, Dr. Miller says, is that Grace's tumors are hormone-receptive, so she might have good luck with the new medication he's prescribing. "I know someone who's been on this medicine for five years," he tells us. "Of course, every case is different."

But I'm trying to be like Grace, who only hears the good news—or at least pretends to. On the way home, we discuss our embattled president's press conference after his Oval Office bust, and how cool and calm Clinton is during the nightmare he's unleashed on us all. "I read somewhere that he can just put his troubles into little boxes and store them away. Unlike Nixon, who fell apart on TV," Grace says. "I guess I'm the same way."

I'm free this Friday afternoon, so I decide we should get pedicures. Neither of us has had her feet pampered since we were married, we realize—which for Grace means it's been twenty-five years.

A half hour later, there we are in another kind of waiting room, this time with Asian women in white coats.

"We're touring the Orient," I say. The best part of this indulgence is all the female chattering. While our feet are pumiced, creamed, and massaged, Grace and I slip in and out of conversations with suddenly intimate strangers. "Make sure you hire my balloon guy for your daughter's bat mitzvah party," she tells the woman who's having her legs waxed. "Look at all the fun I've been missing," she announces to the room at large, while a beautiful Korean woman paints her toes a glamorous shade of crimson called "A Peony for Your Thoughts."

Mine look amazing in "Barefoot in Barcelona." I've seen the major Gaudí landmarks there, which Grace would so adore. When she's better, I'll take her.

32.
dusk

THE THIRD CONTRACTOR has come, walked around the apartment, banged on walls, scratched his head, and gone. Marty has measured every room and window and made sketches, but we still can't find a plan that will give us more light and storage without having to move the bathroom or completely gut the kitchen.

"Back to the drawing board," Marty says, about to stay up late again working on another plan. His patience is admirable. He'll work forever on a tangible problem there's an actual chance of fixing.

"Can't you take a break and come to bed?" My attempt at a different kind of renovation.

"Why don't *you* put some time into this, if you think it's going too slowly?"

"Maybe there are other ways we could change things around here," I suggest, but he thinks I'm questioning his draftsmanship, and gives me an exasperated look.

Instead of explaining what I mean, I go to bed and read *The Romance of Remodeling*. I should be reading how to remodel romance instead.

*   *   *

SINCE WE'RE NOT in the mood to go away alone this winter, Marty agrees to take Joey and join my parents on Virgin Gorda.

A less-than-private getaway will at least force us to cover up our malaise.

My parents are crazy about Marty, so they're raring to go. Marty, Joey, and I fly to San Juan and then Tortola, where a water taxi speeds us loudly toward the island. While Marty chats with an investment banker who'll be sailing his own yacht from island to island, Joey lies in my lap staring up at more constellations than he's ever seen.

"There's Cassiopeia, and Diana the huntress," I point. "And there's Orion's belt."

My worries melt into wonder in the sultry, starry night, and I feel some long-forgotten optimism. I've rented a round, two-bedroom house on the water for our week of tropical togetherness. "I brought my negligee," I whisper to Marty, and he squeezes my hand halfheartedly. He'd rather be home trying to keep his business going, but he's always been at his most cheerful on a warm island, so I'm hoping for the best.

We spot my father in his legendary palm-leaf hat, pacing the dock. He and my mother love the ritzy accommodations. "Just like *Lifestyles of the Rich and Famous*," she says.

The trip is officially grand. Our deck surrounds the house so we can follow the sun. Joey chases lizards and stares at the iguana warming itself on our private pier. Marty likes driving our rented Jeep all over the dry, rocky island. But he's suffering from some kind of ennui he won't admit to, so we can't talk about it.

My mother's in her glory, skinny-dipping in our private pool. We buy provisions in a tiny store and she and I cook breadfruit and red snappers in coconut oil. Even my father finds little to complain about, except how much everything costs. There are only a few brief father-daughter skirmishes.

One afternoon Marty and I take off for a secluded beach where we lie in silence against huge boulders, breathing in the dreaded aloneness, eating grapes. If we could figure out what's wrong between us, we could move on. He puts suntan lotion on my back mechanically but won't let me return the favor. His bald spot will get burned, but I keep my mouth shut.

We haven't held one another in the water since Guadeloupe, three years ago.

I'm reading a novel about a man who lies in bed at night thinking about whether to leave his wonderful wife. Instead of explaining why he's so unhappy, he keeps singing her praises. I feel a kinship with this oddly sympathetic narrator, even though he's not admirable.

Marty holds my elbow as we climb back up to the road after our swim. We're so kind to one another it hurts.

Each night we drink Marty's margaritas and look for the elusive green flash at sunset. After dinner, Joey keeps himself busy drawing. In another season of our nation's discontents, Clinton's now charged with repugnant and ludicrous acts. In Joey's picture, a kid points at a constellation. "Look, Mom," the cartoon boy says. "There's a new constellation called The President's Zipper!"

※   ※   ※

"WE COULD BE HAVING a great life," Marty says to our therapist, succinct as ever. He's about to go away on a short business trip, and I've been looking forward to his absence. I'm safe and cared for—for the first time in my life. But when I think about the future, I can barely breathe. I'm the only person Marty ever really talks to. My depressions are more overt than his, but perhaps more fixable. There's not enough oxygen, and I'm worried we'll suffocate. I'll never tell anyone I saw our adjacent tombstones in a dream. Is commitment another name for claustrophobia?

⁜ ⁜ ⁜

BACK HOME, SOCCER season takes over. After the other team fires a shot right past him and the game is lost, my little goalkeeper tries not to cry. Any blow to his small ego hurts me more than it hurts him. I feel a kinship with any other mother of a goalkeeper. It isn't their fault if the team lets them down, but they take the rap. Joey and I drive home through luscious spring countryside, discussing Chaplin's *Great Dictator*, which we watched the night before.

"Do you think he made the movie so people would get over the war?" Joey asks. "So they could laugh after so much awful stuff?" His face is red and dirt-streaked, but now he's chipper again. Full of insights, hungry to know everything, to have as many lives as he possibly can, my kid makes me envious.

Write about a room, I tell my students on a day when I'm distracted and not well prepared to teach the class. They save the day for me. Laura writes about her father's music room, which she wasn't allowed to enter. She remembers standing in the doorway, studying him while he played classical guitar. Her parents were strangers, always away.

Allen writes about the jail cell he slept in after he was arrested in a small Midwest town. He'd hitched a ride with suspicious-looking characters. Kyoko describes a veranda where she made love with a man of twenty-five when she was a schoolgirl of seventeen:

After we wrinkled the sheets that first time, I realized I didn't love him. I was only practicing for when my real lover came along. I was ashamed that I had hurt him. Salty tears fell into my tea.

If I had the courage, I'd write about our bedroom where the sun wakes me every morning, first deep pink, then white. I'm usually asleep when Marty goes to bed these days, and he's still unconscious when I leave in the morning to get Joey to school.

The future tense has evaporated from our conversations. I'm craving solitude the way I used to crave our closeness and our heat.

One summer, years ago on Martha's Vineyard, I'd see an elderly couple walk slowly each dusk across their sweeping lawn to watch night fall. Their house faced the sea. When they came close enough, I caught their enigmatic smiles. I watched their sunset romance from the shed where I wrote, so envious of their luck. I knew I'd been looking for all the wrong things.

33.
mildew

PATRIOTS' DAY, WHICH commemorates the Revolutionary Battle of Lexington and Concord, is also Marathon Day in Massachusetts. Grace and I are spending the double spring holiday at the hospital. To add to the confusion, this year it's also Passover.

"It's just as well," she says. "I wouldn't know whether to fire a cannon, run twenty-six miles, or make matzo ball soup." With a horrible look on her face, she chugs down a gallon jug of white, chalky stuff for yet another photo shoot of her failing innards. Her face is as white as her beverage.

"The pharaoh could have used that stuff for the eleventh plague," I say. I found myself perusing the Mortality section of the library the other day and I skimmed through Kübler-Ross, but I didn't bring it home. Which stage is Grace going through, denial or anger? What about me?

I stare at the runners on television, a magnificent, proud Kenyan woman in the lead. "I have to start thinking about who's going to take care of the boys," Grace says casually while she's getting dressed. "In case I can't."

I'm relieved that she's finally brought this up, but she's caught me off guard, and the question's way beyond my expertise. If I have time after I bring her home, should I stop at the library again to research the subject? Then I realize books have their shortcomings.

Who would take Joey for me? Jake or Marty?

"If Jerry and Sam would move into the house, the kids could stay where they are." I'm silent. "But Louis will have a hard time with that. He flips out about the gay business."

"I guess we don't all get to have our way," is the best I can come up with. I stare at the sweat-drenched Kenyan as she breaks through the tape in downtown Boston and receives her olive wreath.

Grace is running her own marathon while the rest of us try to keep up. As we walk back to her car, she mentions she's now in stage IV, slipping it into our conversation as if it's a small detail she forgot to mention. I try not to react, but she's definitely thrown a wrench into our conversation.

"But at least we don't know which part of stage IV," she tries to soften the blow. "So what's new with your family, Ruth?"

"Joey spilled poster paint on Marty's new suit."

"If you call him on that magic phone you bought for me, he'll forgive you." I don't remind her that the phone hasn't exactly worked the way we wanted it to.

⸱ ⸱ ⸱

IT'S FINALLY AUGUST. As usual, I've packed too much stuff for the Cape, even for two cars. Joey rides with Marty this year, and we arrive with three bikes, Marty's sunfish, and more books than I could read in a year. There's a cookout on the beach this evening and I'm hoping Marty will make an appearance.

"The cottage looks terrible," he says, shaking his head. Our sweet landlord doesn't do much to take care of it, but that's never interfered with my blissful summers. Marty points out peeling paint around the windows and porch screens.

"Let's put on our suits and go down to the beach for free hot-dogs." I try to take his arm.

"I'd rather get things organized up here. I'll unload the cars."

After Joey and I are back and he's in bed, Marty wants to talk about having the wood trim on the cottage repainted. "I already called Bob, and he said he'd pay for everything if we buy the paint and hire the painters."

Now that we've tabled our apartment overhaul (no plan seems worth executing), he's itching for some home improvement. "The wood should be protected from the weather," he says, "or the place will really fall apart."

"Are you sure you want to bother? It's your vacation."

"Bob said we can change the color."

Marty and I don't usually like the same colors, so I'm relieved that he's happy with the dusty sage-green sample I bring back from the hardware store. So far, so good.

Joey's really on his own this year, putting in brief appearances for sandwiches, snacks, and the bathroom. I'm playing decent tennis and have been cooking us wonderful meals: swordfish, lobster, and mussels. I swim in the bay, in the ponds, even in the ocean, and catch up with my Park girlfriends.

       .   .   .

AFTER I ASK AROUND about painters, friends recommend a young couple who've worked in the Park for years, and their estimate is lower than the one the painting company Marty found in the Yellow Pages gave us. We have to stay within our landlord's budget, so the decision seems made.

The cheerful team finally starts, only a few days late. Soon there are ladders all around the cottage. The painters' soft brushstrokes are audible in our silence. They eat sandwiches in the shade, laughing, while we have stilted conversations about whether to have scrod or bluefish for dinner.

"I'm thirsty!" Joey shouts as he streaks past us with sandy feet.

"I just swept that floor," Marty barks. No point mentioning that a beach house is supposed to have a little sand in it. Joey pours his orange juice so fast it spills on the floor, but I mop it up before Marty notices.

"They're doing a terrible job," my perfectionist husband says dourly after inspecting the painters' work. I follow him outside. "Look at this, Ruth. They call this prep work? They hardly even sanded." I'm not sure what isn't right, so I keep my mouth shut. "I wanted to wait and get more estimates, but you were in your usual rush."

I follow him slowly around the house while he runs his hands over sills and doors, frowning. I did want to get the painting over with as soon as possible so we could enjoy the cottage without people staring into it all day long. But the painters have a good reputation.

"Betsy Smith says they did a great job on her place."

"The whole point is to get rid of the mildew and prevent it from coming back. No wonder their estimate was so low."

When he's out of earshot the next day, I mention the mildew issue to the painters. "My husband's a little worried," I whisper.

"He's worrying for nothing," the man assures me. "There won't be a problem."

"If there is, we'll come back and fix it," his wife adds. They've been so physically close to us for two days, I've bonded with them. *He can't trust anyone these days*, I want to tell them. *He's not usually like this. But he has a lot of pressure at work so he's taking it out on your paint job.*

We can't leave someone we like, so we find ways to dislike the person we blame for our unhappiness, I read in the book about divorce I've been secretly devouring, hiding it under my pillow.

Marty wakes up a few mornings later and announces, very calmly — as if he's talking about getting the car washed — "I'm going home."

Does he know I've been sitting on the porch since dawn, wishing him gone? But as soon as he reads my mind, I change it.

"Will you please just take a walk with me?" I'm sweating, frightened, trying to resist his fight or flight mode. One of us in panic is enough.

Marty dislikes walks, even on a good day, but he agrees to go around the tennis courts. "You need this vacation. If you're upset about having the painters around, we can ask them to come back and finish up after your vacation is over."

If I could apologize for whatever I'm accused of, would it be enough? My weak effort at peace fails.

We let things fall apart.

I watch him drive off into the heat of the day as if I'm watching a film I already know the ending of.

LATER ON, NUMB with shock, I bike to my favorite beach and sit on the jetty, watching intact, or intact-looking, families enjoy themselves. That night I retreat to the backyard hammock and stare at the stars. Joey's watching movies in the community house, and I won't have to update him for a while, so I allow myself some peace, at least for now. For the first time this summer I notice fireflies in the woods.

After I get Joey to bed, I call my cousin Gert, who's been expecting this. "You haven't sounded happy in months," she reminds me.

Grace calls the next morning, in the middle of her own *mishegas* about Louis's baseball uniform. I can hear him shouting at her. "He's mad because I'm too cheap to buy him a new one when this one is fine." When she runs out of steam, I finally dump my news in her lap.

"Let me get this straight. He didn't think the painters were doing a good job and then he did *what?*" I feel as if I'm telling her someone else's story, and I know this isn't a good sign.

"He liked the color you picked out. That was where we left off the other day. On an optimistic note. You agreed on moss green."

"Sage."

"OK, whatever. The point is you *agreed* on it."

"That was a surprising victory."

"He'll come to his senses. Give him a few days and he'll drive back." If only I could believe Grace's indomitable optimism.

I wake up early the next morning thinking about the summer I was nineteen, hitchhiking through the British Isles with an Australian girl named Rita I'd met via a bulletin board. We both wanted to do the same trip, so we teamed up.

Rita and I had very different ideas about how to spend our days and argued constantly. We were in the lush, late-summer Lake District, and it was dusk. My companion was nervous that we'd be too late to get into the youth hostel in another town and insisted we take the next bus. I wanted to stay and wander through Wordsworth country. I was finally breathing in the poetry of the place I'd so longed to see.

The next thing I knew, I watched the bus disappear with Rita staring at me through the window. I'd get a later bus and catch up with her. After I asked for the schedule, however, I found out that was the last bus of the day. My terror came on strong.

"Go on and hitch a ride," said the grizzled, kind bus dispatcher. "No reason to be afraid around these parts."

Who'd sent him to me? I'd never hitched a ride alone, but I knew I had to follow his advice. The story had a fairy-tale ending.

"Oh look, Veronica. Another American to rescue." The English couple who picked me up turned out to be wonderful new friends. We spent that evening sailing across Lake Windermere, then shared a great meal and found a cheap bed and breakfast. My stick-in-the-mud companion, meanwhile, was putting her hair into rollers and eating a cheese sandwich in the youth hostel.

⁕　⁕　⁕

OVER THE NEXT few weeks, Marty and I talk on the phone a few times. I don't hide my light mood, but I know it's a dangerous kind of happiness. The joy before the inevitable fall.

"We need to talk." My usual line.

"I'll come back for the weekend."

I grill marinated sweet-and-sour salmon, sauté sugar snap beans, and slather sweet corn in butter. I even make the peach crumble Marty likes for dessert. We keep things pleasant until I go to sleep early—playing it safe?—leaving the guys playing Monopoly.

"How about letting me take you out for blueberry pancakes at Grumpy's?" I ask Marty the next morning, with actual love in my heart. It's his favorite way to start a Saturday, and rarely mine, so it's an unmistakable peace offering.

He glares at me. Instead of looking unshaven in a handsome way, his face is full of darkness. "I *wanted* to *sleep*," he growls. "I worked hard all week. You're so insensitive."

I'm too surprised to answer. In another lifetime he would have grabbed me to him and then bounded from bed to dress and get to Grumpy's before the crowds. As angry as I've ever seen him, he pulls the covers over his face as if it's a cold winter morning.

Which it is.

Joey's already playing beach Frisbee, far away, and it's a Sunday without the painters, so we're alone. We try to talk, but we're speaking different languages. My theory is that he's given up on joy. His is that I'm insatiable and can't accept what is.

When we take a short break to sit outside, I spot some good friends who've just arrived at the Park, and I greet them with a hug. After they leave, Marty's angry that I embraced Susan and Mark and have hardly touched him. I'm guilty as charged, but he could have come toward me as well. Once we get to the heart of the matter, we hold each other and cry. We can't find our way home.

34.
dogs

NOW THAT MARTY and I are having separate summers, I worry about Joey. Always considerate and responsible, Marty talked to him before he left, explaining he'd be gone for a while. But after a few more weekends go by, Joey wants to know where Marty is, and when he's coming back.

"We're taking a little break. We need some time apart." How am I supposed to explain what I can't make sense of?

"Why?" Joey wants Marty to put new wheels on his skateboard. I've rehearsed this conversation in my mind, with friends, and with the pinch-hitter therapist I've seen a few times in Hyannis. But I still don't have the right words to protect my kid from deep and most likely permanent disappointment.

Except for Max's death and Gracie's sickness, Joey's been sheltered from sorrow. He'll think, rightly, I could have prevented it this time. I should have.

"We stopped being nice to one another. I'm sure you could tell." I take a breath, planning to launch into a philosophical discussion.

"Oh, that's just what happens when people get married," he says, before running off to something more important.

I read an article in the local paper about a woman with psychic powers, about her own difficult emotional journey and how she discovered she could see deeply into lives. I know it's crazy, but I'm desperate for any kind of help.

Sally the psychic lives close to the Park, so I bike over for a sunset appointment. Her house is a Cape Cod ranch with a lovely garden. She and her huge Great Dane are standing in the open doorway.

"Sunset is an excellent time to delve into the unknown," she'd said on the phone. I'm not really the psychic-consulting type, but I can't think of anything else to do between therapist appointments and talking to my friends.

"Is there anyone who has passed on that you would like to contact?" Sally asks, taking me by total surprise. Instead of Max, so recently gone I don't want to bother him, I mention my Aunt Justine, who lived in New York. She'd been an early bohemian, a role model who broke free of conventions by not getting married. We were always very close.

Sally closes her eyes. "Does she have red hair? Was she an actress?" She's close enough; Justine was a costume designer. I feel chilled, as if by a sudden wind. "She says she wishes you could meet her in a restaurant. I think it's a French restaurant." My aunt and I loved to spend too much money on lavish meals.

For the next few hours, skepticism melting, I learn about the spirit world. Souls travel together through different lifetimes, friends and family have shared other incarnations. Husbands and wives have been brothers, parents to one another; parents and children have known one another over many existences, in many different relationships.

"So why are you here?" Sally stares at me a little too intensely.

"My marriage feels over. I've behaved badly and I'm afraid of losing everything, but it's too late to get it back." My vision is blurry with tears.

This blond stranger, dressed in turquoise silk with too much jewelry, studies the photograph of Marty she asked me to bring. I picked the one we chose for our wedding invitation: Marty and I with our arms around Joey, all of us laughing.

Sally closes her eyes and waits for information. "This man was your mother. You needed him to nurture you this time around. Your mother in this life wasn't warm." I nod at the sense she's making. "But it could be time to leave the nest."

She gestures to me to be patient while she waits for more truth from her mysterious source. I don't care if she's making everything up. I hang on her every word.

"You had such a lasting, deep love in a previous lifetime, you may not need it in this one." This doesn't sound at all right. Sally must have her spirits tangled up. "You and your son were lovers. He was a woman and you were a man."

This is a lot to absorb, but the surprise rings oddly true.

"Your son has had many, many lives." I'm hearing way more than I can take in. "Encourage his spiritual life. Your son sees auras. He's wise beyond his years."

Sally assures me that Joey will be fine as long as I am — which any decent therapist would say. "He's good friends with his dad and his stepdad, but you're the one he counts on."

When the Great Dane yawns, my session's over.

If we do get that chance to live over and over until we get things right, it takes some pressure off things now.

◦ ▪ ◦

I SPEND A LOT of time on the glider, trying to read Thoreau for the fall semester's course, but mostly staring into space. I walk the beach a lot, casting out for understanding, like the night fishermen at Nauset who wait for the ocean to send them rare striped bass.

I'd convinced myself Labor Day would keep receding into the

future, but now it's a week away. Will Marty be home when Joey and I get back there? Do I want him there? I drive into Boston to drop Joey at his dad's for the first week of school, then find myself walking into a real estate office in Brookline. After they show me a few dark, overpriced apartments, I almost rent the least terrible one. I drive home to get a check, but when I see our beautiful view of the pond and the skylight in my kitchen, I can't go through with it.

I get back to the Cape just in time to help my neighbor make potato salad for the ham and bean supper, the swan song of the season. No one asks if my husband is coming. That night I drink enough beer to dance by myself to scratchy fifties music. At the end of the weekend I clean the cottage and pack up all our stuff, including the bathing suits Marty forgot, his baseball hat, and six bars of soap.

When I get back home, Joey's toys are stowed away and my side of the desk Marty and I share has been cleared off; it looks like he lives alone in the apartment which used to be all mine before he moved in. There are pears for me and grapes for Joey in the refrigerator, a more generous welcome than I expected: a sign, at least, of his ambivalence.

Which is how I'd describe myself. How can I want him to still want me when I don't want him? For the first few days I behave like a guest, not taking up too much physical or psychic space. I fold the towels carefully and remind Joey to put his dirty clothes in the hamper. I feel a more defined unhappiness than before I left, but it's no worse than all the dreading.

Marty and I master a safe kind of status quo, treading lightly, talking only about practical details. Now and then we give one another a friendly hug, probably for Joey's sake. I cook or he cooks or one of us brings home take-out. We make no plans for more than a few hours in advance. I pray he'll leave for work before I need the bathroom. No more morning small talk.

I spend as much time as I can at the college, giving my students extra conference time and attending every faculty meeting. After dinner and dealing with Joey, I retreat to the office, trying not to mess up my part of the desk.

No news is good news, I'll tell Grace if she asks.

       *   *   *

JOEY'S BACK IN the swing of school, soccer season, tap dancing, and piano lessons, although I doubt he's oblivious to the change at home. He spends a lot of time playing basketball with his buddies on the street. Marty reads to him at night, more often than he used to.

Now that we're beyond the pale, I complain more audibly about the television noise. I go to bed as early as I can and choose a book from my growing, disorderly stack: *Living an Authentic Life, When Things Fall Apart, The Trouble With Marriage*. For fun, I have a biography of Frida Kahlo.

I consider reading Marty a moving paragraph from *Making Your Love Last*: "By choosing safety over passion, we turn love into boredom. Desire depends on the unknown." I'll never shake my faith in the power of the written word. But by the time he joins me, I'm asleep.

One Saturday, out of domestic habit I suppose, we buy a new toaster oven and plant tulip bulbs in containers on the roof, with no idea who'll see them bloom. I'm teary watching Marty and Joey outside sawing wood for a basketball backboard.

"Will we still be friends — not just for Joey's sake?" I ask when Marty comes in for some coffee.

"Of course," he mumbles, his first, but necessary, lie.

There are other places to sleep, but neither of us moves out of the bedroom. This is how we're slowly taking leave of one other, spending those few dark, horizontal hours side by side. Sometimes, experimentally, we soften and speak gently, touching toes or hips anonymously in the dark. We make love once, by accident.

I meet a friend at a reggae club one night — out of spite? One toke of someone's joint brings me all the way back to that enticing, falsely profound bliss. I stay out past two without calling, like an arrogant teenager.

"Didn't you think I'd worry that something happened to you?" Marty says when I get into bed. I'm glad he's angry, but have too much pride to say so.

We try another session with Melanie, the down-to-earth therapist, which will probably result in that dreaded stage called closure. "He won't come alive," I mumble. "I want him to want me enough to take a risk." I have no idea what I'm saying. They both stare at me. "I'm tired of being the only one who wants there to be *more*," I try again.

"Why does life always have to be exciting and unpredictable?" Marty wants to know. He thinks I won't be happy without fireworks. But all I'm talking about is being alive instead of dead.

"I don't want any more life than we already have," he glowers. "You want to control me. You'll never be satisfied." All of us know he's also talking to his mother. Or at least the therapist and I do.

"He's locked up," I look at Melanie. "All I can see is flat infinity."

"Can you find the richness in his silence?" she asks.

"I've looked hard for it," I say. *Could I look harder?*

"There's nothing wrong with either of you," she says as we leave.

[2 7 2]

BETWEEN MY CLASSES, I still drive Grace to her legions of doctors.

"Exciting news, Ruth. The Dana-Farber now has valet parking!" I've brought a stack of my students' essays for us to correct while we wait. Grace reads one out loud to me, about a trip to Beijing: *Our waiter showed us a wire cage with three snakes in it. They were writhing around and hissing a bunch just like snakes do. After the chef cut off their heads, their mouths kept opening and closing like they were still breathing or trying to bite us.* I'm glad Grace picked a funny essay, because it's not going to be her favorite day.

Next, I watch her make a terrible face while she drinks two more quarts of scary white barium cocktail before another CT scan.

"Those snakes sound pretty good to me," she laughs.

"I'll split that stuff with you. They'll never know." They won't even give my friend some water to get the taste out of her mouth. When no one's looking, I slip her some chewing gum.

The Nuclear Medicine waiting room has been redecorated in depressing greys. Decor is *all* when you have to stare and wait and worry. "Do you believe this disaster?" Grace laughs. "I'm sure their high-paid decorator was never sick."

Our next stop, the upscale radiation wing, is gorgeously appointed in exotic blond wood with brightly painted glass panels, granite, and stainless steel everywhere.

"Even the magazines up here are classier," Grace points out. "What's the latest news at home?"

"We go back and forth." I feel trapped inside a burning building, scared it's just as dangerous outside. "This will be Marty's second failed marriage, so I think he feels worse than I do."

"Oh, my little Ruthie." This land of agonizing doubt is unfamiliar to her, and I know she wants us to survive. She's right that I've raced to an awful conclusion. That I'm too far gone to consider any other possibility except the inevitable. She thinks I have a choice. "We were fine when we had projects: taking trips, planning the wedding, cleaning the cottage, making plans to fix up the apartment."

"So your last project will be a divorce? I've never said you were nuts before and I don't want to say it now—or ever—but you can't do this to yourself and Joey."

But I can't not do it, which I keep to myself.

* * *

THEN MORE BAD news: my well-adjusted kid seems to be falling apart just like everyone else. I've been searching his face for signs of distress. He's rude and annoying and I can't set him straight with any conviction because I feel responsible. He shouldn't have to live with so much bad weather, trapped in our ambivalence. He complains about his dinner and refuses to show me his homework or talk with either Marty or me for longer than a few seconds. I wonder what he's telling Jake.

It's bad enough fighting with my kid, but when Jake overhears us, I know he's sure it's my fault. I have no idea what's bothering Joey, but tonight he's at his most unpleasant. He refuses to eat the chicken I reheated because "it's gross," then almost breaks the plate I make him wash a second time. We watch a television program about the sculptor Alexander Calder, but he pouts all the way through it. Finished giving orders for the night, I go up to bed, leaving Joey alone.

In the morning he hands me the drawing he made of Calder-like figures with geometric heads and wiry animals chasing one another. Joey often wakes up a different child than the one who went to sleep. He's forgotten we were enemies.

※ ※ ※

GRACE IS FEELING good enough on a bright October Saturday to suggest we take the boys to the crafts festival at Larz Anderson Park. We bribe them with five bucks each to come with us. Marty's still asleep, so I try to keep Joey quiet while we have breakfast. Weekends are always tricky.

After perusing earrings, scarves, and pottery, Grace runs into some friends and I go off to get us hot cider. When I return, she's deep in conversation with a Japanese woman who's selling handmade origami boxes. "Look at this one." She points to a silver octagonal box. "Marty would love that." She's caught me off guard. She's right. He'd like the object's perfection. "Buy it for him. Maybe it'll turn things around." She flashes me her instigator smile.

I haven't told her Marty's going to look at apartments today. That it's a little late for peace offerings. But I plunk down my seven dollars. I can give him the box for a housewarming gift.

I invite my parents to visit the following weekend while Marty's away. It's time to tell them what they already practically know but don't dare bring up. I say what makes the most sense to me this week. "It just didn't work. We're not nice to one another anymore." Instead of being comforted by them, I have to deal with their shock and hurt and disapproval. I've made another terrible mistake in a life full of them. *How can you do this to us?* is what they're thinking.

※ ※ ※

MARTY PUTS OUR situation so succinctly: "We can't have what we want." We go through every phase of disintegration, pleading to bickering to tears, but as soon as we let go, there's an aching kind of relief. And even, by surprise, some offbeat humor. One night, while sorting through our finances, one of us says something funny and we both crack up. When Joey hears us laughing, he comes into the office where we're scrolling through tax documents and gives us a puzzled look; then he goes back to watching the more understandable world on television.

Marty finds a place he likes on a pond in the suburbs. "I bought a leather chair," he announces cheerily the day after he signs the lease. I'm sure it has those dreadful brass studs, like the chair I talked him out of buying once. Marty's sedentary nature was always obvious, but it rankled me more as our caring faded.

He's spent so much time in my armchair that it needs reupholstering. I'm not even controlling my judgments anymore. "And now you can sit in it as long as you want," I say, stooping all the way down to snideness. Later, I apologize.

"The last week is the toughest," he consoles me. He's been here before. His tenderness makes me want to beg him to relent.

*　*　*

I'VE BEEN WORRYING what to do on the day Marty leaves so Joey and I don't have to watch movers carrying my marriage out of the house forever. When I read that the Bay Colony dog show is coming to town, and that it opens at eight a.m., I'm relieved we'll have a place to go.

Early that morning, I get Marty and Joey to pile onto our bed in a last family sandwich hug. Then I get Joey into the car before the moving van pulls up. We spend the next three hours watching Airedales and Cavalier King Charles Spaniels jump through hoops and swivel their hind quarters around fancy gates. It's like the doggie Olympics. The grooming area is as big as a football field, crowded with baroquely coiffed poodles being blown dry and unhappy, beribboned schnauzers having their beards combed.

This seems to distract Joey, but it doesn't work for me. I've thought about getting a dog, to fill up the holes in our hearts, but I'm careful not to say so. I'm not a dog person, and can't imagine even more solo responsibilities than I'm going to have. Ironically, a few days ago, Joey noticed a small terrier without a collar wandering around in front of our building. I let him bring the dog inside and called the Humane Society. Joey named him Linus. The dog's timing was impeccable, and if his owner hadn't turned up, I'd probably have given in and kept him.

Joey likes the frantic, wire-haired terriers. We discuss the different breeds in detail. "I want a dog like Linus," Joey says after we leave.

"Mutts are the best," I tell him. "It's nice to take in a dog whose parents fell in love." He gives me one of his odd looks, as if he thinks love's overrated.

The apartment doesn't feel very different when we get back. All Marty took—besides his Art Deco dresser—was a mahogany table, his vintage oak liquor cabinet, and the burl desk, nothing hard to part with. Then Jake picks up Joey and I'm really alone. I've gotten through several grueling weeks with a suspicious amount of sangfroid, but this is the acid test. All I know is I'm not crying.

I'm not dancing, either.

"You must miss that dresser something terrible," Grace says. Marty's precious *ongapatchka*—hideous—antique, which always reminded me of a passage in *Look Homeward, Angel*, when someone with nicotine-stained fingers carries a coffin by its silver handles.

I move on to the latest squabble with Jake, a refreshing

mini-crisis. "He brought Joey back the other day with only one soccer shoe," I tell Grace.

"*Another* lost shoe?" I'd forgotten that one of Joey's sandals disappeared at Jake's last summer, never to be seen again. Grace remembers my life better than I do.

"He needed it for the soccer game that afternoon, so I asked Jake to look for it. 'If the shoe were here, I would have sent it home with Joey,' he said, annoyed I was disturbing his work—*and* questioning his word. I had to beg him to check his car, which is where it was. Then he acts like the whole thing was my fault!"

Then we get to the real portion of our conversation. "I'm fine, honest," I tell her. It's hardly the same as her first night without Max, but she can tell I'm in bad shape. Grace always says that no matter what's happened to someone else, you still have the right to feel awful about your own problem.

"Now we can finally go out and look for guys together," she says. "Just give me a few days to find my panty hose."

Before Grace got sick again, I did have the crazy idea of fixing her up with someone. Maybe I could find a man who'd walk her through the shadows. I couldn't stand the idea of her going to all those family functions without an escort. ("Every time one of our relatives farts, they throw a party," Max told me once.)

Curious about the prospects, I looked through the personal ads again. There was a widower who sounded perfect for Grace. "I'm used to being someone's best friend and would like to share my mostly happy life," the guy said when I called. Modest and caring.

Was I practicing for myself? Will I ever be brave enough to jump back into shark-infested waters?

35.
catching air

WHEN MARTY COMES OVER every few weeks to see Joey, we have more to talk about than we did once our end was in sight. He wants to know how I'm really doing, and I want to know the same, until he mentions—bad form—he's dating someone. But even that doesn't upset me as much as I thought it would.

I make snow angels on the new, firm mattress I bought for myself as a separation present, luxuriating in its cool expanse. I let Marty take the soft one. Another thrill: I can open the bedroom window for some fresh night air.

I turn the music up louder than Marty liked and use the fireplace for the first time, since he couldn't stand the smoke. I invite friends and their raucous kids for messy spaghetti dinners. I'll crash eventually, but for now Grace's conveniently short attention span has rubbed off on me, and I'm not worrying about anything. Well, not counting the fact that I haven't written a sentence since who remembers when.

Grace and I have stopped going to Chinatown. It got harder and harder to believe that Dr. Lee's frantic qigong arm-waving and all those needles were killing off enemy cancer cells. When I find out that the young man Lee had supposedly pulled from the jaws of lung cancer finally lost his battle, I keep the bad news to myself.

Even Grace's "real" doctors seem to be out of ideas.

We rarely broach her situation, sticking to current events, movies, and books. There's enough day-to-day surviving to cope with to ignore the bigger picture. Grace's friend Marion, president of the temple sisterhood, has asked the rabbi to help her make some decisions. I assume that means figuring out who can finish raising the boys. Before Marty left, I considered asking him if we could do it, but we were in no shape. Taking in the boys myself seems beyond daunting. But I think about it.

I remember Grace telling me about Rabbi Drexler's love of musicals. "Which play should our theater group put on next?" he asked her.

"I'd go with *Annie Get Your Gun*. Your wife will be fabulous in it!" ("The rabbi's wife has a Broadway voice," she assured me when I bought a ticket to see Max in *Fiddler*.)

I find out later that when the rabbi and Grace finally get together to discuss dire matters, they veer off into Jewish mysticism and Israeli politics. "Our girl is such a charmer, the rabbi just couldn't stay *on task*," Marion reports to me in frustration. The rest of us can't do it, either.

❦   ❦   ❦

SINCE GRACE AND I have been hungry for live music, I buy tickets for Cassandra Wilson at Symphony Hall. It's hard to get out on such a frigid night, but I know it will be good for us. "I'll just wear that old Balenciaga," she says on the phone while we're both throwing together some version of dinner for our kids. "Don't forget your tiara this time, Ruthie."

By the time Joey and I stop fighting about whether he can eat in front of the television, I don't have time to find my lipstick. Grace and I show up in matching outfits: baggy jeans and polar fleece. "I hope the Authority isn't here tonight," I say.

"I remember her distinctly saying that if it's below ten degrees, anything goes," Grace says. We finally find a semi-legal parking space, then walk as fast as we can on icy sidewalks. After we see ourselves reflected in a store window, we can't stop laughing at how bad we look.

"Thank God they let us in," she says as we join the soigné crowd in the ornate, Brahminesque, and acoustically perfect hall. "There's Beethoven." Grace points to the row of marble busts on high. "I'll bet he wasn't such a great dresser, either."

※　※　※

I HAVE NO PLANS for our first Chanukah and Christmas without Marty. My parents are fortunately in Florida, my cousin's too far away in California, and everyone I know has a family to join, whether they want to or not. Grace's in-laws have descended on her, supposedly to help her manage, but she'll end up tiring herself out to keep them happy.

"At least divorce takes care of the annoying in-law problem," she says enviously, helping me count my blessings.

I'm reading *Breakup* by Catherine Texier, a Parisian transplanted to the East Village whose husband cheats on her and then walks out. Her paragraphs are lacerations, shrieks, and assaults against the odious prick who makes love to her in the morning then runs off to meet his girlfriend for lunch. I must be a jerk for losing a decent guy.

On my worst days, I blame myself for committing a self-destructive crime out of sheer hubris. On merely bad days, I list the reasons we're not together: my illusion that life should be wonderful, his hypochondria. He used to like my liveliness and I used to like the way he calmed me down — the qualities that did us in.

Rhonda convinces me to spend more money than I've budgeted so Joey and I can go skiing with her family in New Hampshire. I'm sure she's picked the perfect mountain with the best snow, and failing that, the best snowmaking. She and I have drifted apart over the last few years. But I need to remember that gliding through life is actually possible, and she seems to really want our company.

I reserve a room at the cheapest lodge I can find: shared bathroom, family-style meals, and only a mile from the mountain. Even though Rhonda was leery about my choice, I love the authenticity of the place and its cast of colorful characters. She's staying in a snazzy ski-in-ski-out hotel on the mountain with an outdoor heated pool, a gourmet restaurant, and a spa.

There are a lot of reasons not to like the sport: its appalling expense, the long, cold waits for the lift, not to mention the terror of actually coming down an icy mountain. But whenever I've faced down my fears on a perilous slope, forgotten courage has seeped back into me. These days I could use some. I'm praying that the splurge, and Joey's joy, will cheer me up. He's both careful and fearless and can't wait to get out each morning, while I steel myself for the ordeal.

Despite all Rhonda's research, there isn't quite enough snow, which means I'll fall even more than usual. Skiing is counterintuitive. Instead of leaning, petrified, back into the mountain, you're supposed to throw yourself *down* it and trust you'll glide through the turn and float safely up into the next one. You have to believe you can conquer gravity by diving into the danger.

My hands are numb and my face feels frostbitten, but every time I get safely down the mountain, I take the chairlift back up again. I tell myself there's nothing wrong with falling, but it doesn't help when I do. At least I'll feel entitled to a beer or two in the hot tub as soon as the sun drops down and the snow takes on a bluish cast.

Rhonda and I take a few runs together, but we're mostly on separate schedules. I'd imagined we'd have time to talk on this trip, that such an old friendship would warm me, but after Joey and I visit her hotel several times for lunch she still refuses to visit mine.

"Come down here for lunch," I say when the week's almost over. I want her to see the funky décor and meet our new friends.

"That's silly, Ruth. The food's better at my place." She doesn't mean to be insulting, but her entitlement is showing. We make a date to meet later at the lift line, but I get there too late.

She calls me later, fit to be tied. "Where were you? I stood there freezing for ten minutes in the cold." I don't mention how many times I've waited longer for her, in worse temperatures. I probably could have gotten there on time, but she'd annoyed me all week and I didn't feel like rushing. I lie and say I'm sorry.

"I don't think we should make any more plans that you're just going to change," she announces haughtily before we hang up. I feel punished and angry. Now I remember why our friendship has wilted over the years. Rhonda's a wonderful listener, but the high price for her kindness is that she makes all the rules and berates me for breaking them.

I remember Gertrude Stein's way of putting it: *when the flowers of friendship faded, friendship faded.* I've lost a husband and I'm about to lose Grace, so I have no patience for a friend who cares more about the quality of her lunch than my feelings.

That night I leave Joey playing checkers by the fire and retreat to our room. I stare out at the mountains and let myself cry. I read the spiritual book I brought by Pema Chödrön, a Buddhist nun. "Practice gentleness and letting go." Instead of a break from the sadness at home, I'm feeling worse.

The next day the wind blasts me so hard I can't get out of the chair lift once it stops. Without a choice, I inch to the edge, extend my frozen legs, and fall toward the fear. On my perilous way down, I'm forced to catch a little air. I get back to the Slalom Inn feeling practically Olympic and decide to relax in the hot tub. But on my way to our room to change, someone stops me. "Your son had a little spill," he says. "Go to the lobby."

I race downstairs and ask someone at the desk to call First Aid for me. "Where is he? How do I get to him?" I plead, shaking.

One of the cooks says he'll drive me down the road, so I follow him out to his Jeep, still in my ski boots. I think he's hitting on me during the three-minute ride, but I can't be sure of anything because I'm in the kind of altered state you see in bad movies. In the middle of worrying about Joey, I can't stop wanting Marty to be back home where I can call him for help.

Jake will have me drawn and quartered for negligence.

"We were about to close up shop for the day," the paramedic says when I get there. "Then this little straggler comes in, *on his own*, and says he *thinks* he did something to his arm!" Joey's on a stretcher, white-faced, and his right arm looks blue — and limp.

"I'm really sorry, Mom. I tried some wicked moguls, and they were icy." Joey already skis better than I ever will. I can't even catch sight of him on the mountain, probably a good thing.

It's his forearm. Or his wrist. He can move his fingers — a good sign — but he can't rotate his arm — a bad one. He doesn't make a sound while three different people examine him. Even when he was very young, no matter what he did to himself, my stoic boy would try not to show that it hurt.

The closest X-ray machine is an hour away, and the clinic will be closed by the time we get there. So they tape up Joey's arm, give him some aspirin, and tell me to get him back to Boston. He keeps saying he's OK, that he can't believe he messed up. I don't believe him when he says it doesn't hurt. "I don't need a cast," he snarls. *"And stop asking me questions."*

We get a ride back to the lodge and I pack us up, look out at the silvery mountains one last time, and pay our bill.

36.
reunion

I LEAVE RHONDA a message that Joey did something to his arm so we're taking off and that I'll talk to her soon, even though it could be longer than that. I was ready to go back before we had to, but Joey's upset he's missing his last day to ski.

He sleeps the entire four-hour trip south. With nothing to do but drive and think, I realize my head and stomach ache. Winter darkness seeps into me. I try listening to a book on tape but my racing thoughts are too loud to hear it. I fiddle with the radio to pick up whatever music and news I can stand. A Mozart cantata gives me a few minutes of solace before static drowns it out. I stop for gas and a bag of potato chips.

When I finally get home, I make Joey stay in the car while I run into the house to call the doctor so she can order X-rays. I call Jake. He insists on meeting us at the emergency room, so I pray he won't antagonize the doctors. I remember when my cat, Molly, hurt her paw and Jake hounded the vet until he agreed to examine the cat immediately. It wasn't an emergency, but Jake had become scarily overprotective. I felt sorry for the vet, who was being so unfairly pressured, but at the time I was in a pregnant fog and couldn't take the situation on.

I make a peanut butter sandwich for Joey and grab an apple for myself. We get to the Children's Hospital emergency room only a few minutes after Jake does. Joey's wrist is fine, but his forearm is badly twisted. No broken bones, but he needs an air cast. He likes the fact that it's electric blue, and that he can take it off whenever he wants.

"Good thing soccer season's over," Jake tells him. So far he's been pretty civil toward me. Maybe it's his I-told-you-so version of compassion for my single-again state. Jake didn't think Marty understood Joey's true nature and I never told him he wasn't far from the mark.

To cheer Joey up, we all walk to an Italian restaurant. I can't remember the last time the three of us were together. After dinner, Jake says he wants to make sure Joey's OK, so I tell him to meet me back home. Marty would unpack the car for me and do a load of laundry, but those days are over. Jake has put Joey to sleep by the time I get three loads of our stuff up the stairs.

"You look like you could use a drink," he says, pouring me some red wine. Soon I'm on the floor staring at the ceiling, crying from relief. It's a shock to feel this close. We're overdue for a truce, although I doubt this will turn out like that, even while I'm undressing. Ski socks, ski pants, turtleneck, long underwear. Jake looks exactly the way he looked the first time I saw him naked, and has the same effect on me, as if time hasn't moved since then.

What the hell, I think. He's the father of my child.

My sore, tired body catches rare air.

⁖   ⁖   ⁖

THERE'S A MESSAGE from Marty when I finally listen after Jake leaves. "I have a Chanukah present for Joey. Why don't you both come over for dinner?" He says something about missing us, but he mumbles it, so I can't be sure. More than the words, I listen to the surprisingly soft tone in his voice before I go back to sleep.

It's a good thing Grace calls and wakes me up, because I have to teach the following day and I've hardly prepared. "Oh, I'll help you," she says. "I'm starving for some entertainment. How was the ski trip? How did Rhonda treat you?"

I tell her about Joey's accident and promise to bring him over later so he can show off his cast. "I'll bring some coconut squares from Rosie's. What else do you need?"

"Cat food, milk, paper towels. Oh, and what about dinner?"

I know Grace will be brilliant at deconstructing the Rhonda debacle, so I tell her my tale: Rhonda's baronial ski lodge versus our funky but endearing accommodations. The weathered ski bum who helped me with my turns, then expected something in return. Rhonda making Joey and me wait while she had her state-of-the-art ski boots adjusted, and finally our serious rift.

"You'll be friends again," she laughs. "Rhonda's always high maintenance."

The boys come inside when it's dark and we let them watch *Annie*. I make us more tea, and mention to Grace that Jake was on good behavior, leaving out the details. I'm not sure why, but sex has never been one of our topics. I have a feeling Grace already considers me a bit too free in that area, so I don't want to give her any more evidence.

But she somehow knows what happened. It's worth my embarrassment to see Grace speechless for once, with such a befuddled expression. I know she's not really judging me, but our different histories are showing. "I know it was a strange thing to do. But it's better than dragging someone home from a bar," I confess.

"Yeah." Long pause. "I guess just *strange* is better than some stranger."

But the truth is, I'm still on sabbatical from coupling. When

Joey and I go to Marty's house for lasagna, I don't even look around for evidence of his girlfriend. His apartment gleams with light and water views. I'm happy for my soon-to-be ex-husband, now so rightfully returned to the soothing order of his life before we met. I'm jealous he has his own assigned parking space, but that's about it. I'll have to tell Grace that the silvery origami box she made me buy looks perfect on his mantel.

⁂

I THROW MYSELF into the new course I've finally gotten permission to teach: *Lit and Women's Lib*. I'm starting with an essay by Germaine Greer, not because I want to impress my department chair with the fact that I once worked for her, but because I still admire her smarts. Books, toys, and clothes lie in piles, and without Marty to keep the kitchen organized, I can't find anything. Joey and I take turns on the ladder trying to install a new light fixture over the kitchen table.

"Marty could do this in ten minutes," he complains. As in, *Why are you so pathetic that you don't have a husband to help you*. I give him a *please be quiet* look, hoping he doesn't see my wet eyes. But, when I finally get the light to work, my smart-ass kid sings me a chorus of "I Am Woman."

Before Marty moved in, I loved my condo. After fourteen years in my fifth-floor East Village walk-up, I felt like a queen here, with a washing machine only three flights down instead of two blocks away.

Now it would be nice to do the laundry in my kitchen.

"You need more windows," Grace says. "And maybe some shelves."

"Shelves! What a brilliant idea!"

"You're my only friend who hasn't renovated."

Without Marty complaining about it so much, I can finally move forward on that front. I find the shelter magazines we shoved under the bed and start to study them.

"Call my cleaning lady's cousin Ryan," Grace says. "Back in County Cork, he was a master craftsman."

Ryan turns out to be a lovely fellow, so reasonable he's hard to resist. "No problem," he says after all my complaints. Unlike Marty, he listens carefully to my ideas and gracefully adjusts them to reality. I'm part of a team again, without the emotional backlash.

Soon I'm practically living at Home Depot. I make friends in Woodwork, Flooring, Electrical. I miss Marty's common sense, but I'm dizzy with so much freedom. I haul bags of knocked-down plaster out to the dumpster I've rented. I help Ryan load his truck with lumber and sheet rock. I stand in line with the real contractors at the Boston Building Department and pull my very own yellow permit.

"I like my room the way it is," Joey whines, understandably upset after I put all his stuff in boxes in the hall. I've heartlessly deprived him of his wonderful stepdad, and now he has to live in an earthquake zone.

"Oh, and while you're at it, Ruthie, please get rid of that ugly pine paneling," Grace pleads. "I know you could paint it over, but it'll be better if you take it off. Do it for me."

Visibly weaker by the day, she has her own enormous project planning Louis's bar mitzvah and figuring out where two hundred people are going to sit. We struggle to create sociable groups: school friends, family, temple friends, neighbors. "I know!" she exclaims. "I'll seat people according to how they're redoing their kitchens. I can have a Formica group, a Corian group, and, of course, the *crème de la crème*, the ones who've chosen granite."

37.
the museum of bad art

JOEY AND I HAVE moved from our noisy, filthy construction zone of a home to the Cape cottage for a month. This summer Coach Ted has hired my twelve-year-old as his official assistant, and Joey's thrilled that he gets to wear the keys to the community house around his neck. He helps run the little kids' games, empties garbage cans, and paints fences. His favorite task is choosing the videos for movie nights.

I drive back to Boston a few times a week, bringing Ryan supplies from Home Depot before visiting Grace.

"My hair had just gotten gorgeous again," she whimpers uncharacteristically en route to her latest oncologist. She's undergoing yet another wicked round of chemotherapy. "When everyone at the hospital knows you by your first name, you're in trouble."

I search for something positive to say and come up empty. But I feel courageous — or desperate — enough to stay quiet and wait for Grace to spill more sorrow. She gives me a new, more frightened look and I pull her to me. Her moans reverberate inside me. Time stops. We're finally out of words.

Our drive to Dana-Farber is strangely quiet, and we browse in the upscale gift shop without much to comment on. Grace buys flowers for her favorite nurse, and I buy myself a straw hat intended for those with hair loss.

In the middle of all this medical combat, Grace is taking the boys to Disney World. "I'd prefer Florence or Lisbon—almost anywhere else on the globe," she says. "But they're the only kids in Brookline who haven't done Disney."

She phones me from Orlando. "I get to stay in bed while the boys run wild. They wear beepers so I can keep track of them. I'm thinking of relocating down here. Who knew we could all be so happy?"

"You'd better come home. I'm in charge of the Wayward Park auction this year, and I'm a nervous wreck. Last year they raised $6,000."

"Do you want me to donate Aunt Sadie's candy dish?"

Marty made me feel stupid when I volunteered last summer, but I belong to this community and want to do my share.

"You're a big *macher* now," she laughs. "If you do a good job, we can use you at the temple."

This is stressful territory for me. But since it's the forty-third Park auction, the regulars have things pretty well under control. Mrs. Gunderson always makes her Swedish meatballs, and several women bring baked goods and coffee. A man who's at least ninety almost kills himself climbing a ladder to plug in the microphone, but he's insulted when I try to get him to come down.

There's a committee for the Friday night silent auction cocktail party, complete with wine in boxes and cheese balls. Joey helps me make posters and carry white elephant items to the community house. I almost forget to formally invite Mr. Ripley to be our auctioneer, even though he does it every year.

I'm also supposed to beat the bushes for big-ticket donations:

golf clubs, lobster dinners, whale watch cruises. But after all my worrying, great donations come pouring in the day before the auction. There's a crisis about a damaged kayak, and I have to refuse an ancient rowing machine. Joey and his friends are "runners," delivering the auctioned items to the buyers in the audience and bringing back the cash. Mr. Ripley shamelessly cranks up the bids, his repartee still superb even though his eyesight and hearing aren't what they used to be. By tradition, the more prosperous among us pay handsomely for paintings and crafts by the artistic Parkies.

The Tiffany cut glass bowl Marty and I got for our wedding, our least favorite gift, makes a hundred bucks for the Park.

Not even counting the extra profits from Park t-shirts and cocktail glasses, we net $7,467.98, which the treasurer posts proudly on the bulletin board. Folks who've never even nodded to me before give me big smiles and slap me on the back.

"It's about time you let a Jew run things around here," I joke to a select few.

"It would be nice if they were willing to spend some of the money," I tell Grace. "The community house could use a bathroom, but everyone has always used Mrs. Richardson's facilities next door. Isn't she tired of all the traffic?"

But this is Yankee territory at its most parsimonious. There were weeks of discussion before the members voted in favor of new curtains for the community house. *Use it up, wear it out, make it do, or do without* is the New England adage. I do admire this anti-consumer spirit. But—I'd never say it—a swimming pool would be fabulous for those sweltering, low-tide afternoons. The new resort down the road has one, but we're a long way from that sort of hedonism.

* * *

GRACE AND THE BOYS finally come by bus to visit us, the first time she's been to the cottage since she came with Max when he was so sick. This time it's Grace who's resting on the glider. Since she says she's feeling good enough, I drive her to the lovely town of Chatham, where our mission is to peek inside the windows of the house her friend Margie has just bought. We discuss every room we can see, and agree that the place is way overdone.

"Chintz is just too grand for a summer house," Grace says.

We end up at the beach café of the Chatham Bars Inn, leaping as quickly as usual from one topic to another during the pretend-normal afternoon, over chicken salad and iced tea. Then I suggest we stroll down to the water, fifty yards away. "I can't walk that far," Grace says.

My hopes for her go out with the tide.

* * *

MY BOY IS SO AT home in the Park, flying out the door to a friend's house or a basketball game. He befriends a comical Belgian girl who speaks no English and teaches him to say "You have a big penis" in Flemish. Most nights his gang has an illegal campfire on the beach, where they watch shooting stars.

What else do adolescents need but one another?

"I love you, Joey," I hear one of the girls call out as he finally heads for home, way after his curfew.

The hard part is being around all these apparently happy families without a requisite husband, at least on weekends. I invite everyone I know to visit, to keep away the blues. I stay busy doing laundry, getting rid of insects and spider webs, sawing ugly branches off bushes, hauling in food and cooking it. I even polish up a few short stories. I drive back roads to solitary sunsets, pink-sky nights with fireflies and stars and silence. Sometimes I cry and sometimes I don't need to.

      ¤   ■   ¤

WE'VE MOVED BACK into our torn-apart home, where even Joey complains about the disorder. Our electricity is intermittent, every-thing's in boxes, and I've set up a primitive kitchen on our small deck. On the first day of classes, I can't find my briefcase or my toothbrush. Joey won't do his homework without the computer.

Grace calls me several times a day for progress reports, espe-cially enjoying the latest installments about Aldo, the new plas-terer I hired after the first one disappeared. "We get along really well," I report. "I listen to his girlfriend problems and he's helping me choose colors." Soon Aldo convinces me to let him paint the place.

Even Joey can tell Aldo's odd, but so am I these days. One night I actually think about going out with him. He doesn't think four different shades of cappuccino in one room is crazy, and he's happy to discuss the way the light hits the walls at various times of day. Marty would have wanted to paint everything beige.

I run out for endless sample quarts of various colors to slap on the walls, then gallons of Sandy Beige, Egyptian Linen, and Mocha Cream, plus soda and sandwiches for Aldo to keep him going, since his schedule is erratic. But progress is slow. One day he calls and says someone ran into his truck. A few days later his red Corvette breaks down, then his uncle needs help fixing his porch.

I sneak into a faculty meeting late, in a wrinkled dress. "I renovated last year and managed to teach at the same time," my chairwoman informs me, snippily. I refrain from mentioning that's because she could afford a contractor.

When I get home, Aldo has left me a note saying he has to finish someone else's place before he can get back to mine.

"You have to fire that new boyfriend," Grace says. "Call my cousin Ellen. She knows a million good painters." The new painters look around, shaking their heads in disbelief. They seem very sorry for me. Aldo's plastering and painting are so lousy that most of it has to be redone. Once I actually look, I have to agree with them. I've been too crazed to notice.

When Aldo finds out he's been replaced, he goes berserk and threatens revenge. He actually uses this word, but doesn't get any more specific, so after he retrieves his tools and ladders, I have scary dreams for a few nights. Then Ryan reports that someone stole his power saw, which I have to pay for.

When I stop fuming long enough to ask Grace how she's doing, her tone's a little too flip, not a good sign.

Marion, who's a nurse, fills me in. "It looks like the docs are out of secret weapons. No one's suggesting any more treatments or drugs or protocols or procedures or studies."

"The current genius on my case doesn't see much 'forward motion,'" Grace tells me the next day, when the boys aren't around. "I asked him, 'Does that mean there's no *forward* to go to?'"

He was afraid so.

But Grace and her legions are orchestrating Louis's bar mitzvah anyway. "I have to keep *hocking* him to write his speech," she says, and when I go over there to help Louis, she's busy ordering tablecloths, talking to the caterer, and researching klezmer bands from her catalog-covered couch. A nurse is giving her an infusion for the pain in her bones.

She calls me at my office while I'm talking to a student about his James Baldwin paper, so I apologize and say it's an emergency.

"*Oy*, Ruth. The bar mitzvah is next week and I just realized I need something to wear."

Thrilled to be the designated personal shopper, I rush through three more conferences and drive straight to Grace's, praying we can accomplish this mission before the stores close.

"Remember all those book club discussions about mother-of-the-bar-mitzvah-boy outfits?" I ask Grace. "Suits versus dresses, hemline lengths, heel heights, appropriate jewelry. Too bad we didn't listen!"

"I have about an hour's worth of energy," she warns me. So I work fast, grabbing whatever looks possible in Macy's. Luckily, Grace really likes the multicolored silk patchwork dress I almost didn't take to the dressing room. This means we have enough time on the way home to stop at my place so I can show her the progress.

After I help her climb the stairs, Grace lets out a gasp of pleasure in my living room with its new skylight and bookshelves. "You've made a miracle here," she assures me. "But you need a window near the dining room table. That won't cost so much, Ruth. Do it for me."

Grace's Aunt Charlotte and I are the bar mitzvah centerpiece committee. Since Louis's torah portion is about Noah, Charlotte and I go with toy wooden boats and animals on blue shiny paper. The night before the event, about twenty of us set up the temple's party room. During a heated discussion about how to fold the napkins, I whisper, "Who knew there were so many options?" to Grace.

"And I put *you* on the decorating committee?" she laughs.

LOUIS'S CEREMONY, on a brilliant, warm Columbus Day, is beyond moving, for good and awful reasons. He leads our prayers in that beautiful sanctuary in the woods where I notice the story of Exodus depicted in the modern stained-glass windows. Who among us isn't wondering when we'll be back?

I laugh with Grace's amazing variety of friends and we watch her hold court, hugging, laughing, so tuned in to everyone's fast-breaking news. And we dance as if there are no clouds in the sky. The queen sits on a chair while we circle our *hora* around her. If only Max were here and the years had gone as he and Grace had so modestly planned.

"What do you think Louis would like for a gift?" I ask Grace.

"Find him an angel to sit on his shoulder and show him right from wrong."

❊ ❊ ❊

A FEW WEEKS LATER I run into Grace and her brother Jerry and the boys at a movie theater we call the Cheap Dedham. It has terrible seats but the price is right. The first time Grace took me here she was thrilled to introduce me to the Museum of Bad Art—in the basement, on the way to the restrooms! She led me past the astonishingly awful paintings and sculptures, most of them rescued from yard sales and trash bins.

"Look, there's always something new on velvet!" I exclaim. MOBA's credo is: *Beyond the merely incompetent, this art is too bad to be ignored.* Grace loves playing the snooty docent. "Let's study 'Poodle in Green Miniskirt.' Notice the depth of feeling in her eyes. And if you glance to your left, there's a full view of the urinals."

Grace and the boys are going to see *The Matrix*. I'm here for *Go Fish*, an arty but lighthearted lesbian film. But after a few minutes of sitting alone, I sneak into her theater and sit down next to her. While Keanu Reeves leaps from building to building, we whisper our bar mitzvah postmortems. "I forgot to tell you," Grace laughs. "The Authority loved those adorable arks you made. 'Who was your *centerpiece person*?' She was begging, Ruth. But I told her you were booked for the entire season."

38.
bras

WHEN I STOP AT Grace's a few days later with chicken soup from the expensive deli, she's flipping through a book about Monet. We study his Rouen cathedrals and his haystacks, but her enthusiasm is weak. Her hair's grown back in flattering short curls, but her cheeks have disappeared, and her eyes seem to sink deeper every time I see her. No more wry smile, no more twinkle. No more hearty laughs. Others tend to her, getting her to eat, helping her shower. Alice and Marion are taking turns staying overnight. My friend is surrounded by saints. When one of her lawyer friends arrives to help with her will, Grace submits to the indignity without a quip.

But talking to the boys, the cruelest job, is hers. She keeps procrastinating, even though the rabbi's been trying to move her in that direction. "I can't do it," she tells me during a midnight conversation. I help her rehearse. We finally come up with: "Uncle Jerry and Sam are going to move in. They love you as much as Dad and I do. You'll grow up and have happy lives and we'll be so proud of you."

Who could have that kind of courage?

"They were relieved to finally hear it from her mouth," Jerry tells me the next day. "Isaac held his younger brother. *That* was a first. Louis said, 'I don't believe you.' But he's the one with the amazing fantasy life."

[299]

"I did it," is all I hear from Grace, who stays upstairs in bed now, not even sitting up. "Does the pastry chef have the day off?" she mumbles when I give her toast.

"I'm only following orders."

"You should know better." She's wearing the blue nightgown I gave her, and gives me a weak but definitive Queen Elizabeth wave before she goes back to sleep.

But when I call that night, the real Grace answers the phone.

"How's my new window coming along?"

"I ordered it yesterday, a custom size, which is costing me extra."

She fills me in about a recent town tragedy: another family in her neighborhood has lost a father to another kind of cancer.

Is talking about others' tragedies a way of dealing with her own?

"How are the boys?"

"Don't get me started."

My cue to pull a joke out of the air. Even if I dared to broach somberness, Grace would duck any heavy topic I could possibly hand her. *Is it still my job to make her laugh?* I segue to my latest apartment crisis, which I know she'll enjoy.

"I spent hours scrubbing the refrigerator with a toothbrush," I groan. "But when I finally plugged it in, it didn't start." My tiny turmoil makes her laugh, so I milk the story for all it's worth. "OK, so I buy a new refrigerator. No big deal, right? Just another $700. They deliver it—but *it's too large for the space.* Now Ryan has to rebuild that side of the kitchen."

"I guess I have competition in the catastrophe department."

"No matter how bad it gets around here, you always have to outdo me."

"You're right, Ruth, you found me out. I want to win the prize."

A pause. "I'm on the cutting edge. The avant-garde of affliction." Another pause. "Maybe we should call it the Tragedy Track?"

During a lull in our dark nonsense, she finds a way to slip in, "You know how much I love you, Ruthie." Whenever I've told her the same thing she's said it back. But this time she started it.

May her words stick to my heart so I can hear them any time I want.

"They cut the hole for that window and you were so right, it's totally worth it."

"Now the afternoon sun will just *pour* in. But you need curtains. Ask Marion. She knows someone."

        *   *   *

THE NEXT THREE or four days are a brand-new phase of bad. In all my falls, Grace was there to catch me. I can barely eat or feed Joey. I forget to wash his soccer uniform, and I get lost driving in familiar territory. I call Grace's house for updates, stop by to help the boys with homework, load her dishwasher, sit on her bed when she's up to it. Meals arrive magically, and Jerry and Sam run things more efficiently than the Stein household has ever experienced. The rest of us keep ourselves manically busy taking care of the kids, paying bills, answering the incessant phone. When we run out of things to do, we talk about how horrible life will be without Grace to enliven it. Everyone else is as dependent as I am on this remarkable, ordinary, brilliant friend to pull them through their lives. Who's going to find us babysitters, interpret current events, tell us what to read, help us make every single decision from miniscule to major? Make art out of all this endless raw material?

Now the self-designated gatekeeper, Alice, tries to dissuade me from going into Grace's room, but whenever I stop at her door, she waves at me — too weakly now to mimic the Queen. "Ruthie," she whispers when I bend down to hear. "This isn't any fun at all."

"That depends," I say, copying Clinton, "on your definition of fun." It's the last time I see my friend smile.

*   *   *

"ALL YOU DO IS yell at me," Joey shouts when I ask him to put his dishes in the sink. "You drive like an old lady," he says in the car.

I lose it, blurting out too harshly what I still haven't exactly told him. (To keep it from being true?) "My best friend is dying. You can't be rude to me — *ever* — and definitely not *now*." He's quiet all the way to school.

Then comes the morning I rush out of exercise class, skipping my usual swim. Without calling the house first to see whether it's a good time or not, I head toward Brookline. I had dreamed Grace was better and I want to see for myself.

There are so many cars you'd think it was another party. I join several of her friends and relatives standing in the cold November sun, not talking much. The kids have been called home from school. A nurse comes outside: "No one expected it to happen this fast."

We hold one another. A woman I realize is Grace's therapist cries along with everyone else. She's been making house calls for weeks. Rabbi Drexler arrives and joins our huddle. I can tell he's angry with his God.

Somehow, on autopilot, I teach two classes that afternoon. The Expository Writing group tries my nonexistent patience: incomplete essays, unread chapters. When it's time for Creative Writing, I'm not sure I'll get through the two hours, but I need to keep busy.

When class is over, not ready to go home, I invite some students to have tea. Jen, an oboist, talks about breaking up with a girlfriend who's jealous of her love of music. Sandra, who's risen from welfare to data entry to honor student, describes the joy of watching her daughter win a swim meet. "I can't even swim!" she says.

I'm never this silent. After they notice, I tell them about Grace. It's my turn to need support from them, and the words come out before I can stop them. My students know more than I do about the trenches, and their compassion is immediate. They describe their own hard losses. "My brother died of diabetes at twenty-seven," Sonya says. "It's been five years and I still talk to him as if he were sitting next to me."

"My daughter died when she was three months old," says a normally quiet man who sits in the back and never shares anything remotely personal. I listen to their consolation and let my tears fall without feeling embarrassed. (I'm sure the professor who's teaching the Chaucer class across the hall would disapprove if he heard us.) It's like call and response: their details, mine, then theirs. One woman, an aspiring actress, had been friends with the comedienne Madeline Kahn, who died in a car accident this week. Grace would have known the names of her movies, and recited Kahn's funniest *shticks*.

⠶　⠶　⠶

I STOP AT GRACE'S again on my way home. Marion tells me the boys are in temple with Jerry, the observant Jew, and Sam, the Protestant atheist. I go upstairs to my friend's always-overflowing bedroom, expecting her to be there. I can hear her joke about the mess.

Did you see that ridiculous book review about Emily Brontë?
Come over here, Ruth, and tell me how you are.

I sit on Grace and Max's king-size bed and take in her collections: books, photographs, cards, earrings, magazines everywhere. Sam once named her Our Lady of the Catalogue.

I find Grace's date book and notice several pages of notes at the end, probably scribbled in waiting rooms. Since the rabbi asked me to find some of Grace's own words to include in his eulogy tomorrow, I take the book home.

Joey wolfs down the sushi I picked up, and it looks like we've forgiven each other our latest trespasses. His report card isn't great, but I hide my disappointment. Right now, the kindness in his eyes seems more important than anything he could learn in school. I get away with a quick kiss, the power of which he'll never know.

After dinner I tell him as gently as I can that Grace is gone. His still-small face doesn't know what to do with this information. He tries to hide his awkward smile, knowing it's wrong. *I love this child.*

"So now Louis doesn't have *any* parents?"

I nod.

"Who's going to take care of him and Isaac?"

"Uncle Jerry and Sam will be wonderful to the boys."

Joey walks away, then comes back. Did she hurt a lot? Were you there? Will she be buried near Max? Out of questions, he sinks to the floor, holds his knees, cries softly. That face I so rarely see even sad is drenched. I sit next to him and gently touch his head, envying the directness of his grief.

I read as many of Grace's scribbles as I can decipher: observations and descriptions of patients, nurses, and doctors. Lists and lists of things to do for the boys, doctors' phone numbers, recipes for Max to try.

On one page, titles of the women's magazine articles she had to scribble down: *Make Lettuce Last Longer, Show Stress Who's Boss, Instant Great Hair Gratification.*

I hear Marty's familiar knock. I'd called him earlier and left a message, but I wasn't sure what he'd do with the information. We sit through a long silence together. When Joey joins us on the couch, we discuss the funniest Stein stories.

"Remember the day Max volunteered to help me pick up the piano?" Marty asks. Max's jovial generosity had surprised him, since they hardly knew one another. But Max's hidden agenda was to have lunch at a restaurant nearby, always his favorite excuse to do anyone a favor. This is how Grace described him in her notebook: "That look of ecstasy on his face when he lifts up the lid of a pot and smells the meal. Eating is his bliss."

"I envy the way you find such amazing friends," Marty tells me before leaving.

I have just enough time before the funeral the next morning to run out and buy Joey a pale blue Oxford shirt. The red one he wears to his friends' bar mitzvahs won't do. I hardly ever have to buy him dress clothes since Grace has always given me the suits and shirts her boys have outgrown, and even their hardly worn loafers.

With no idea what to wear, I want to call Grace for advice. "What do you suggest for a cocktail party around the temple president's pool?" she once asked me. "Should I go with the Chinese silk pajamas, or my vintage clam diggers? What does dressy casual mean, anyway? Why don't they just make up their mind?"

"I wasn't invited, Grace. I'm too jealous to help you."

I open my closet door and listen. *A somber occasion calls for something classic. That deep magenta skirt and blouse you bought secondhand would be perfect. Did you get around to having it cleaned? And Ruth — I'd change those earrings.*

Marty drives up while I'm sitting on the steps and feeling the sun. I'm so grateful he's taking Joey and me to the temple. Did his girlfriend convince him to buy the new suit?

One of my silliest days with Grace comes back to me. We'd spent the afternoon at Max's parents' place at Nantasket Beach while Max and the kids were at Fenway Park. We swam and talked and read and swam some more, eating huge tuna fish sandwiches and lots of potato chips.

"I need some new bras," she said on our return trip when we passed a Wal-Mart. I stifled my urge to get her to wait until we passed a better store, but she knew I was thinking it. "Their bras are fine," she assured me. "Just cheaper than anywhere else."

The next thing I knew we were in the same dressing room holding blue, yellow, and pink 38Cs and a few beige 36Bs for me. After baring our torsos, there in the ugly fluorescent glare what we saw in the mirror was terrifying: our breasts were not only sandy, but covered with seaweed.

"We look like we're in a horror movie," she shrieked. We laughed so hard we were afraid someone would bust in and ruin our fun.

Grace bought the baby blue ones, two for $8.99.

39.

the best seat
in the house

IT TAKES THE FUNERAL to release me. I've been wanting to share my grief with others, and the temple in the woods feels like my own by now. I remember the first time I took Joey there, on a Saturday morning, when Grace invited us to the *tot Shabbot*. She may have still been hoping I'd become a member.

The rabbi talks about Grace and Max's endless generosity of spirit. "If you knew them," he says, "you were changed." Then, in an unsteady voice, he reads the sentences I chose from Grace's notebook:

"It's a mistake to have only one life. We should be given three tries, like in baseball. Next time I'll definitely be a painter."

Dear Marion, another best best friend, comes to the *bimah*. "Well, Grace, here you are, in the temple you loved, surrounded by several hundred of your closest friends and family, in your favorite front-row vantage point. You always had to have the best seat in the house."

The Gracie-esque wit causes the entire sanctuary to sigh in unison. She's comforting us all, as usual.

"You loved each one of us the most," Marion continues, "and you taught us almost everything we know:

1) Why talk when you can break into song?

2) Gossip is a vital source of wisdom. Imitate everyone's accent and expressions perfectly to enhance your performances.

3) Make sure everyone you know knows everything about everyone else, whether you have permission to spill the beans or not.

4) Give advice liberally.

5) When you're upset with someone, reward them with a devilish act, like grabbing their lunch from the school fridge and dumping it gleefully into the garbage pail, knowing that everyone else will get so much pleasure from your naughtiness.

6) Make your family everybody's family and your friends everybody's friends.

7) Die peacefully, with great dignity."

Joey and I walk away from the crowd at the cemetery, through that field of stones marking the departed. His still-short arms reach all the way around me.

*　*　*

INSTEAD OF STUDYING modern dance and living in Paris, instead of loving and leaving or losing a dozen men, Grace simply got on with her life. "She always has that perfect 98.6-degree mental temperature," her cousin Roz once told me, both of us envious. "When a person has quiet confidence and no fear in the world, but is not overly egotistical or self-involved, they're perfectly in balance. It's like the temperature on a glorious day: you don't notice it because it's perfect."

*　*　*

I BUNDLE UP AND HEAD for the arboretum. To tire myself out, I climb the steep way up Bussey Hill, where the long view toward the Great Blue Hills rewards me. The noise of the city outside these few hundred acres is comforting. Most people have companions, or at least a dog. A teenage boy and girl sit back to back, their eyes closed.

Grace and I always took the more gradual corkscrew route, winding our way slowly to the top. But we were too engrossed in rapid-fire banter to appreciate the scenery.

When the wind stops, I realize my heart is pounding. I sit on a stone bench to catch my breath and stare at the ominous-looking clouds.

I can't imagine no Grace.

"Find an opening in the clouds," I remember the psychic telling me. "Stare into it until you feel like you're traveling straight through, toward somewhere else."

Before I knew Grace very well, I confessed how lonely I was without Jake — even though we fought so constantly. She couldn't really relate. She'd never been alone — maybe not even for one night.

But she wanted to dispel my gloom. "Stand up." She pulled my arms. Suddenly, I had no idea why, we were doing the box step to the slow version she was humming of "Life Is a Cabaret."

"This is what Aunt Sadie says they did at her assisted living. If anyone got sad, they hummed something and fox-trotted around the room. Sadie said it worked every time."

What good is sitting alone in your room, I hum. *Come hear the music play.* Then I scan the sky for a place to see through, until I feel like I'm falling — up.

Past what seemed like all there was.

* * *

Acknowledgments

∗   ∗   ∗

MY DEEPEST GRATITUDE to E and M for making my family theirs.

Believers and helpers along the way: Nancy Aronie, Donald Barthelme, Paul Bresnick, Cynthia Clarkson, Ellen Davies, Maggie DeVries, Susan Duff, April Eberhardt, Francine du Plessix Gray, Lawrence Haydu, Deb Hordon, Merrily Kaplan, Michael and Suz Karchmer, Barbara Kline, Lillie Mae Law, Nancy Lester, Elaine Markson, Pam Pacelli, Ellie Rhymer, Elizabeth Rhymer, Marcia Trahan, Frederic Tuten, Barbara Valliere and Iris Weaver.

Carole Robinson is the best friend and editor anyone could have, Kathleen Westray the best book designer and Harry Teitelman the best son, artist and jokester.

Many thanks as well to Boston's Grub Street community of writers.

SUZ KARCHMER

Jill Teitelman

has taught writing at the Sorbonne, The School of Visual Arts
and Simmons College. Her stories have been published in *Chicago
Review*, *Transatlantic* and *Story Quarterly*. She has produced public
affairs programs for television and National Public Radio and has
been a MacDowell Fellow. She lives in Boston and on Cape Cod.

Visit www.saving-gracie.com

CPSIA information can be obtained at www.ICGtesting.com
Printed in the USA
BVOW082238091012

302601BV00001B/22/P